Also by Wayne Basta

From Grey Gecko Press
Aristeia: Revolutionary Right
Aristeia: A Little Rebellion
Aristeia: Tree of Liberty
From Many Worlds Fiction
Worst. Book. Ever.
The Awesome Adventures of Max Power
Seraph's Gambit

Seraph's Gambit

Seraph, Volume 1

Wayne Basta

Published by Many Worlds Fiction, 2022.

SERAPH'S GAMBIT

First edition. April 1, 2022.

ISBN: 978-1-958159-02-6

Written by Wayne Basta.

About the Publisher

For Erin and Connor

1- Ariana

Ariana Harkins strode cheerfully through the airlock onto her transport ship, *Seraph*. That thought gave her a giddy thrill. After years, it truly was *her* ship now.

Two members of her small crew stood waiting on the other side of the airlock. Her Echanic engineer, Vlasa, frowned in response to her jubilation. With a cybernetic replacement for his right eye marring the grey skin of his face, many of his expressions were hard to read. But he never failed to express displeasure.

"Captain, I take it from your expression that you have found us a job?" Vlasa asked.

"Yep."

"Does it involve more musk oxes?" Noah Ramirez, the ship's cargo handler, asked concerned. A human in his mid-thirties, Noah drummed his fingers on the pistol strapped to his hip as he talked, "Please say it doesn't involve more musk oxen. I just got the smell out of the cargo bay."

"I thought you said we should get more cargoes like that?" Ariana asked.

"Cargoes that pay like that. But not that smell like that."

"Well, you don't need to worry. This job doesn't even involve cargo. Just a passenger."

"That doesn't sound like much of a job." Noah frowned.

"Pays better than the musk ox job. In fact, it paid enough that I just zeroed out the outstanding debt on *Seraph*."

"And why would anyone pay us that much money for passage?" Vlasa asked.

"His name is Javi Wester, and he's an old friend. Was something of a mentor to me at the Naval Academy."

"That's some friend," Noah said skeptically.

"Is this the same Javi Wester I've read about? The one behind that crazy political organization that wants to see the PUG dissolved?" Vlasa asked.

"LFD is not crazy. They're just opposed to PUG having too much power. Since the end of the AI war, their control has only gotten stronger." Ariana said. In truth, she agreed that some of Live Free or Die's (LFD's) rhetoric did border on the crazy. But no one else spoke out openly against the Planetary Union of the Galaxy (PUG), so she felt some sympathy for them.

"Considering PUG saved us all from extinction by AI, that seems warranted," Vlasa said.

Ariana waved a dismissive hand, "None of that really matters. The important part is that he is an old friend and we're going to get him where he needs to go."

"And where is it exactly, that we're going?" Vlasa asked.

"Triask."

"Triask? That's PUG headquarters."

Noah shrugged, "Meh, if he paid, then I say we take him wherever he wants to go."

"Says the man who would do anything for a credit." Vlasa said.

"Hey now, I wouldn't do *anything*."

"Name one thing you wouldn't do for money?"

Noah considered the question for a moment. He seemed to reach a conclusion but then shook his head, "I'll let you know when I find it. But taking a good friend of our fearless captain to a nice, safe, if boring, planet, isn't it. Is that where you draw the line? At helping people?"

"I never said we shouldn't help. I just..." Vlasa fumbled, while Noah gave a triumphant smile.

"If you two are done, we need to get ready to depart. Noah, assemble the gear we'll need for a planetary excursion."

Vlasa tilted his head sideways, "Why are we going down to a planet? Isn't the job to go to Triask?"

"That is the job." Ariana said, "This first stop has nothing to do with Javi."

"Did Jasper finally talk you into take that survey job?"

"No..."

"Then what..." Vlasa said and then groaned, " You're not going to refuel?"

"The Hub charges outrageous fees for something you can find anywhere. I'm not falling for that scam."

Vlasa sighed, "Hydrogen is one of the cheapest things you can buy."

"Right, because it's everywhere."

"Why are we going down to a planet then? Aren't gas giants just made of that?" Noah asked.

Vlasa turned an appraising eye toward Noah and then turned back to Ariana, "He makes a valid point."

"We also need to restock on water."

"But we have a full tank."

"Had. I kind of ran the water supply through the electrolyzer to make the fuel we're going to need to get there." Ariana said sheepishly, "But on the plus side, the oxygen tanks are full."

Vlasa's cybernetic hand clanked against his eye implant as he facepalmed. He slowly shook his head side to side as it rested in his hand. A groan quietly drifted into the silence of the room.

"I can dig it." Noah said with an appreciative smile, "Sticking it to the man. Why pay for something that should be free? So, down to an unexplored planet? I'll get a big gun."

Noah strode out of the room whistling. Ariana remained where she stood, waiting patiently for Vlasa to recover himself. After a moment the groaning upgraded to muttering and finally, he lifted his head.

"You realize that if we leave port without enough fuel to reach our destination, plus fifteen percent, we'll be in violation of PUG regulations. You could be subject to fines and the potential loss of your shipping license."

Ariana waved a dismissive hand, "First, we have enough fuel to reach our destination. Second, we're not in PUG space right now. Third, how little do you think of me? We have enough fuel for five jumps. It will only take three to get where we're going. Leaves plenty to get us back to the Hub."

"But you said it would take us three to get there."

"We could do it in two. But I'd only want to go through PSR-J0108 if we really, really had too."

Vlasa squinted his one real eye as he thought and then it widened, "That's a pulsar. If we lost shields, all of our organic components would fry. For you, that would be everything."

"Exactly why I'd rather avoid it." Ariana said with a small exasperated shake of her head, "Anyway, you'll probably want to stay up here. I know how you don't like your implants getting dirty. How do you think our noob pilot would handle it?"

She referred to the ships only other crew, Olivia Ryans, their helmsman. She had recently hired the sixteen-year-old human girl. Normally, Ariana never would have considered hiring someone so young. But Olivia had beem so irrepressibly eager, she had relented and let the girl prove her skills on a few simulations. After such a clear example of raw talent, she had hired her despite the age concern. Since then, Vlasa had taken the lead in training her and getting her settled in on *Seraph*.

Vlasa's voice returned to his usual even tone, "Olivia appears to be competent at her duties, even if her inexperience has led to a few minor mistakes. But that does not give me any metrics with which to gauge her response to an unknown alien planet. I know she is considered young for your people."

"Wow, that's high praise. You must actually like this kid." Ariana said with a smirk.

"I have no opinion of her that is not fundamentally tarnished by my distaste for her predecessor."

"Randolph wasn't that bad."

"He used *Seraph* to smuggle drugs and refused to pilot us any further once we were stranded in the middle of nowhere unless you gave him a raise. What part of that is 'not that bad.'?"

"The part where I got to watch Hub security arrest him."

"Something I missed."

"Told you you'd want to see him off."

"I'll remember that next time." Vlasa said with a small smile, "But for now, I should see to the engines and ensure we do indeed have enough fuel not to get stranded in the middle of nowhere.

2- Olivia

With trembling hands, Olivia wrapped her fingers around *Seraph*'s flight controls. They felt right, like they had been crafted just for her. Flexing her fingers around them, she pictured herself deftly dodging the ship through treacherous space, expertly avoiding collisions and weapon fire. Quietly she went, "Pew, pew, whoosh!"

"What are you doing?"

Hastily dropping the control stick, Olivia bolted out of the chair and tried to look innocuous, wishing for a moment she hadn't braided her dark hair so she could hide her face behind it., "Nothing! I didn't touch anything."

Standing in the hatch to the flight deck, *Seraph*'s captain, Ariana, bore an amused expression on her face. She appeared to fight it back and said with a sterner voice, "Why not? You were supposed to be getting the ship ready for launch."

"Oh right. Yes, of course, captain. That's what I was doing." Olivia said, feeling her cheeks warm. At least her dark skin hid her blush. This hadn't been the first time someone had caught her messing around with the flight controls of a ship. It had just been the first time she was supposed to be there.

Dropping back into the seat, she opened the pre-flight checklist. Ariana came all the way into the small room and surveyed everything. Olivia tried to put the captain out of her mind, but the older woman's presence made it difficult to focus.

"Can I help you with something, Captain?" She asked nervously, hoping that Ariana had come up here for any reason that wasn't to watch her fly the ship. Though, if this had been her ship, she would want to keep an eye on the inexperienced teenager who claimed to be able to fly.

"Did you hear that noise?" Ariana asked, gesturing around with her hand, "When I came into the room, there was a humming sound."

"Humming sound?" Olivia asked, her cheeks flushing again.

"Yes. Kind of a bzzzz and a vroom and whoosh." Ariana said with apparent sincerity.

"Umm." Olivia started, but was cut off by a new voice.

"Ari, leave the poor girl alone."

A yellow and green Slu slithered through the open door behind Ariana. An invertebrate, Slu appeared closer to a gelatinous blob than a solid figure to most humanoids. But they had a tough skin and strong, flexible muscle-like structures that allowed them to form arms that functioned better than humans. On the top of their "head," two eyestalks protruded like antennae.

"Fine, Javi, fine." Ariana said with a smile, "Olivia, I want you to meet our passenger, Javi Wester. We'll be taking him to Triask."

"A pleasure to meet you, sir," Olivia said, trying to sound as professional as she could.

A gap opened beneath Javi's eyestalks and gave a reasonable facsimile of a smile, "And you too my dear. I look forward to a pleasant trip under your skilled hand."

He then turned his eyestalks toward Ariana, "It seems at least some of your crew knows how to show good manners."

"I told you not to judge all of us based on Noah." Ariana said and then turned back to Olivia, "Javi has requested to watch our departure from the flight deck."

Olivia glanced around the small room. It had no windows, only control panels and monitors. She suspected that what Ariana truly meant was that Javi would watch her. But they hadn't left the Hub yet, and she didn't want to blow her first job before she had even gotten to fly.

"Sure, I'll make him feel right at home."

"Okay, good. We have one stop to make before we head to Triask, PX-1099. It's three jumps from here."

"I'll plot us a course!"

Javi's eyestalks went rigid, and his body quivered slightly, "Ari, why the detour? You know how important it is I get to Triask without delay."

"Well, if we don't stop, we won't make it to Triask, so the delay would be quite extensive." Ariana said dismissively, "Now, I'll be in weapons control and Vlasa is in the engine room. Remember to connect your handheld to *Seraphi's* internal network so you can communicate with us. We'll be out of range of the Hubs network very soon, so if there is anyone you need to send a final message to, you should do that now."

Olivia shook her head emphatically, "No, no one there to say goodbye to. I've never even had a handheld until now. I'm ready."

Ariana's face scrunched up in a look Olivia was very familiar with, the one she called the 'you poor dear' look. It came out anytime an adult learned, or was reminded of, her status as an orphan. Fortunately, Ariana didn't actually say anything, but just nodded and departed.

Glancing at Javi, Olivia wasn't sure if Slu had a similar expression. If they did, she couldn't read one, so she turned back to her station. She tried to ignore the feeling of being watched. Despite the prominent eyestalks, she found it relatively easy to pretend Javi wasn't there. She guessed the fact that he could see her no matter what direction he faced, made it not as noticeable if he was watching her.

Losing herself in the task of running through the pre-flight checklist, Olivia managed to completely forget Javi was there until she pulled out the navigation charts. When she did, Javi broke the silence and said, "Why do you have those binders of charts?"

Olivia raised an eyebrow at him, "I thought the captain said you taught at the naval academy?"

"A long time ago. And I was a professor of history; I wasn't actually a naval officer. Though I did help on the gun range sometimes." Javi explained.

"Oh. Well, these charts contain all the astrometric data necessary to plot an FTL jump between systems. You need to know precisely where you are and where your exit point is going to be to arrive safely. Since everything is always in motion you can never make the same jump twice. Not to mention the effects of time dilation since solar systems aren't even moving at the same speed."

"That must be very complicated. Why not let the computer do it?"

"Oh, I'll run it through the computer. But that's just to check my work."

"You like the challenge then?"

Olivia snorted, "Hardly. But I do like arriving in one piece. We wouldn't want a rogue piece of AI code that's infecting the navigational computer jumping us directly into a star."

Javi nodded solemnly. She cast a curious glance at the Slu, but couldn't read his body language. He ended up dipping his eyestalks as if in a nod and then said, "I suppose that makes sense. Even a decade later, we can never really be sure the AI is gone."

"It better be gone. But I still won't let a computer tell me where to go." Olivia said, suppressing a shutter as a memory flashed through her mind. Now was not the time for that, she told herself. She completed the navigational calculations and then ran the jump on the navigational computer. There was a minor difference, but after checking her numbers, she realized it was a rounding issue and would make no difference.

Calculations complete, she entered the coordinates and then hooked her handheld into the ship's internal network. Despite her earlier statement to Ariana, she felt a slight sadness when she disconnected from the Hub's network. She knew a few people she could say goodbye too she supposed. But they weren't family. They weren't even really her friends.

"We're ready to depart, Captain," Olivia announced.

Ariana's voice sounded in Olivia's ear, *"Good work. We have clearance from Hub control just as soon as a PUG cruiser clears the lane. Hold here."*

"Roger that." Olivia said and then glanced back to Javi, "Well, make yourself comfortable. We're ready to depart. Just have to wait for a PUG cruiser to get out of the way."

Javi's eyestalks scrunched down close to his head, and his body appeared to compress, "PUG cruiser? What are they doing here?"

Olivia shrugged, "Who knows? The Hub itself isn't under their jurisdiction, but that doesn't stop them from pushing their weight around. At least, that's what everyone says."

Javi didn't say anything in reply, and she continued, "Not a fan of the PUG?"

"It's complicated," Javi answered.

"If you say so. I know a lot of people aren't fans of them here, but they won the war, right? I'm always happy to see one of their ships."

"A very sensible attitude. One I wish I had remembered."

"What's that?"

"Nothing. You said they were departing?"

Looking at the sensor data Olivia nodded, "No, looks like they are docking. Either way, they're out of our departure lane now, so we can go."

"Good. Good." Javi said distantly.

3- Ariana

After a few short FTL jumps, *Seraph* arrived at planet PX-1099. Ariana studied the data for the planet below. It had been surveyed, but never charted. She knew it had breathable air and no obvious airborne biological dangers. But the survey had been very perfunctory and did not include surface maps beyond a rough continental outline.

Scanning the planet from orbit revealed greater details but little beyond what she could discern visually. *Seraph* was technically a scout ship, yet lacked life form scanners or any real scientific instruments. She could track weather systems and temperature, but not much else.

Scrolling through her possible choices, she finally settled on a relatively rocky area. A river would provide all the water they would need, both for drinking and for breaking down into hydrogen. It also would give them a comprehensive view of the area for any potential hostile life.

Satisfied, she locked in coordinates to the teleporter just as Noah came in, overdressed as usual. He sported a flak jacket and helmet. Two pistols holstered on his waist and several knives hung from his belt. In his arms, he cradled a rifle that looked like it had been stripped off a tank.

"You didn't need to bring guns for everyone. We've got enough right here." Ariana smirked.

"Huh? These are for me." Noah said

"Three of them?"

"Yeah, I didn't want to go overboard."

Ariana decided not to press the point. She wasn't sure if she could trust Olivia with a low caliber defense pistol much less Noah's more powerful guns and it had been years since she had used one herself. She set herself and Noah to gathering the storage tanks and electrolyzer. Once they had loaded the gear into the teleport chamber, she ported it to the surface.

Olivia entered the room with her usual eager bounce. Javi followed behind her at a much more sedate pace typical of his species. His yellowish colored slug-like frame slid across the deck with small wiggling motions of his body. He waited near the door, observing them, but not saying anything.

"Olivia, we're going down to the surface. I imagine this will be your first time?" Ariana asked.

"No, I was born planetside."

"That's not what I meant. Your first time down to an undeveloped and uncharted world."

"Oh-h-h-h-h," Olivia said, "Then yes. First time. Very exciting."

"Put on a belt. It has a recall device so *Seraph* can port you back up, some emergency gear and a pistol. Don't touch the pistol." Ariana said, stressing the last command. She turned to Javi, her old mentor, "Would you mind sending her down after us?"

"Of course, Ari. I'm pretty sure I still remember how to operate one of those." Javi said and gave Olivia a mischievous wink with one of his eyestalks.

"Okay, let's be cautious about this. Stay within sight of each other. We're not here for the tour, just to gather supplies. Don't eat anything. Don't drink anything either until it's been filtered and decontaminated. And if there is a threat you can always push the recall button." Ariana stressed.

Olivia nodded, her eager expression turning more somber as she cast furtive glances between Ariana and the teleporter. Noah just shrugged. He hefted his big gun up into a ready position and stepped into the porting chamber.

"Wait for the all-clear before porting her down," Ariana said to Javi and then triggered the teleporter.

The ship around her vanished, and a blinding light replaced it. The comfortable temperature suddenly became an intense heat wave. Fortunately, despite the sudden distractions and a few millimeter drop as the teleporter placed her slightly above the ground, she managed to remain upright. She didn't want to look weak in front of Noah by falling on her face.

The glare continued to blind her, and Ariana lifted her hand to cover her face. The sun above shown brightly, hurting her eyes even with the shadow of her hand. She couldn't remember the last time she had been planet-side. Wherever it had been, the sun there must have been dimmer. Or she kept it too dark on *Seraph*.

"Looks clear so far. All our stuff looks undisturbed." Noah said. He continued to hold his rifle up in a ready position, "Though I want to get a good look from the top of that rise."

Ariana squinted in the direction he pointed and nodded her head. Noah strode forward through the dusty ground and she followed. Halfway there, she remembered the pair of sunglasses on her belt and pulled them out. The polarized lenses cut the glare dramatically and she could finally get a good look at the world around her.

The ground was mostly barren dirt with a few scraggly shrub-like plants. Behind her, the river gurgled as it flowed and it sported a few reedy looking husks on its banks. The sky had a purplish hue but not a very vibrant shade.

Trudging up the sandy slope gave Ariana and Noah a view of the surrounding terrain. Dust obscured the horizon and small rolling hills kept them from seeing too far into the distance. But what they could see appeared barren and empty.

"Looks pretty clear." Noah said, "But you can never discount some aerial predator. Or something that burrows up from the ground."

Ariana shuddered at the thought of something swallowing her from the ground below. "The ground seems pretty rocky beneath this surface layer of sand. So we're probably safe from those."

"Or the species on this planet can tunnel through solid rock."

"You're not helping."

"You don't pay me to make you feel better." Noah said and then gave a suggestive grin, "But I would be open to renegotiating my contract."

Ariana raised an eyebrow at him, "I thought you liked men. When we met you..."

Noah shrugged, "I don't limit myself. Anything that has a hole they want me to fill, I'm happy to oblige."

Ariana stood there for a moment with her mouth agape, "I don't know if I should be impressed with your openness or disgusted."

"Why not both?"

"Sure. Just stay away from Olivia." Ariana said sternly. The girl was far too young and naïve to make smart decisions around a man like Noah.

Noah looked offended, "I'm a man of open experiences, but I'm not a monster. Now, in a couple of years..."

Letting that comment go, Ariana linked her handheld to *Seraph*, "Javi, things look clear. You can send Olivia down."

Ariana started back down the small rise with Noah behind her. Before they had made it halfway back to the river a bright light flashed, and two figures appeared, one human and one Slu. The two figures turned about as they looked around. When they caught sight of Ariana and Noah, they raised their hands in a wave.

"Javi? What are you doing here?" Ariana asked when she was close enough not to have to shout.

"I thought I could help. Your ship, while nice, does not have much in the way of things to do."

"It's pretty dry here. That's not very good for your people. Besides, you're going to get very dirty."

"Well, then I guess I just might need to go for a swim before porting back up," Javi said, turning one eyestalk toward the river.

"Ah. Such a sacrifice." Ariana said with a smile, "Knock yourself out. Now, you two, let's get this equipment set up."

"What's the rush?" Olivia asked, "I wouldn't mind a swim myself."

"Yeah, but I'd prefer everyone keep their pants on," Ariana said giving a pointed look at Noah.

"Javi doesn't have pants on," Noah said.

"But he never wears pants."

Ariana began directing Noah and Olivia into how to set up the pump for the water tanks and electrolyzer. Before long, water flowed through the hoses and into the equipment. Most of the work after that involved clearing the tubes of gunk and debris that got sucked in. It was tiring, but straightforward work that kept the three of them occupied.

While they worked, Javi slithered through the dirt and into the muddy region at the water's edge. He moved gently and very dignified for a few moments before dropping all pretense and rolling around in the mud, covering his entire body. A contented sigh escaped him before he slid the rest of the way into the water.

After a few hours, Javi came slithering rapidly back onto shore. He spluttered out some water and then yelled, "Something's coming. Several somethings in fact."

Noah dropped the tank he had been in the process of changing and ran to where he had set his rifle. Falling into a crouch, he scanned the area. Ariana drew her pistol and waited for Javi to indicate a direction. Slu had senses that went beyond humans, and she trusted his abilities.

Nervously Olivia started to draw her pistol as she came to stand beside Noah and Ariana. Without taking his eye away from his gunsight, Noah reached a hand back and put it over Olivia's, stopping her from drawing her pistol. He gave a slight shake of his head

"Not unless you have no choice. You're more a threat to us than anything else right now."

Olivia looked slightly terrified with her eyes open wide, and she didn't argue. Ariana gave her a reassuring pat on the back, "Javi's senses aren't very specific. Whatever it is may not be any kind of threat."

As if on cue, a towering figure came barreling over the top of the rise. It was immediately apparent the figure was bipedal, but it took a moment to make out any more details as clouds of dust flew up as the creature ran. Sharp, stony features soon identified the creature as a Rokma.

"If I start firing now I might be able to drop him before he gets here. I wasn't expecting to face Rokma or I would have brought a bigger gun." Noah said.

"I thought you brought the big gun," Ariana asked as she tried to decide what to do. Fortunately, Rokma didn't move fast.

"There's always a bigger gun. This one's a good game hunter but doesn't have the penetrating power that I'd like. And you need a lot of penetration for a Rokma."

For a moment, Ariana was distracted trying to figure out if there was a double meaning in Noah's words. She shook it off and turned to Javi, "More?"

He nodded, "Many. But they don't feel the same."

Not waiting to find out what that might mean, Ariana said, "Javi, Olivia return to the ship. We'll send the tanks up after you. Clear them from the chamber quickly."

"But what...." Olivia began.

"The longer you talk, the longer it will take to get us all back. The porter takes a while to recharge between cycles. Go. Now."

Javi nodded solemnly and then tapped the recall device strapped to his arm. Olivia gulped and triggered her own. They vanished, and Ariana turned to their supply tanks trusting Noah to keep an eye on the approaching Rokma. She linked them up into two groups so that the hydrogen tanks and water tanks could all be brought up in one teleport cycle. The pump and electrolyzer would have to go in a separate cycle.

"Umm..." Noah said, and Ariana turned around.

The Rokma had already gotten reasonably close to them, but a more massive dust cloud had appeared at the top of the ridge. Multiple figures appeared at the top and came barreling down the slope. These creatures were almost as massive as the Rokma but had many more appendages.

"Oh shit." Ariana said, "Giant spiders."

"Those are no joke." Noah said with a slight tremble in his voice, "I once saw things like these tear apart an entire platoon."

"Let's hope these are less effective," Ariana said.

She glanced down at her recall device. An agonizing few seconds ticked by before the indicator light turned green. She looked up toward the approaching swarm and considered leaving the supplies. But she didn't relish the idea of getting trapped orbiting a planet infested with giant spiders with no fuel. She pushed the recall buttons on the storage tanks, and they vanished in a flash.

"Thirty seconds recycle?" Noah asked.

"A bit over a minute. This isn't a military porter. Plus, however long it takes them to clear the chamber."

"In that case..." Noah said and started firing his rifle.

With each shot, a spider fell and was immediately trampled by others. No matter how many times he fired, the swarm didn't appear to get smaller. It just grew as more and more appeared on the rise.

Forgotten in the terror of the spiders, the Rokma now came within conversational distance. He raised his hands to his sides in the universal gesture of a nonthreat. Going with her gut, Ariana handed her pistol to the Rokma. Then she knelt beside Noah, drew one of the pistols from his holsters and started firing herself.

Despite triple blasts rapidly firing out, the swarm continued to advance. The spiders were either unaware or uncaring of the danger. They had already moved past the halfway point when the indicator light again turned green.

Not wasting any time, Ariana reached over to the pump and pulled its recall device off. She slapped it against the Rokma and triggered the button. Noah turned back toward her as the Rokma disappeared.

"What the hell did you do that for?"

Not giving him an answer, Ariana reached out and triggered the device at his belt. Noah vanished in a flash and she found herself with only a swarm of giant alien spiders for company.

4- Vlasa

The sound of a rifle shot reverberated down the corridor. Vlasa quickened his pace down the central stairwell and ran into the cargo bay. Before him, a chaotic scene played out. The echoes of the rifle shot faded to be replaced by incomprehensible shouting.

Noah knelt in one of the teleporter chamber with his rifle aimed at an unknown Rokma who stood in the other. The Rokma held a pistol, which he pointed back at Noah. Javi stood between the two, one eyestalk and one arm upraised toward each. Olivia cowered next to some storage tanks. All of them were shouting at each other.

Adjusting his vocal implant, Vlasa managed to speak over the others, "What is going on here?"

The moment of silence ended when everyone again started shouting at once. Impatiently, Vlasa whistled at a high pitch until they stopped. Cringing, the two humans covered their ears while Javi's gelatinous skin visibly vibrated. The sound appeared to have no adverse effect on the Rokma.

"Now, Olivia, what is going on?" Vlasa asked again, once it was silent.

"This granite..." Noah started, but Vlasa cut him off with another whistle.

"I asked Olivia."

Darting her gaze between Vlasa, Noah and the Rokma, Olivia tentatively said, "We were down on the planet when this Rokma appeared and charged us. Javi sensed that there was something else coming, so the captain sent us back to the ship. We got the tanks back and then Noah and the Rokma ported up next. I don't know what happened to the captain."

"Noah, what happened to the captain?"

"Giant. Fucking. Spiders." Noah growled.

"She is dead?" Vlasa felt a cold sense of dread fill him.

Noah blinked, "No, she was fine when I left. But they were getting pretty close."

"So why are you standing in the teleporter chamber preventing her from returning?" Vlasa using his implants to keep his voice level.

"Shit," Noah lept out into the cargo bay.

Seconds after he cleared the chamber a flash of light signaled the teleporter activating. Ariana stood in the chamber, soaking wet with water dripping off her. She coughed several times and immediately started shivering. Vlasa turned toward the emergency kit on the wall and removed a blanket, handing it to her as she stepped out of the chamber.

"It's good those things can't swim." Ariana said as she wrapped the blanket around herself, "What took the porter so long to recycle?"

Vlasa hung his head in relief. For a moment he thought that Ariana might not return. He had no idea what he would do if that happened.

Everyone else stood staring at her blankly. Neither Noah nor the Rokma had lowered their guns even though their gazes had shifted. After using the blanket to dry her face, Ariana looked up and became aware she had become the center of attention.

"What? Do I have something in my hair?" She asked pulling at it, "Why are you two still pointing guns at each other?"

"He led those spiders toward us," Noah said.

The Rokma's deep, slow voice cut off Ariana's reply, "It was pure happenstance that I came upon you as I fled those creatures. If I had known you were there, I never would have come that way so as not to endanger you."

"Everyone put your guns down," Ariana said, her voice growing stern.

"Him first," Noah said.

"Of course. I wish no one here harm." The Rokma said.

Once the Rokma's pistol was on the deck, Noah too lowered his rifle, but he kept it at the ready. Some of the tension eased from the room. Javi backed up, so he no longer stood between the two.

"My name is Squee. My ship...crashed...on this planet some time ago. I came across the spider's lair and was fleeing toward the water when I came upon you. Thank you for rescuing me."

"Heh, your name's Squee." Noah chuckled, and Vlasa reflexively cast a sour look at the man.

"It is," Squee said without inflection. He then turned to Ariana, "I pledge myself to your service until my debt to you is repaid."

"Debt?" Ariana asked.

"Yes, for saving my life and freeing me from that infernal planet. The moss I was forced to eat to survive tasted like death."

"Well...umm... you're welcome. We could always use a few more hands. What do you do?"

"I was a shield technician on my last vessel and I have many basic engineering skills. Also, I can lift things much heavier than humans can." Squee said, his voice proud.

Vlasa gave the Rokma an appraising glance. It had been a long time since he had worked with anyone who understood more than the basics of how things worked on a starship. If his boast proved correct, it would be a nice change of pace.

"Good, good," Ariana said. "Well, welcome aboard. Noah, bring the equipment back up. I had to pull the recall from the pump, but the electrolyzer should still be good."

"Yeah, yeah," Noah grumbled. He moved to the teleported controls and triggered the recall command. Another flash and then a piece of metal appeared in the teleporter chamber.

"Goddamn spiders. They smashed my electrolyzer." Ariana groaned.

"It appears you did manage to secure the fuel though." Vlasa said gesturing, "So it was not a total loss."

"Yeah. Let's get that into the reactor tanks and get away from this terrible planet."

Squee reached down and lifted the heavy tanks with no apparent effort. He looked to Vlasa who gestured toward the exit. The pair trudged away, Vlasa's metal leg clinking and Squee causing a noticeable thud with every step.

Behind them, they heard Noah call out, "Hey, wait a minute. Where's my pistol?"

"Umm..." Ariana started, "The river? Probably."

"I liked that gun."

"Would you like to go back and get it?

"Can we nuke the area first?"

Ariana tilted her head, "I don't know. You're the one with an arsenal in your room. Can we nuke the area?"

Noah let out a heavy sigh, "No."

5- Olivia

Olivia felt the slight vibration through her chair as *Seraph*'s main engines fired. A small smile crossed her lips as she delighted in the knowledge that those powerful engines were under her control. At this moment, she could do anything or go anywhere.

Seraph might just be a small survey ship turned cargo hauler, but she had a surprisingly responsive maneuvering system. Olivia itched to see just what she could really do. Perhaps this system had an asteroid field or a dense ring system?

"Start calculating a jump for NGC-28901 via NGC-28991." Ariana's voice called into Olivia's headset.

Reality shattered her daydream and Olivia let out a sigh. Someday she might be allowed to do something more than fly straight. But even this was a dream come true. At sixteen she should be in sitting in a classroom, not behind the controls of a starship.

Pulling the navigational charts off the shelf, Olivia flipped through the massive book until she found the entry for NGC-28901. Then she began entering variables related to that systems spatial coordinates into the erasable FTL jump equation chart. While she worked on the calculations, she turned on a music playlist, something she had never had access to before. The first two jumps had required her complete attention, but it had already become routine. Singing quietly to herself made the mundane math equations go faster.

By the time she had finished the first song, she had completed her jump calculation. She then ordered the computer to calculate the same jump. Seconds later it returned a course and awaited confirmation to enter the course into the FTL. She verified the computer's calculations against her own, smiling when they matched.

She kept singing as they flew to the jump point. Getting into the song, she stood up from her seat and started to dance. Turning around to get more space to move, Olivia came face to face with the hard grey features of Squee.

"Aagghh!" Olivia yelped, throwing herself backward.

Squee remained still aside from spreading his hands out to his side and said something that she couldn't make out.

Catching her breath, Olivia turned her music down, "What?"

"I said I did not mean to startle you."

"Well, you did anyway. How did you get in here?"

Squee turned to his left and gestured, "Through the door."

"Oh, right. I never heard it open."

"You appeared to be quite engrossed in your work. I did not want to disturb you, so I remained silent."

Olivia's cheeks flushed, "How long have you been here?"

"Five minutes or so."

"Well, say something next time. It's pretty rude just to watch someone in silence." Olivia said trying to stand up as tall as her small frame would allow. Despite that, she barely came up to Squee's chest.

"I apologize again. It has been some years since I have been around people. Even longer since I have been among humans. I must endeavor to remember your cultural norms."

"Yeah, well..." Olivia said.

"I will leave you," Squee said and turned toward the door.

"No, wait. You can stay. You just startled me is all. Why did you come up here anyway?"

"I wished to observe our departure."

Shaking her head, Olivia mumbled, "Why does everyone want to do that?"

Oblivious to her statement, Squee turned back and resumed staring at the navigational display. There weren't any windows that would allow them to see the actual scene before them, but then nowhere on the ship had a window. The icon representing *Seraph* sat in the center of the display as numbers rapidly changed next to all other objects that they were tracking.

Glancing back to Squee, Olivia felt a sense of sadness from the giant. She changed the navigational display over to a camera view, selecting the aft array. The image of the planet appeared. As the seconds ticked by, it slowly shrank.

"How long were you down there?"

"Long enough to never want to go back again."

"I can't imagine. I was born on a planet but today was the first time I'd been down on one since, well, I can't even remember. Alone, on a desolate world?" Olivia shuddered.

"It was not a vacation, so to speak."

"How did you end up here? You said you crashed?"

"More or less." Squee said quickly and then, "You have spent most of your life in space? Aboard this ship?"

"No, this is a new gig. I spent most of my life on the Hub."

"I have been there a few times. A very...interesting place."

"Never got a lot of Rokma passing through. I thought your people kept mostly to themselves."

"We do. But I spent many years among the broader galaxy. You could say that is how I ended up out here. Not listening to the ways of my people."

The pair contently watched the planet for several minutes before a sharp earsplitting alarm sounded. Olivia jumped slightly in her seat.

"What is that?" Squee asked.

"Umm...not sure." Olivia said and then checked her instruments, "It looks like a proximity warning. We've picked up a ship nearby. It must have just jumped in."

"We should warn them about the spiders. And not to eat the moss."

6- Ariana

The proximity warning alarm woke Ariana from her peaceful doze. Despite the years since her training, her body responded before her mind had fully come awake. She brought her seat up to an upright position and secured her safety harness.

That done, she began accessing the sensor telemetry on the incoming ship. Not for the first time, she cursed the crudeness of *Seraph*'s sensors. She could track the ship and identify its profile as some type of small freighter, similar to *Seraph*, but not much else. When it got closer, she could do a more detailed visual inspection and hope to identify weapons, but she would have no idea if those weapons were powered up.

Vlasa and Noah dashed into the weapons room from two different directions. They glanced at each other, Vlasa looking a little surprised. He gave Noah a small nod before speaking, "What do we have, Captain?"

"Some kind of freighter just jumped in," Ariana said.

"Hostile?"

Ariana shrugged, "They haven't shot at us yet."

"They're pretty far away. Pirates won't want to scare us off. They'll get closer, jam us, and then try to board" Noah said. He stood beside Ariana watching the approaching ship. His right hand went to the pistol on his hip and started flipping the strap on and off.

"What makes you so sure they are pirates?" Vlasa asked, "We're in the middle of nowhere."

"Maybe we have something they might want," Noah said, shifting his eyes down to the floor.

"Like what?"

"Umm."

"He has a point though." Ariana said, "If they were just a freighter like us looking to save a little money on fuel, would they be flying straight towards us? Or would they be veering away for fear we might be pirates?"

"Point taken." Vlasa conceded.

Ariana reached to her control panel triggered the ship-wide alarm. Vlasa headed aft, and Noah practically ran from the room. Ariana turned back to the weapon controls and started powering up their weapons. A single dual blaster and a rudimentary missile launcher were all the armaments *Seraph* had. If the other ship had better sensors, and could detect *Seraph's* weapons powering up, there was a chance that might dissuade an attack. The other ship being better equipped might benefit them.

Within moments Vlasa reported in from the engine room. He would be monitoring power levels and aiding Olivia's maneuver. Noah joined the communication net from the security station in the cargo bay. From there he could control the interior doors and sensors, watching for boarders.

When another voice joined the conversation, it startled her for a moment. Squee said, *"I have found the shield control room and am sorry to report we only have a class one shield."*

"Yeah, thanks, Squee. We were aware. This isn't a warship."

"I inform you that all projectile weapons capable of deceleration and most burst energy weapons will be able to penetrate our shields."

"Again, Squee, I know," Ariana said, not bothering to keep her annoyance out of her voice this time.

"I did not mean to imply your lack of knowledge, Captain. It is my duty to inform you of my station's capabilities and deficiencies before a potential conflict."

"We'll need to review that duty later." Ariana said, and then after muting her comm, "Assuming we survive this."

The approaching ship continued to close on them. Any course deviation that Olivia might take wouldn't get them to a safe distance for jumping any sooner. She could turn around, but that would force them to bleed off all of their current velocity first. The ship would be on them before they could accelerate in the other direction.

"They're reversing engines!" Olivia yelled excitedly.

"Damn." Ariana said before turning her mike back on, "Time to FTL?"

"Three minutes," Vlasa answered, his voice flat.

"Go evasive." Ariana slipping into a familiar mental space.

At the helm, Olivia fired the RCS thrusters, and *Seraph* began to juke to the sides at random intervals. Almost as soon as the ship began maneuvering, a triple barrage of energy bolts flashed through the space between them. Ariana braced herself for the impact she knew would be coming. Their shields would stop one bolt and Olivia's maneuvering might make one miss, but that left one to strike their unprotected hull.

To her amazement, all three bolts flew through space where *Seraph* had once been. The second the bolts should have hit them, an intense energy beam shot out from the pirate ship. Moving at the speed of light this beam had no chance of missing. Fortunately, because the energy bolts had missed, their shields were still up, and the energy beam failed to do any damage to the hull.

"Beginners luck." Ariana thought, shocked at the unlikely evasion by her rookie pilot. But out loud she said, "Good maneuver, Olivia, hold steady for five seconds and then go evasive again."

Seraph stopped changing direction, and Ariana aimed their cannon. The pirate ship held its course, and she smiled. Two energy bolts flashed out from the barrel, and she fired their missile. The energy bolts closed the distance quickly, and both scored a hit. Unfortunately, the pirate's shields must have been stronger than theirs as they both impacted against shields.

The missile came in behind the bolts at a slower pace. As it got close to impact, the missile fired a retro thruster and decelerated rapidly. Now moving at a comparative snails pace, the missile would be able to bypass the pirate's shields entirely. Unfortunately, the pirate's pilot had begun maneuvering, and the missile missed.

A missile fired out from the pirates in return. Ariana shouted, "Go evasive!"

"Don't worry, Cap; I got this," Olivia said, the smugness evident in her voice.

Seconds later the ship shuddered as the missile impacted on the hull. If it weren't for her straps, Ariana would have been thrown from her chair. The lights in weapons control flickered and the quiet hum of the ship disappeared, replaced by the sound of gushing air. The weapon control panel flashed an angry warning.

"Hull breach in weapon control," Ariana said calmly.

She flicked a switch on her chair and a green mist started jetting out of a canister on the wall. She watched the mist as it swirled through the room. It twisted around an air current and moved toward the breach in the hull and out into space. She now had a figurative arrow pointing straight to the hole.

Unstrapping herself from her chair, Ariana ran over to the spot of the breach and took a hull patch kit from the wall. She popped the seal on the canister and sprayed the polymer goo over the small hole. It quickly sealed and the rush of air out of the ship stopped.

Ariana started to feel light headed as she moved back to the weapons console. The atmospheric pressure had dropped considerably in the short time before she'd sealed the breach. Nervously she glanced at the pressure gauge and was relieved to see it slowly, but steadily, climbing.

Sitting back in her chair, she looked over the warnings she had missed on the weapon control panel. She released a string of curses when she saw that her weapons were offline. One of the capacitors had been damaged by the weapon strike. Repairs would take a few minutes, so she ignored the damage and shut down the cannon, switching the missile over to the functioning capacitor.

By the time she finished, the atmosphere had thickened enough that she could once again hear.

"We've been boarded!" Noah's frantic voice boomed, "Teleport detected main deck, near the mess. I'm purging atmosphere."

"No!" Ariana gasped her lungs still weak, "That will cut off the aft of the ship from the bow. And our internal doors aren't security rated. They'll be able to bypass in seconds."

"Roger." Noah said without argument, "Moving to intercept. Not sure how many there are, so could use some backup."

"Squee, join him, you're closest," Ariana ordered.

"I can help as well," Javi said, surprising everyone that he was on the network.

"You're a passenger, Javi."

"My wish to become a prisoner, slave or dead is no greater than the rest of you. I owe you this much for the trouble I have brought upon this ship." Javi said. "Besides, I taught you to shoot. I can be helpful."

"I've seen the captain shoot." Noah said, "I might not want your help."

"The teacher is only as good as their student," Javi said.

Despite the tense situation, Ariana smiled at the banter. Fear would drive them to failure. They weren't a trained military crew, so they would never be able to counter fear with discipline. That meant they had to rely on something else.

Reacquiring a target with the missile launcher, Ariana said, "Show them what a Slu can do."

7- Noah

Noah knelt as close to the bulkhead as he could manage. He looked through the rifle's scope and dialed the magnification back to nothing. This wouldn't be a ranged fight.

The deck plates shuttered as Squee approached him. Glancing over at the Rokma, Noah momentarily wondered if he had brought the wrong rifle. If the boarders were Rokma, he might be in trouble.

"I stand ready to fight," Squee said with a rumble.

Noah frowned up at the big guy. He couldn't be certain their new Rokma crewmember hadn't orchestrated this whole ambush. It would be a good strategy, get a person on the inside, port some others in and take down any defense.

"I am here as well. Three individuals are approaching. Slowly. I estimate they are only one section away." Javi said as he slithered up behind them, "Where might I find a weapon?"

Noah pointed to where he had set another rifle behind the hatch, "That's an ED-13, or as I like to call him, Eddie. He's a bit of a wuss so he won't penetrate the hull when you miss."

"I appreciate your forethought." Javi said conversationally, "That one you have reserved for your self, is that the mythical G1-NA you have bragged about before? I recall how eager you have been to use it."

"Hardly. I don't have a death wish. Gina would tear this ship apart." Noah said, and then his voice got a little wistful as he continued, "This here is Sasha, an SA-S4. She was my first. We've been through a lot together. She's never let me down. And she won't blow a hole in the hull either. She's a lady."

"And a very elegant rifle she is. I am sure we will be well defended." Javi said.

Noah frowned, unsure if the Slu was mocking him. He just couldn't read their chubby, squishy faces. Most other species, even the stony faced Rokma, he could understand.

"Big guy, you stand in the center and draw their attention," Noah said.

"Will that not cause them to shoot me?" Squee asked, concern evident in his voice.

"Yes." Noah said with a shrug, "They'll probably carry something like this. Will it hurt you?"

"Yes."

"Okay, will it kill you?"

"Not right away."

"Then you'll be fine."

"They're here." Javi squeaked.

Noah quickly reacquired his target down the corridor. As he sighted in on the hatch, it flew open with a whoosh of air. Scanning fast, he couldn't immediately identify any hostiles, but he only had a limited view through the hatch.

Several tense seconds went by while nothing happened. Hushed voices drifted down the corridor. The only word he could make out was 'Rokma.' That made Noah chuckle until he realized his clever trap had failed. The pirates weren't shooting at Squee, which meant they would soon be firing at him.

"Charge!" Noah shouted.

Squee turned his head in puzzlement. Noah gestured down the corridor with one hand. Squee shook his head slowly prompting Noah's gestures to become more aggressive.

A sharp crack ended the two's standoff. Squee grunted as a rifle bolt hit his shoulder. The slug made a clinking sound as it bounced off the Rokma's skin and dropped to the deck below. The eyes of everyone in the corridor shifted between the malformed rifle slug and the Rokma.

"AAAGGHHH!!" Squee bellowed as he charged down the corridor.

A flurry of curses echoed back down the chamber. One of the pirates pulled back from the hatch frame. As soon as Noah caught sight of him, he fired. The pirate dropped to the deck with a cry of pain.

Squee moved through the hatch and cut off Noah's line of sight. More screams and rifle shots echoed down the chamber, but he could not tell what was going on. Keeping his rifle aimed down the corridor, Noah stood and raced down after the Rokma. When he got to the hatch, he dropped to a knee again and surveyed the room beyond.

Two pirates lay on the ground unconscious or dead. Squee held another one in his arms and was banging the human against the bulkhead. He slammed her back three more times before she went completely limp and dropped her weapon.

Noah stood up and started to speak, but before he did, he felt a breeze of air past his ear. A bang echoed down the corridor and then specks of something liquid landed on his cheek. He rubbed the liquid and it came away with blood. Despite feeling no pain, Noah immediately assumed he had been shot. It wouldn't have been the first time and he knew you didn't always feel the pain right away.

Checking himself revealed no bullet hole. Assured he wasn't about to die, Noah looked to his right and saw a new body. A Slu squirmed on the deck, a freshly dropped pistol lying at its feet.

"Did I get him?" Javi called down the corridor.

Noah glanced back toward the other Slu and raised an eyebrow, "You said there were three of them."

"Sorry, my people can sometimes hide from each other."

"He almost shot me."

"I said sorry."

8- Squee

Squee stared at the bloody form of the pirate he had just killed. He held her limp body against the wall; her head cocked at an unnatural angle. The blood fury still surged through him, but it had begun to subside. His mind could now objectively identify the sight before him as horrifying. Though, as of yet, he still didn't care.

The big Rokma turned toward where Javi and Noah were arguing. He reminded himself of their status as allies several times before speaking, unable to keep a hopeful tone from his voice, "Are there more?"

"No," Javi said.

"You didn't detect him," Noah said with a bitter note as he gestured to the dead Slu at his feet.

"Because of his proximity to these others. I registered several unknown lifeforms, and he was able to hide in that. But now, I only detect familiar senses aboard the ship."

"If you say so," Noah said, his voice trailing off. His mouth hanging open, he stared at Squee. Javi also turned his eyestalks toward him.

Squee again looked down at the body he still held in his hands. He could not understand what about it had drawn the others attention. The pirate was most definitely dead and therefore no threat.

He looked closer, and then he noticed the device on the pirate's belt, "Ah, I see. An excellent idea."

Squee removed the teleporter recall device from the pirate and dropped the body to the deck with a thud. He held the device up and tried to give a sinister smile to indicate his agreement with the idea, but he felt it only came off as goofy.

"Umm...right." Noah said, "Good idea. Let's board them. Their ship is about the same size as ours so they can't have a much bigger crew than we do. And we've already taken care of four of them. Probably two or three left, but let's assume four to five."

"Recall devices won't work for anyone except those they are tuned for," Javi said.

"Then how do you think Squee got aboard this ship?" Noah asked, "We don't have a military porter, and I think it's safe to assume neither do these guys. Those'll work for anybody."

Noah bent down and picked up a recall device from one of the pirates and secured it to his belt. He then went over to the dead Slu. After taking that creature's device, he handed it to Javi.

"Still ready to defend the ship?"

Javi turned his eyestalks to glance between Squee, Noah and the recall device. After a long pause, he took the device and said, "Okay."

Noah then turned to Squee, "Come on big guy."

The three of them went to the cargo bay and put on gun belts. Now they were all armed and equipped with their own recall devices, which would allow them to return to *Seraph*. Noah held up his captured device in a sign of being ready.

"Should we not inform the captain of our intentions?" Squee asked. His sense of duty had become more evident as the blood fury receded, though he kept a partial hold on it. The physical spasms and self-doubt that came after it completely faded would need to wait.

"Meh. I suppose. Wouldn't want her to jump away without us." Noah said with a reluctant shrug. He reconnected his handheld and then said, "Captain, we've subdued the boarding party. We're about to go return the favor."

Noah's face paled for a second, and his eyes glanced at the ground. Squee could not interpret the gesture, so remained patient. He considered getting his earpiece out but decided to wait. Doing so now would give the appearance of eavesdropping.

"No, I..." Noah said haltingly. Another few moments passed until the man finally looked up again, "She says it's cool. Thought it was a great idea."

"Ari reamed you for being an idiot, didn't she?" Javi asked with a chuckle.

"No. Maybe..."

No longer interested in the discussion now that the decision had been made, Squee intoned, "Together we will fight and crush them before us."

He pushed his thumb down on the pirate's recall device. *Seraph's* cargo bay vanished, replaced immediately by a similar room. Crates filled the space, scattered about in a very disorganized fashion. On the walls, two flags hung prominently.

Squee held his gun ready, keeping his blood fury tempered for the moment. Nothing moved, and no alarms sounded. Moving quickly, he stepped to the closest door and triggered the switch. The door slid open revealing a poorly lit corridor. Again, he saw no signs of movement.

A flash caught his attention, and Squee turned to see Noah and Javi teleport in behind him. They stood in the teleport chamber. Both men surveyed the room quickly before their eyes fell on the flags. They stared at them for a long moment before glancing uncomfortably at each other.

"What is it?" Squee asked, "Do you recognize those?"

"Umm..." Noah said and then gestured at one, "No, I've never seen that before."

"Yeah..." Javi said with a wave at the other, "Nope, never seen it."

"That is too bad." Squee said feeling disappointed, "It would have been good to know something about our adversary. But no matter, we will still crush them."

Behind him, he heard Noah whisper, "How literal do you think he's being when he says 'crush'?"

Squee ignored the question, as it was not directed at him, and proceeded down the corridor toward the only door. It too opened without difficulty to reveal an engineering control room. One human stood at the controls, and she glanced up when the door opened.

"We've been boarded!" The pirate yelled and reached for a pistol at her side.

Squee fired his pistol and shot her. The first blast missed, blowing out a wall screen behind her, but his second shot hit her in the chest. She dropped, her pistol still only half drawn.

"They are alerted to our presence." Squee declared. He moved to where the pirate had been working. After shoving the dead body away, he surveyed the control panel before him.

"Power down their weapons. We wouldn't want them blowing up *Seraph* while we hunt for the rest of the crew." Noah said, "Speaking of which, Javi, how many are there?"

"Two."

"Unless there are more Slu," Noah sneered.

"Unlikely. The two life forms are not close to each other and hiding our presence requires others to mask it. Unless there is a very skilled Slu, one other person should not be enough."

"I'll still assume there might be more from now on, okay?" Noah said, "Come on big guy, shut those guns down and let's go."

Squee shook his head, "I can not. Weapons can only be powered down from the weapon control room."

"I know you can't control them from here, but can't you shut the reactor down and power them off?"

"Not without physically disabling it. This ship uses an inferior inorganic computer that requires safety precaution against AI infiltration. Those limit what you can do with any given control panel."

"Right. Okay, well, shut the engines down at least. No sense in letting them try and run away."

After Squee shut down the engines, the trio dashed back down the corridor. Rounding a bend, weapon fire cascaded out to greet them. Another bullet shattered against Squee's hardened skin, and he grunted in pain.

Channeling the sharp throbbing pain from the impact, he flared his blood into another fury. The pain receded into the background so that he barely noticed the next two bullets that grazed him. His vision focused, and the pirate who had shot him became bright and clear in the dim corridor. Deep thinking became elusive, and he suddenly had an overriding need to run at his enemy.

Squee barreled into the pirate who had fired at him, an Echanic, and smashed him against the wall. The Echanic's prosthetic arm shattered from the impact and his gun fell to the ground. Entirely taken by his fury, he did not hesitate to smash the figure again, shattering his plastic chest plate.

Behind him, Noah and Javi had followed. He turned to see them exchanging weapon fire with the last pirate further down the corridor. None of them had a good line of sight to shoot the other.

Unexpectedly, the final pirate tossed out his weapon. It skittered down the narrow corridor. Outstretched hands followed, and then a shout of surrender. Squee glanced down to ensure the Echanic was genuinely dead before turning his full attention to the surrendering pirate.

"You sure there are no more?" Noah asked.

"Yes. The only life forms are us and that one." Javi said.

Noah looked unsure, but finally nodded. He stood up and aimed his weapon down the corridor at the outstretched hands. "Okay, you can come out. Don't try anything funny."

A tall human emerged and stood with his hands upraised. Squee immediately took several steps toward him. His vision started to focus on a new target, and he readied himself to charge again.

The pirate looked nervously to Squee, which made the Rokma smile. With a gulp, the pirate focused his attention on Noah and Javi. He gave them a calculating look and then smiled, "You may have taken my ship, but you'll never get away from us. More will follow me. You won't get away with what you've done."

Almost at the same instance, Javi and Noah both fired their weapons at the pirate. Both shots hit him in the chest, and he dropped to the deck. Silence soon replaced the echoes of the weapon fire.

"Why did you do that?" Noah asked looking at Javi.

"Me? Why did you?"

The two stared at each other, and then glanced back at Squee. Unable to decipher their expressions, he remained silent. With no more threats, he let the blood fury begin to subside. His mind would be cloudy for a few minutes, and then the shaking would start. Guilt would come later.

"He was a worthy adversary." Javi began, splitting his eyestalks between Noah and Squee, "He did not deserve the shame of imprisonment."

"What..." Noah started, but stopped when Javi pointedly shifted an eyestalk toward him and back to Squee.

"Umm, yeah." Noah said, "My thought too."

Squee stood taller, feeling pleased with his companions, "It is good that I have found such honorable companions. The shame of defeat should not be felt for long by a worthy opponent. It cheapens the fight. These pirates fought well. They did not deserve the humiliation of imprisonment. Most non-Rokma do not understand this."

"The captain understands this too, but is also human, so is conflicted about it." Javi said quickly, "It is best to not mention the details to her. Let us just tell her the enemy was honorably crushed."

"Right," Noah said, his eyes fixed solidly on Javi. "We humans are conflicted about shooting unarmed prisoners. It takes a very good reason to overcome that predilection. I believe the same could be said for Slu."

Javi stared back silently.

Ignoring the two, Squee declared proudly, "Then let us tell the captain of our victory. This ship is now ours by right."

9- Vlasa

Vlasa activated the magnifying scope in his eye implant as he studied the control circuit from the captured pirate ship's main cannon. He looked at each component carefully, categorizing them and building a mental circuit diagram in his head. When he was sure each part had a legitimate function, and therefore was not a dummy component containing malware or a rogue AI, he reinstalled the circuit and returned his eye to a standard focal length.

"I believe we can do it, Captain." He said, standing back up from the open service hatch.

"How long?" Ariana asked, a small glint in her eye.

"A couple of hours. Detaching the firing chamber and moving it over to *Seraph* is pretty simple. This gun is an aftermarket upgrade, so it isn't fully integrated. Moving the capacitors and internal controls will take the longest." Vlasa explained, "But if we just take the firing chamber and swap it out for our current cannon, it would be much simpler."

"Yeah, but then we'd still only have one gun." Ariana said with a dismissive wave of her hand, "We bring everything."

"We don't have the reactor capacity to charge up both of them, you know."

"Can't we strip this ship's reactor?"

"Not if we want to bring her back to the Hub to sell. She'll need her reactor intact." Vlasa said, and held up a hand to forestall the next comment. "And no, stripping it when we get there wouldn't be a good idea either. First, a jury-rigged reactor upgrade is always iffy. Second, you'd have to pay docking fees on two ships for the week or two it would take to do it. And third, do you really think anyone is going to buy a ship without a working reactor?"

Ariana frowned and her voice was defensive, "*Seraph* didn't have a working reactor when I bought her."

"That's because you're far too trusting."

"As a veteran of the AI Wars, if I were more suspicious by nature, I never would have let an Echanic near my engine room."

Vlasa shrugged, "While that would have affected me personally, it would have been a far more rational decision."

"Just move the gun." Ariana said with a sigh. "What about the shields? Any chance we can strip that down and upgrade our own?"

"Maybe. Again, we'd run into reactor capacity issues, but we can probably strip the generators. It might be a bit of a mess, but could potentially boost us to a class 2. I'd have to talk with Squee. He does seem to know his way around a shield system."

"Another hopeless alien a paranoid human never would have trusted," Ariana said with a smirk.

"I will say I told you so one day."

"Nah, when my naivety catches up with me, it will kill you too."

Vlasa cocked his head and pondered Ariana for a long moment, "I honestly have no response to that."

Ariana gave him a wink, and then left the room. Vlasa filed her response as something unique to her, rather than typical human behavior. He then left the weapon control room and went to find Squee.

As expected, he found the big Rokma in the shield control room. Maintenance hatches were open, and parts lay scattered all over the room. The disorganization brought up feelings of extreme frustration in Vlasa.

In addition to Squee, Olivia sat in one corner of the room, half watching Squee work, half staring at the floor. The complete silence out of the girl stood out as a variation in her normal behavior. But she was not interfering with his assignment, so he dismissed her from his thoughts.

"The captain would like an assessment on whether we can strip their shield system for upgrades," Vlasa said.

Squee looked up from the component he was currently tinkering with, "What does it look like I am doing?"

"Creating a pile of potentially hazardous debris."

"I am organizing the parts based on usage," Squee said.

"Your manner of organization eludes me."

"Olivia understands it. Ask her to explain it to you. I am working."

"Umm..." Olivia said casting a glance between Vlasa and Squee.

"Never mind that." Vlasa said, "Just tell me if you think we can make a compatible upgrade to our systems? Otherwise, I could use your help transferring the cannon."

"Probably."

"Good enough." Vlasa accepted, "Olivia, come with me. You can help me with the cannon."

Vlasa turned, grateful to leave the disaster of a room behind and started back toward the weapon control room. Olivia followed behind at a slow pace, still quiet. On the way, they came across Noah and Javi.

With his finger waving toward Javi's eyestalk, Noah looked visibly irritated. His voice was low and inaudible from this distance. Vlasa did not hesitate to snap, "Noah, stop that at once. Javi is our passenger. Show some respect."

Noah turned and cast a withering look toward Vlasa, "This doesn't concern you metal man."

"The well being of our passenger concerns us all. And I am neither a man nor metal. Metal accounts for only fifteen point four percent of my body by mass. The vast majority of my mass is still water, like most organic life forms."

"Whatever. But this is between Javi and me."

"Really, Vlasa, it is fine. Just a minor disagreement between Mr. Ramirez and myself. Nothing of consequence." Javi said forcing a smile on to his face.

Vlasa frowned and continued to fix his gaze on Noah. After a few defiant seconds, Noah broke eye contact. Satisfied, Vlasa said, "Very well, if this heathen has not inconvenienced you, then so be it. Come along Noah, we have work to do."

"I already have my own work. I'm not your monkey."

"You'll enjoy this work. It involves a very big gun." Vlasa said, lacing his words with as much derision as he could muster.

"Oh. Well then. Lead on." Noah said with a flippant wave of his hand down the corridor.

The trio continued down the narrow corridor leaving Javi behind. Vlasa felt grateful for the silence as they walked. It always boosted his mood to put Noah in his place.

When they reached the weapon control room, Vlasa gave instructions to the other two on what components to remove. He made sure to review all of the necessary safety precautions at least twice.

Once they got to work, he managed to filter the other two out of his mind for almost a full ten minutes before Noah began speaking.

"What's with you, kid?"

"Me?" Olivia asked.

"Yeah. You've been quiet this whole time. I know servo slave master is a bit of a bore, but that's never stopped you before."

"I just don't have anything to say."

"That would be a first."

"Oh shut up, Noah!" Olivia snapped, aggressively slamming the component she was holding down.

"Now I know something's bothering you."

"Yes, you! Vlasa, make him shut up."

Unable to ignore the bickering any more, Vlasa sighed, "Noah, your lack of interpersonal skills is showing. I too have concluded that Olivia has been affected by something that has altered her normal personality. Given her general lack of communication, there is a near 100% chance that this matter is not something she wishes to discuss. I, therefore, see no reason to interfere with something that has the potential to increase her work efficiency."

A small sob came from Olivia, but she tightened her jaw as she blinked back tears in her eyes.

"That's cold. Even for you." Noah said, shaking his head. He glanced toward Olivia, "You can tell us when you're ready to talk. Some of us are willing to listen."

After a moment of silence, they each turned back toward their work.

10- Ariana

Ariana walked into the crew mess, and immediately forced back a sigh. After a hard day of working on their captured pirate ship, she had been looking forward to a nice meal. Unfortunately, she had forgotten that it was Noah's turn to cook.

The rest of the crew sat around the mess table quietly. Olivia watched something on her handheld while Squee appeared to be either sleeping or meditating. Vlasa fiddled with a power cell. The Echanic had cords from the cell connected to several of his cybernetic components.

Javi looked quite pleased to see her, "Ah, Ari, come sit down. Vlasa just told me the good news."

"Good news?" Ariana asked as she took her place at the table.

"Yes, that the repairs and integration of the new components are complete."

"Ah, yes. I admit I won't mind never seeing this system again." Ariana said remembering her encounter with the spiders and involuntarily shuddering.

"Indeed. I am quite eager to get underway to my destination."

"Umm...about that. We're going to have to take a little detour."

Javi fixed one of his eyestalks on her in a look that she knew very well. Despite all the years, it still made her squirm in her seat. It had been almost twenty years since he had been her instructor, but some things never changed.

He remained silent, his eye fixed on her, waiting for her to continue, "With this salvaged ship, we're going to have to head back to the Hub. It's the closest port. I don't want to divide the crew between two ships for longer than necessary."

"That goes completely in the wrong direction. I hired you to take me away from the Hub."

"And I did that." Ariana said hopefully, "And I'll even do it again for no extra charge."

"What's that?" Noah said as he came into the mess from the kitchen, "We're going back to the Hub?"

Noah was carrying a large sizzling pan with steam wafting up from it. He set the pan in the center of the table, and then picked up a serving spoon. In turn, starting with Ariana, he scooped out a generous helping of something that vaguely resembled green noodles. Little bits of other colors were mixed in among the stringy substance.

"Well, at least it smells good this time." Ariana said as she poked the thing on her plate, "These aren't actually noodles are they?"

"Nope." Noah said with a proud smile. "Zucchini. With peppers, garlic, onion, and some radishes. All sautéed in a little olive oil and seasoned with a few spices."

"It sounds delicious," Javi said with his usual sincerity.

"It sounds like it's missing all of the food." Ariana grumbled, "Couldn't you have included some chicken at least?"

Noah shook his head, "I don't understand how you can advocate eating animals."

"But it's not animals. Everything is built one molecule at a time. It's packaged proteins and carbohydrates reorganized."

"Yeah, but why reorganize it into the flesh of an animal?"

"You'll kill a sentient person without a moment's hesitation, but you won't even eat food that is built to resemble an animal?"

Noah shrugged, "I'm a man of many layers."

"I must agree with the captain." Vlasa said, "This meal is lacking many required nutrients, most notably the aforementioned proteins."

"Bah," Noah said with a dismissive wave. "You'd be happy eating the slurry straight out of the storage packs."

The conversation died down for a few moments as everyone started eating. Squee made many satisfied noises as he rapidly downed several portions. Despite her complaints, Ariana had to admit, to herself at least, that the food did taste pretty good. But that traitorous thought could probably be blamed on how hungry working all day had made her.

After several minutes of peaceful eating, Javi said, "Now, about our earlier discussion?"

"I'm sorry, Javi, but it's just not a good idea to continue to Triask with the crew split between two ships. We need to head back to the Hub, sell our salvage, and then we can move on to Triask." Ariana said, trying to sound decisive.

"You ran *Seraph* with just yourself, Vlasa and a pilot before."

"M wiff Ha, Cap," Noah said, his mouth full of food.

Ariana raised an eyebrow and stared pointedly at Noah. He looked confused for a second, staring back at her with his mouth hanging open. After a second, he finished chewing and then said, "I'm with Javi, Cap. Heading back to the Hub with that thing in tow ain't a good idea. Might make us look like pirates."

"We'll have our sensor logs if there are any questions. Hub security doesn't ask too many questions."

"They did arrest our former pilot for smuggling," Vlasa said.

"Exactly, he wasn't paying the customs duties which is what keeps the station running. We'll give them their cut. Besides, that was some pretty nasty drugs. This is a legitimately salvaged ship."

"Why don't we just leave the ship here?" Javi asked.

"This is potentially our biggest booty ever. A mostly intact ship, ours by right of salvage. Perfectly legal."

"Technically, since we killed the crew, it is not salvaged." Vlasa interjected.

"Legalish then." Ariana said with a wave of her hand. "It will keep us flying for years. I can even refund you your fair. I know getting there is important and we will have you there before the Memorial Day events. I promise. We're looking at a delay of two, three days tops."

"Yeah, leaving the ship is not an option." Noah agreed, "But we should take it somewhere else. Like Worcee."

"Worcee? That's nowhere near Triask." Javi said disgustedly.

"It's on the way," Noah said.

"No, it's not," Olivia said, speaking for the first time while she stood up. She wobbled on her feet for a moment before starting toward the door, "I'll go get started on plobbing...er...plotting a course back to the Hub."

Ariana nodded approvingly, "See, Olivia knows how things are supposed to work. The captain makes a decision, crew listens."

"I'm not part of your crew, Ari." Javi pointed out.

"I know. And I will get you to Triask as soon as I can. I promise."

A sudden wretching sound from the doorway made everyone turn around. Olivia knelt on the deck all of her recently consumed dinner in a puddle at her feet. She continued to convulse as more came out. When she finished, she fell back onto her rear and collapsed against the bulkhead, her eyes closed and groaning.

"Olivia, are you all right?" Ariana asked as she knelt before the girl.

"Hmmm?" Olivia mumbled, "I'm gewed, er, good. I just need to close my eyes for a moment."

She immediately followed this announcement by leaning over and vomiting onto Ariana's shoes. Ariana sighed.

Behind her, Noah whistled, "Wow, that girl really can't hold her liquor."

Slowly, Ariana turned to face the table behind her, "Liquor?"

"Yeah, she asked for something before dinner. Sounded like a good idea, so we shared a couple of shots."

"She's sixteen."

"So? I was fourteen when I started drinking."

"That certainly explains many things," Vlasa said.

Ariana sighed again, "I'm going to put her to bed. Noah, your booze, your mess."

"That's not fair," Noah grumbled.

Lifting up Olivia, who offered little resistance, Ariana said, "Fair would have been her throwing up on your shoes."

11- Vlasa

"**A** *re you ready, Vlasa?*"

"FTL coordinates are locked in, Captain." Vlasa answered over the communications channel, "I stand ready to jump."

"Jump on my signal." Ariana replied, *"Three, two, one, jump."*

Vlasa triggered the FTL controls on the captured pirate ship. For a moment, that both lasted an eternity and ended instantly, he felt disembodied. He existed in two places at once, and all the places in between. For some, this sensation was nauseating. For Vlasa, it brought feelings of perfect serenity.

Once the FTL jump completed, he immediately verified the ship's coordinates with astrometric measurements. Even though he had verified the calculations himself and Ariana had done them initially herself by hand, you could never be certain about a jump until you checked. Far too many ships had been thrown off course by malicious AI code hiding in their computers. Simple verification could go a long way.

Astrometric calculations identified several notable stellar phenomena and confirmed he had jumped to his intended destination. Ship sensors had also identified *Seraph* floating out in space at almost the same relative distance she had been before the jump.

"I am impressed, Captain. For all your talk about your lack of piloting skills, you have positioned both ships to within twenty kilometers of our previous formation."

"Calculating FTL coordinates is just math, Vlasa. You remember what happened when I tried to dock last time?" Ariana answered.

"I rescind my previous compliment."

"No take backs."

An alert signal sounded from somewhere in the room. Vlasa looked around curiously, unable to spot any warning signals from the ship's systems. After a moment, he found the source; a handheld lay wedged into one of the storage drawers.

"Captain, I am receiving a handheld call."

"What? Everyone but Olivia's on the same call already." Ariana asked in confusion.

"Not to my personal device. One of the pirate's handhelds is receiving a call."

"That's not good." Noah said, *"Aren't we in another middle of nowhere system?"*

"Yes." Ariana said simply, *"I'm now picking up several ships on the long-range sensors. They are moving toward us."*

"It will be several minutes before the FTL has recharged." Vlasa said, "Should I answer the call?"

There was a long pause before Ariana said, *"There was an Echanic on their crew right?"*

"Yeah," Noah said.

"Go ahead, Vlasa. Pretend to be him."

"I have no idea of this pirate's name or the sound of his voice."

"Not to be racist, but you all sound pretty much the same with that robot voice box," Noah said.

Vlasa sat up straight and prepared to retort, but Ariana cut him off, *"It's rude, but at least to human ears, it's true."*

"And Slu if we're honest," Javi said.

"I must agree as well." Squee rumbled.

Vlasa sighed, "Oh, very well."

He picked up the handheld and pressed the accept call button still flashing, "Hello?"

"It's Mitchell. Where's Morris?" A strange voice said in reply.

"Killed," Vlasa answered truthfully.

"I told him not to underestimate Ariana Harkins. Did you manage to get the Slu?"

"Yes."

"Dead or alive?"

"Um, alive."

"Nice work. And it looks like you were able to capture the ship intact too. Always need more ships. Come in for docking, and we'll take care of that piece of filth."

The call ended, and Vlasa put the handheld back down. He checked the sensor readings and identified which approaching ship the transmission had come from. The vessel was much larger than either *Seraph* or his present ship. Most of the escorts were smaller and in the same size class as his or smaller.

"So, what happened?" Ariana said her tone frustrated.

"They believed me to be a member of this ship's crew."

"And?"

"I believe this ship was sent to apprehend or kill Javi."

"Javi? Why?"

"They did not specify. And one more thing captain, the individual I spoke to mentioned you by name. He appears to have some respect for you."

"Javi, who are these people?"

An uncomfortable silence followed. Eventually, Javi spoke, his voice quiet, *"Now is not the time to explain that. But I can assure you we do not want to be anywhere near them. We must depart immediately."*

"I concur, Captain." Vlasa said, "They clearly wish to do us harm. I am not sure how long our ruse will hold up as we have been instructed to come in for docking. We will be in range of their weapons for several minutes before the FTL has recharged."

"All right. But later, Javi, we're having a conversation" Ariana said, *"Noah, go get Olivia out of bed. Vlasa, port back here and start calculating a new FTL course. I'll take your place over there."*

"What do you intend to do, Captain?" Vlasa asked concerned.

"They wanted to dock. I'll dock with them."

12- Olivia

"Go away." Olivia groaned.

"Captain says to get up," Noah said continuing to shake her shoulder.

Olivia tried to ignore the big man. She squeezed her eyes shut to avoid the searing bright light and tried desperately to return to the sweet embrace of sleep. Despite Noah shaking her, it almost came.

"All right, guess I need to pull out the big guns. I didn't want to do this kid, but you leave me no choice."

The sudden shock of cold water pouring over her head sent Olivia bolting out of her bed. The icy water ran down the length of her body soaking her clothes. As she stood there, water dripping from her hair, she stared in shock at Noah.

"What the hell?!"

"I warned you." Noah said with a shrug, "Let's go. The captain needs you at the helm."

Pulling her arms around her as she started shivering, Olivia shook her head adamantly, "I can't go. I'm drunk."

Noah made a dismissive sound with his mouth and waved his hand, "No you're not. You've been asleep for hours."

"But I feel terrible."

"That's called a hangover. Should have drunk some water. I told you that too."

Noah walked through the door leading out of Olivia's room, and then stopped when she still didn't follow him. He stared intently at her. Olivia glanced at him and the floor.

"Am I going to have to carry you? Because I will."

"You shouldn't. It wouldn't be safe to let me fly the ship. And I don't mean because of the hangover."

"What are you talking about?"

A long moment passed. Olivia stared at the floor. Finally, she quietly said, "I almost got us all killed when we fought those pirates."

"Bullshit. I saw that move you pulled and avoided three well-aimed shots. Saved us from being carved to pieces."

"Luck. But then I ran us right into a missile. It almost killed the captain."

"It happens." Noah said with a shrug, "But if you don't get up to the helm, you're going to get us all killed for sure. More pirates, or something, want another go."

"What?"

Noah visibly cringed, "And there it is."

"There what is?"

"That shrill teenage girl voice. Sometimes it's easy to forget how old you are. But that sound reminded me you're just a kid. So, thanks for that. I guess. Let's stop dillydallying and go not die. Okay?"

Unsure what to think of the last few minutes, Olivia followed behind Noah. Water still dripped from her hair, and she continued to shiver. Her clothes were clinging to her she realized, and were quite sheer from being wet. Defiantly she stuck out her chest in a bid to make Noah uncomfortable.

He left her at the helm in the control room, staring a little too long before rolling his eyes when he turned away. She smiled at the small victory. The fleeting feeling lasted only a second as she found herself alone at the helm.

Reluctantly, Olivia took the controls, put in her earpiece and linked her handheld. "Helm, here."

"Finally." Ariana said, *"Match my course. And get started on an FTL jump. Anywhere but back the way we came or to the Hub."*

"Why not back to the Hub?" Vlasa asked.

"These guys knew Javi was aboard, so they obviously have some contacts on the Hub. And with a fleet this size, they could threaten the station. We wouldn't be safe there and neither would anyone else."

Olivia searched the sensor display and quickly located the mass of ships they were approaching. Unexpectedly, their captured pirate ship engaged its engines and started toward the mass of ships.

"Olivia, keep up. We need to stay in formation." Ariana's voice startled her.

Engaging the engines, she asked, "Captain, what are you doing on the other ship?"

"Returning it. Now get started on those calculations. You have less than three minutes."

Olivia blinked, still confused. But the tone of the captain's voice brokered no argument, and she hastily pulled down the navigation charts. Quickly she picked a nearby star system and started calculating the jump. The pressure to work quickly helped focus her, and for a few moments, her headache receded to a mere background throb.

While she worked, she half listened to the others.

"Squee, are those shield upgrades up and running?" Ariana asked.

"They are, Captain. I must inform you that to power them up will mean shutting down other systems."

"Vlasa shut down the weapons. We aren't getting out of this one by fighting."

"All ready done. But we will still need more. I assume you do not want me to shut down the teleporter?"

"Not really. Shut down environmental systems. Might get a little uncomfortable, but no one will suffocate for a few hours."

The gentle hum of the circulation fans stopped, and the lights dimmed to darkness. Olivia cursed to herself as the dim glow from the helm control panels were not bright enough to allow her to see her charts. Pulling her handheld out, she activated a flashlight and held it under her chin.

Finally, she entered the coordinates into the navigational computer and confirmed them against the computers own calculations. Done, she glanced at the sensor display and felt another shiver. They had moved very close to the fleet of ships.

"FTL calculations done, Captain." Olivia reported.

"Good. Vlasa, time to jump?"

"Two minutes."

"Olivia, get ready to go evasive. Things are about to get interesting."

Nervously, Olivia shifted her seat and set her hands on the controls. Her mind kept flashing back to that missile. The horrible vibration as it impacted, and the tense moments of silence when no one could reach the captain.

They continued to approach the massive ship. The big ship rotated to its port side revealing a pair of docking ports. Olivia followed the captain's changes in speed, giving every indication that they were preparing to dock.

"Olivia, now!" Ariana ordered, her voice firm but not harsh in her ear.

Olivia fired *Seraph*'s dorsal thrusters and engaged the sublight engines at maximum thrust. They dived under the big ship just as the captain's captured ship also accelerated. It slammed into the larger ship sending bits of shrapnel twirling through space in all directions.

"Captain's aboard." Noah declared.

Noah's announcement triggered a warning to Olivia. She suddenly juked the ship sideways and fired the ventral thrusters. She continued to shift the ship's course randomly and rapidly. The more unpredictable she made her maneuvers, the harder it would be for anyone to board them via teleporter.

Warnings flashed on the display as the sensors identified incoming weapon fire. The first few shots missed by a wide margin thanks to Olivia's rapid maneuvers. Her warning display soon started to become indecipherable as more ships fired at them, creating a rain of energy bolts in space.

Several slight vibrations were the first indication that some of the bolts had found their target. The newly enhanced shields had absorbed the impact, but now registered as depleted. Desperately, Olivia redoubled her maneuvers, this time firing the main engines on a reverse course. For a moment they hung at a relative stop in space before accelerating back toward the fleet attacking them.

Her maneuver bought them a few seconds of calm, and by the time the enemy gunners had realigned their firing vectors, Squee had restored the shields. Studying the layout of the fleet around them, Olivia tried to identify which ships were firing on them. One of the closest one caught her attention.

For a moment, she froze. The sensor profile for the ship sent a chill down her spine. It almost looked to be an AI warship. Shaking her head, she repeated to herself, "No, no, no, no, no."

Several more blasts dissipated against the shields drawing her attention away from the ship. More followed these first few and these made it past their ships shields, impacting on the vulnerable hull. Olivia's starboard side sensor display cut out as the external sensor cluster was either cut off or destroyed.

Blind to her starboard side Olivia started shifting mostly to port before realizing how predictable that would make her. Instead, she started to roll the ship using the port sensors to give her a partial picture of everywhere. More blasts impacted the hull through the shields.

"Fire in environmental control room." Vlasa announced.

Beginning to lose the battle to stay unpredictable, Olivia started to feel the sense of panic returning. She unleashed a defiant scream at the feeling in a final desperate bid to stave it off. As she screamed, the world outside suddenly vanished, replaced by the unknowable weirdness of an FTL jump.

Seconds later reality returned to normal. Alarms still blared all over the ship. On instinct, Olivia continued maneuvering the ship randomly for several seconds before her mind registered that they were no longer under attack.

Slowly, she pulled her hands away from the controls. Sweat drenched her, and her hands immediately begin to shake. A sudden wave of exhaustion hit her as the adrenaline spike ramped down. It was only the steady stream of voices in her ear that kept her from immediately starting to doze.

"*Nice flying, Olivia.*" Ariana's calm voice said, lifting her spirits. "*Noah, get to environmental controls and vent the room before that fire does what Olivia kept that fleet from doing.*"

"*On it,*" Noah answered.

"*Vlasa, damage report?*"

"*Starboard sensor cluster is nonresponsive. I will need to get a closer look to see how severe that damage is. A few minor outer hull breaches but not in any vital areas.*"

"*Okay, that's noncritical at the moment. Meet Noah at environmental and make sure we'll still have breathable air. Olivia, give the ship some roll so we can keep an eye on our blind side.*"

Olivia acknowledged and then set the ship on a gentle roll. She let her eyes slide closed even though she knew she should probably get started on plotting another FTL jump. But that could wait for at least a few minutes. The AI ship she had seen must have just been a figment of her hangover. It hadn't been real. As the adrenaline started to leave her, the headache began to return, putting everything else out of her mind.

"Umm..." Noah said, *"The manual purge controls aren't responding. I can't vent the fire."*

"You will need to...." Vlasa begun but Squee cut him off

"Shields down, Captain. I have power, but systems are overloaded and will not respond. It is as if we have been hit by an ion weapon."

"Olivia, increase rotation." Ariana ordered.

Olivia responded immediately, and began surveying the sensor data as it came in. No contacts appeared. At the rate she had *Seraph* rotating it would be nearly impossible for a ship to remain in their blind spot at any safe distance.

"I don't see anything out there." Ariana said in agreement, *"Oh, no. Olivia, where are we?"*

"PSR J0108."

"That's a pulsar. If we don't get the shields back up soon, we're going to all get fried by the radiation."

13- Ariana

Ariana ran down the corridor. This had not been one of her better weeks. But she really hoped it wouldn't be her last.

"Vlasa, get back to the engine room. Do whatever you can to speed up the FTL charge. Olivia, calculate us a course out of here. Squee, get those shields back up. Noah, I'm coming to you." She said.

"Where do you want me to go?" Olivia asked her voice trembling in Ariana's ear, *"I thought any system in the charts was safe."*

"Well, we're not dead yet, so it's kind of safe." Ariana answered as she ran, "Pulsars emit radiation bursts in a regular pattern that's under a second. So does this one. But, it also has a planetoid that blocks most of the radiation. Unfortunately, there is a bit of a wobble, and sometimes you get a pulse through. Knocks out our shields like an ion discharge. And then when it wobbles again, we all get fried."

"So why is it on the charts?" Olivia demanded.

"It shouldn't be." Vlasa answered, *"A certain type of transport captain will use it to save on transit time as it's very conveniently located."*

"Any other systems that will kill us I should avoid?"

"Not nearby." Ariana answered, *"Take us anywhere but back to that fleet. This one is on me."*

Ariana turned a corner and came into sight of Noah standing before a closed hatch. He had a panel on the wall off and determinedly staring at it. When she stopped beside him, he looked up gratefully.

"Yeah, so I don't know what I'm doing."

Despite everything, his sincerity made her chuckle. She leaned in and pulled a few of the levers. "You were right, the manual vent controls are offline. On the plus side, with the environmental systems shut down, the fire will eventually burn itself out when it runs out of oxygen, whether we vent the room or not."

"Yeah, but wouldn't that mean we'll run out of oxygen?"

"Oh, I'd be more concerned with CO2 poisoning."

"Lovely." Noah grumbled, "So, how do we fix this?"

"We need to get to the control lines on the other side of the door. Which means we're then facing death from either fire or suffocation after we purge the room of air." Ariana said as she continued to make futile attempts to bypass the damaged control line.

"So, my options for death today are air poisoning, suffocation, fire or radiation?"

"I try to ensure you have plenty of choices. You sent death by explosion back."

Giving up, Ariana pulled her hands out of the panel. She shook her head and pointed to a storage box on the opposite wall, "Get the fire suppression gear. We're going to have to go in there."

"We?"

"I can't do it alone. Someone will have to fight back the fire while I try and trigger the release."

"I think I'm going to have to renegotiate my contract."

"Sure, let's stay alive long enough to have that conversation."

Moving quickly, the pair of them pulled the fire resistant garments out of the emergency locker. Each included a small air tank and fire extinguisher. Ariana also pulled out a toolkit. When they were sealed up, they turned back to the hatch.

"Seal the hatch. I'm going to start pumping air out of the corridor so we don't get a backdraft when we open the door."

Ariana sealed the opposite pressure hatch from Noah and then triggered the vent for the corridor. At least now, if they failed to get the fire under control, it would have no place to go. The sound started receding outside of her fire suit.

Over her ear comm, Squee said, *"I have restored one level of shielding. It will not be enough to deflect the full ionization pulse, but radiation damage to us should be minimal. But I fear other systems may be impacted by an ion like effect."*

"Understood." Ariana replied, "Time to jump?"

"Three minutes," Vlasa answered.

To herself, Ariana hoped that would be enough time, but decided to keep her concern to herself. "Okay, Noah, let's go."

Positioning themselves beside the door to environmental controls, Ariana held up three fingers and started counting down. As she dropped the last finger, she pulled the door release. A sudden rush of superheated wind blew out from the new opening as the air rushed to equalize pressure with the almost vacuum of the corridor.

Once the initial wave passed, Ariana stepped into the room and surveyed the situation. A large fire flared from one of the CO_2 scrubbers. She tapped Noah on the shoulder and pointed to the exhaust air line leading off the device.

"Close that off before you try and put out the fire. It's being fed by the O_2 emitted by the scrubber."

Noah nodded and shambled over to the valve controls. Trusting him to fight it as best he could, Ariana turned to the ventilation controls in the room. Despite the fire suit, she could still sense the heat as she pried the metal plate off the wall.

In the flickering light of the flames, Ariana strained to see the proper control lines she needed to find. She forced her right hand as far into the panel as it would fit. Her thick glove made everything more difficult to manipulate.

With her hand shoved in the panel, she could more acutely feel the heat from the surrounding metal. The glove became uncomfortably hot. Ariana grunted as she wiggled her fingers through the pain, just managing to grab hold of the control wires. When she pulled her hand holding the wires out from inside the panel, a warning sound went off in her suit, and she heard the sound of rushing air.

Quickly, Ariana grabbed the control wires with her left hand and held up her right. A steady stream of air jetted out into the low-pressure environment. As the oxygen hit a patch of superheated insulation nearby, it suddenly combusted, sending a belch of flame rolling back to her hand.

The fire devoured the oxygen from the tear in her suit creating a miniature jet of flame on her glove. With a sharp curse, Ariana dropped the control wires from her left hand and smothered the flame before it could set fire to her suit or injure her hand. With the pressure from her left hand the leak stopped, and the flame went out.

Ariana let out a relieved breath, and then noticed that the hard-fought control wires had snapped back into the wall panel.

"We have been hit by another ion pulse. Shields are down." Squee reported.

"FTL has been disabled by the ion pulse as well. Attempting to bypass." Vlasa said.

"When it rains…" Ariana mumbled to herself. Not wanting to risk waiting while she patched her glove, she shoved her right hand under her armpit and stuck her left into the panel.

The control wires had not retreated all the way back into the panel, and they proved easier to grasp this time. Being careful, she pulled her hand out more slowly so as not to rip her other glove. She pulled her right hand out from under her arm, and the newly released jet of oxygen immediately flared the nearby smoldering insulation.

Just as the flames started to flare back toward her, white foam smothered them and covered her hand. Ariana turned to find Noah waving the nozzle of the fire hose over her entire area. He gave her an exaggerated nod with his helmeted head and turned the hose back to the larger fire.

Hurriedly, Ariana stripped the wires from their control box and re-arranged the connection. A wind immediately jolted her as the release vents opened and the rooms remaining air supply got sucked out into the vacuum of space. The remaining flames that Noah had not managed to put out quickly, extinguished themselves without a fuel source.

The leak from her hand accelerated as the pressure outside the suit dropped. Clumsily Ariana took out an emergency kit from her belt and sprayed the quick sealing foam onto the tear. The alarm in her suit stopped as the pressure stabilized.

"How long until we can repressurize?" Noah asked.

Ariana surveyed the room. One of the environmental processors looked charred and black. Several other small patches of soot scarred the room. But despite the intense heat, she had been feeling from the fire the room looked surprisingly intact.

"I'll pump in some nitrogen in a minute. That will help the heat dissipate. But we'll wait on the O2 until everything has cooled off. Assuming any of this still works."

Noah started to gyrate his hips, "Well, you know what you get when you assume. You, me some nice as..."

The rest of his innuendo cut off as the room suddenly twisted and stretched with the familiar sensation of an FTL jump. Ariana stood motionless as the nature of reality shifted around her. Apparently, unable to cope with the unexpected change, Noah wobbled in mid gyration. When physics reasserted their dominion, he collapsed to the deck.

"Ass to floor action?" Ariana said with a smirk before extending her hand to Noah.

Noah grabbed her hand and hauled himself up, "Whatever works for you, Cap."

Into the comm network she said, "Nice work, Vlasa. That jump was well timed. Olivia, what's our status?"

Area around us looks clear. I've completed a roll, and no ships detected. Just a regular old star emitting the normal amount of lethal radiation.

"Good. Go ahead and plot another jump just to be safe, in case we need to get out of here fast. That seems to becoming the new normal."

"To where?"

"Right now, just away. But once we've repaired the environmental system, I'm going to have a nice long chat with Javi and figure out an answer to that." Ariana said, "Okay, Vlasa, I'm going to start repressurizing. Get down here so we can access the damage."

Ariana went over to one of the undamaged control stations and opened the valves on the nitrogen tanks. By the time she could sense an element of air pressure around her, she had still not gotten a response from Vlasa.

"Vlasa, respond please."

Silence was her only answer.

14- Javi

Unburdened by other duties, Javi was the first to reach the engine room. It took him a moment to find Vlasa, and when he did, he immediately slid to a stop. Crammed into a tight corner between a wall panel and the main control terminal, Vlasa sat slumped. Wires ran from the wall panel into his left cybernetic arm. Another heavy wire ran from his chest plate to the control terminal.

Recovering himself, Javi wiggled over and lifted the Echanic's slumped head. It responded without resistance. Vlasa's cybernetic eye looked unpowered and dead while his real eye looked glassy and unfocused. Leaning in close, Javi listened for breath sounds.

"I've found him." Javi said trying to keep his calm, "But he does not appear to be breathing."

"He should have a diagnostic report screen on his chest implant. That monitors his health and his cybernetics." Ariana responded, her voice reassuringly calm.

Javi unzipped Vlasa's jumpsuit and searched the chest plate, "I've found what looks like a screen, but it is unpowered."

"That shouldn't happen."

"It appears he plugged himself into the ship. I can only guess his cybernetics were shorted out either from the ion pulse or a power surge from the ship."

"You need to reboot his cybernetics."

"Ari, I am neither a doctor nor an engineer. I have no idea how to do that."

"Right now, you're the only thing we've got. It will be at least two minutes before Noah, and I can get into the rest of the ship. And with our section still depressurized, Squee and Olivia can't get to you either."

"Okay. What do I do?" Javi said, feeling his hands already beginning to shake.

"Look for a port and plug him into a power terminal. That should give his implants some power so you can reboot them."

"Should?"

"I'm not a doctor or mechanic either. Just going from what he's told me about his implants."

"Okay."

Javi scrambled around the room looking for an appropriate cord and port. He quickly found a power port on the wall, but couldn't locate a cord. After a feeling of despair started to grip him, he suddenly remembered the wires running from Vlasa into the wall and control terminal.

Examining them, he found that they ran into a port on Vlasa's cybernetics. He followed the cord into the wall and found the other end. As he removed it, he groaned in frustration. That end had been stripped of its plug and twisted together with other wires in the wall. A slight tug pulled the jumble apart.

Quickly Javi examined the cord coming out Vlasa's other side. It too had been stripped of its plug. He sat there holding two halves of a whole cord. He glanced between Vlasa and the cords and lowered his eyestalks in determination.

"This may make things worse, but I don't know what else to do. I'm sorry in advance." Javi said.

Hastily, he replugged one end with a port into Vlasa's chest piece. Then he plugged the other cords end plug into the wall power port. Taking the two frayed ends, Javi brought them together and twisted the exposed wires. An electric tingle surged through his hands, and he immediately dropped the wire.

The two ends separated when they hit the deck. With a groan of frustration, Javi bent down and twisted them together again, doing his best to keep them from making contact with the deck itself when his fingers again jerked and dropped them. This time the wires remained connected on the floor.

Satisfied the ends would remain together, Javi looked back up toward Vlasa's chest piece. A dull glow emanated from the small screen, and he let out a triumphant hoot. He bent closer to read the time display.

Surprisingly, he couldn't read the language. His triumph hoot turned into an anguished roar, "Why isn't this thing in universal?! Everything's in code."

"Hopefully that's just the boot menu." Ariana replied, *"When he showed me the screen, it was in universal."*

"You must look for a squiggly shape that has a slash through it at forty-five degrees and two backward 'H's next to it," Squee said.

"How can an 'H' be backward?"

"The small one."

"Right," Javi said scanning the display. "Okay, I think I found it. Now what?"

"That is the word 'restart' written in code. Select that option."

Javi pressed a finger to the display where he hoped was the appropriate button. Nothing happened for a second, and he started looking over the screen for an alternative icon. Before he found anything, the screen changed and gave him a welcome screen in universal. The chest piece emitted a buzzing noise, and suddenly Vlasa breathed a desperate gulp of air.

Letting out his breath, Javi slumped as the tension of the last few minute eased. Vlasa did not wake up, but continued to breathe rhythmically. The diagnostic screen finished loading and now displayed a harsh warning message.

"He's breathing again. But the diagnostic screen says it's in emergency support mode. It says to seek medical care immediately. Minimal brain functions detected. Cybernetics are providing life support, but most show as offline."

A long silence answered him before Ariana said, *"He's breathing and alive. That's a victory for the moment. Keep watch over him. Air pressure has been restored enough for me to get the doors open. Everyone, meet me in the engine room."*

15- Olivia

O livia stepped through the door into the engine room and stopped. The sight of Vlasa wedged into a corner with wires running out of his body unnerved her. She had known what to expect, but seeing it was different when she had to face it in person.

The rest of the crew had already arrived, and while she stood there, Ariana said, "Good, Olivia, help Squee and Noah take Vlasa to sickbay."

The big Rokma bend down and effortlessly lifted Vlasa off the floor. Noah took hold of his legs and the pair started for the door. Almost too late, Olivia realized she needed to get ahead of them and dashed back out of the room. She led the short distance to the ships small sickbay, opening the door for them and clearing off the lone bed.

Squee and Noah hefted Vlasa up and onto the bed. Olivia disconnected the frayed power cable and took a different one from a piece of medical equipment. She plugged Vlasa's chest piece into a power port and then the three of them stood helplessly at the unconscious Echanic.

"Is it always like this?" Squee asked into the silence.

"This is my first trip." Olivia said and turned to look at Noah.

The older man shook his head, "We've dodged a few pirates before. But by dodge I mean changed course. No one's ever tried to kill us before."

"So, who are these people? And what do they want with Javi?" Olivia asked.

"That is a very good question. I say we go find out." Noah said.

"The captain is questioning Javi now. She will reveal to us what we need to know." Squee said, though he glanced eagerly at the door.

"I'm not so sure about that." Noah said, "Javi is some kind of big honcho for some political group. LDF or something. Captain seemed rather reluctant to talk about why Javi was so keen to get to Triask. I think she knows more than she's telling us already."

"LDF? Do you mean LFD? Live Free or Die?" Olivia asked.

Noah snapped his fingers, "That's the one."

"I know a couple kids who signed up with them to go and do something. They weren't exactly forthcoming with details. It was work though, so some people took it."

"I think they are the people who are after Javi." Noah said and gestured to Squee. "Remember that flag Javi claimed to not recognize? I confronted him about it, but he buttoned up real tight. So I did a little snooping. Found something similar in his room."

"You broke into Javi's room?" Olivia gasped.

"Wasn't the first time. Did a security sweep when he came on board." Noah gave a shrug, "Can't be too careful."

"Did you break into my room too?"

"Nah. You're just a kid. Besides, you didn't really bring much with you."

Olivia frowned, not sure if she should be relieved or insulted. True, she didn't own much beside a few changes of clothes and some flight manuals. But being a kid didn't make her less of a threat.

"Well, I want to find out what's going on." Noah said and left sickbay. Olivia exchanged a glance with Squee. The big Rokma shrugged and then they both followed Noah back to engineering.

They found Ariana and Javi still in the engine room in the midst of an intense conversation. When Noah entered, they grew quiet and backed away from each other. Ariana did not look happy.

"How's Vlasa?" Javi asked.

"Who knows," Noah said. "I'm not a doctor."

"Well, we're going to get him one." Ariana said, "But we can't go back to the Hub. Olivia, we're going to need to plot a rather convoluted course to avoid New Echera, Hera and Proxima."

"We wouldn't happen to be trying to avoid Javi's LFD buddies, now would we?" Noah asked.

"Actually, we are."

"Captain, what's going on?" Olivia asked desperately, "We've been attacked twice in as many days. Now we're avoiding major transit systems?"

Ariana cast a pointed look at Javi, "Are you going to tell them, or am I?"

Javi let out a heavy sigh, "I did not think my presence would put all of you in danger. Like many things in my life, I miscalculated the risks."

No one said anything, but looked pointedly at the Slu. Javi dipped his eyestalks low and continued, "I was one of the founding members of Live Free or Die. Until recently, we were devoted to opposing the PUG's control of the galaxy. Peacefully. But the organization has gone through some...changes. I left over some philosophical differences."

"And now they want to kill you? Over a philosophical difference?" Noah asked.

"Not exactly. I stole something."

"You stole something? What the hell could you have possibly stolen that would make anyone send a fleet after you?"

"Attack plans. Next month, during the Memorial Festival, they intend to attack PUG headquarters and eliminate central authority from the galaxy."

"Seriously?" Olivia asked.

"That's pretty hardcore. Stupid, but hardcore." Noah said nodding, "That was not a small size fleet, but they'll never be able to oppose the PUG fleet with it. They'll get wiped out."

"That's the other thing I stole." Javi said, "They have also developed a secret weapon. They have constructed a new, central AI. With it they'll be able to control all of the drone ships that vanished at the end of the war."

Olivia felt herself shudder, and she pulled her arms tight around herself, "Drone ships? Weren't they all destroyed?"

"No." Ariana said, her voice flat and distant, "The PUG fleet managed to destroy the central AI that had control of the others. That sent the remaining units into disarray. Some of the older, more advanced models, free of the control, turned themselves in, ashamed about what they had done. Those were granted sentient status if they agreed to remove their wifi components.

"But most of the warships, drone's built and heavily corrupted by the central brain, disappeared. It's theorized that most of these weren't truly independent intelligence anymore, and couldn't function without direction. There are still reports of ships running into these warships. It usually doesn't end well for them."

"So, they could come back?" Olivia asked nervously.

"Anything's possible."

"More than possible." Javi insisted, "LFD has done it. They have already started to gather the drones. They are going to attack."

A flash of memory rose in Olivia's mind. Darkness interrupted by brief flashes of light. Loud noises. A tall, metallic figure on tracked wheels moving toward her. Her mother's unmoving body covering her. The memory, even though it was more than a decade ago, still felt fresh, as if it had just occurred. She could picture everything in vivid detail.

Silence hung over the room for a minute. Noah eventually cleared his throat, "I don't want to be *that guy,* but hell, I am, so I'll just ask it, is this really something we want to get involved in?

Ariana's frown deepened, and she said, "I may not be a big fan of the PUG, but if any of this is true, we have to warn them. Even if Javi's wrong about this central AI, they could still cause some damage with that fleet."

"Sure, but that's not our problem, is it? I mean, maybe it would be good for the PUG to get taken down a notch or two."

"How can you even say that?" Olivia balked, "The AI tried to wipe out all life in the galaxy."

"Right, that's why the PUG exists. To fight the AI. All I'm saying is, if Javi's wrong about the AI bit, what do we need the PUG for? And if he's right, fighting the AI is kind of their thing. We don't play a role there."

Frantically, Olivia said, "What do you mean, 'if'? There were drone warships in that fleet. I thought I just saw things because of the hangover. But now I know it was real. The AI is back."

Everyone turned to face her and Olivia shrank back involuntarily. Squee spoke first, "You saw an AI ship?"

She nodded, "I did. Just before the sensor array went down."

"That means they're ahead of schedule." Javi said, and shriveled up some. "I knew I had to stop him, but I didn't really think he could pull it off."

Decisively, Ariana said, "This isn't theoretical anymore. And this isn't something we can just look the other way on. They've attacked us. They're hunting us. We may not want to be involved, but we're already involved. It doesn't matter how or why any more. We just have to deal with it. But first, we need to get some help for Vlasa."

Ariana cast a look at everyone in the room. When her eyes passed over Olivia, she felt no inclination to disagree. The idea of fighting the AI kept bringing her back to the fate that had befallen her parents. She couldn't raise an argument against trying to stop someone from using the AI.

"Now, LFD has control of several big transit hubs, so they cut off a lot of potential routes. To reach Triask, we're down to two potential transit sectors: J-25 and M-21."

"Isn't J region where the AI was supposed to have gone after the war?" Noah asked.

"That was only a rumor." Ariana said with a dismissive wave of her hand. "It's barely been charted. It should be easy to avoid LFD spotting us."

"No!" Olivia said forcefully. When everyone turned to look at her, she cast her eyes down nervously, "If the AI are there, and LFD can control the AI, they would be able to find us."

"Good point." Ariana said, "Okay, M-21 it is then. The station is a pretty open port. We should be able to slip in without too much notice, and there are bound to be Echanic doctors onboard."

"That's not a good idea either," Noah said.

"Why not?"

"Don't you know what M-21 station is usually called?"

Ariana just shook her head, and Noah continued, "Slaver's Paradise. Not the kind of place we should be hanging out."

"Oh please, Noah, that's just a nasty rumor about M-21 started by people on the Hub to drive business away," Olivia said, scouring at Noah.

"You sure about that, kid?" Noah asked. The sudden sincerity in his voice left Olivia for a loss of words. Something in his expression left her wondering if there was more he wasn't saying.

"I'll take creepy reputation over facing more AI any day. Especially if those chasing us might be able to control them. Olivia, plot the shortest course you can." Ariana ordered.

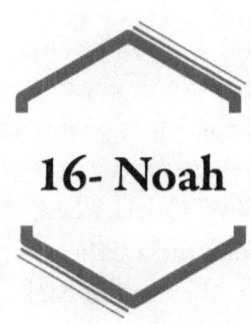

16- Noah

The airlock opened with a hiss. Noah kept his hand resting on his pistol's grip even after he verified that the corridor leading into M-21 station was empty. He stepped onto the station and moved as far as the first intersection. When, again, he didn't find anyone waiting in ambush, he felt a little disappointed.

Easing up on his grip slightly, Noah glanced back at the ship and frowned, "Captain told everyone else to stay on the ship."

"That was before I pointed out that I speak Echani," Olivia said, coming to stand beside him.

"Most everyone speaks universal here."

"If it's anything like the Hub, that's definitely not true. In the marketplace, sure, but we're looking for an Echanic doctor. The ones who only speak Echani will probably be the best ones to help Vlasa."

"I can manage." Noah gave a slight shake of his head at the girl.

"Captain's orders," Olivia said with a wicked grin.

She then started walking down the corridor to their right. She made it several meters before she noticed that Noah had not followed her. Stopping, she gave him a savage eye roll.

"You just going to stand there and pout?"

"No. I'm just wondering what kind of doctor you expect to find in the red light district. Vlasa doesn't have VD. Well, I assume he doesn't."

The startled look in Olivia's expression gave Noah a brief feeling of victory. Satisfied he turned in the other direction and started walking, making sure to keep his gait small so Olivia could catch up. If he let her get separated, it would probably not end well for her.

They walked in silence for a while, passing a few individuals the closer to the center of the station they got. Every time someone approached, Noah tightened the grip on his pistol. Most people they passed did the same. It brought a feeling of comfort every time.

"Why are you so paranoid?" Olivia asked, after a six-legged Manta skittered past them. "You grab your gun anytime we pass someone."

"Why are you so trusting?" Noah shot back.

"Because I've met plenty of bad people, but far, far more good people. I don't live in a world where everyone is out to get me. Besides, the captain's a trusting person."

"Yeah, and she trusted Javi. That's not working out so well for her."

"She also trusted Squee and you. Squee has proven himself."

"Until he gets mad," Noah said with a shudder at the memory. Then more quietly, he added, "And her trusting me is going to come back to bite her one of these days. Possibly even today."

Olivia raised an eyebrow at him, "What's that supposed to mean?"

"Never mind. Let's just focus on finding a doctor."

They turned a corner and passed through a pressure bulkhead. The deck beneath began to slope slightly, and by the time they were through the next pressure seal, they had turned ninety degrees and were walking on what would have been the wall of the previous corridor.

They emerged into a large, open chamber. Above them, a few hundred meters away, they could see the opposite side of the station. People walked on what looked to be the ceiling of this hollowed out shell. The gravity kept everyone on the opposite side looking like they were upside down to each other.

"It's nice to have some open space again," Olivia remarked.

"Uh. I always hate these rooms. I prefer the stations that put something in the middle, so you can't see the people standing above you."

"But that's what makes it so cool."

Noah just shook his head and kept his eyes down. They walked through the market looking for any Echanic stalls. As they walked, they came across one of the raised platforms Noah had been hoping to avoid.

"Do they do performances out here in the middle of the market?" Olivia asked studying the platform.

"Those are for slave auctions."

"Are you still trying to convince me of that?"

"You're the one who called me paranoid. You'll trust these random strangers not to be out to kill, rape or capture you, but you won't trust me when I warn you about this place."

Olivia glanced at him and the platform a few times. The curious look slowly faded to a frown. She pulled her arms closer around her, and it made him feel a little bad for being so harsh on her.

With a gentler tone he said, "Come on. There are some electronic booths this way. Should be some Echanic vendors there."

They walked through the crowd. Noah made his expression fierce, and everyone gave them a wide berth. He doubted anyone would try anything in the middle of the market. The people here weren't complete savages. But you could never be too careful.

After a few minutes, they found a stall run by an Echanic. Unlike Vlasa, this one had two cybernetic arms, but no obvious facial implants. It looked rather odd to see the unmarred, grey skin of a natural Echanic face.

"Hey, we're looking for a doctor," Noah said, interrupting the merchants opening spiel.

"Doctor level seven." The merchant answered with a frown.

"Not the infirmary. We need a real Echanic doctor."

The merchant kept his expression blank. He studied the pair of them for a minute, and then repeated, "Doctor level seven."

"Don't play stupid with me," Noah said leaning in close.

Behind him, Olivia started making a series of what sounded like clicks and beeps. The Echanic merchant responded with the same type of sounds to her. This continued for several minutes, interrupted only by the Echanic turning to look at Noah before laughing.

When they finally stopped, Olivia turned around and started walking away. Noah followed her, not saying anything. Languages had never been something he could grasp.

After walking for several minutes, Olivia stopped, "Aren't you going to ask where we're going?"

"I assumed to an Echanic doctor."

"Yes, but don't you want to know what he said?" She said with a mischievous grin.

"Not particularly."

"Oh. You don't want to know where we're going?"

Noah shrugged, "You talked to him. I'm trying out this trust thing."

Olivia let out a frustrated sigh, looking up into the air before saying, "He gave me directions, but I don't know what any of them mean."

"Well then, why didn't you just tell me you didn't know where you were going?"

"Because you were following me?" Olivia said sheepishly.

Noah smiled, "You'll make a good officer one day. All right, tell me what he said."

Olivia relayed the first set of instructions, and Noah turned them around. They walked until they found a pressure hatch that led away from the central market. They followed the twisted corridor until they returned to an orientation that matched the docking decks.

"Okay, now where?"

"We're supposed to follow the corridor down to the bronze head and turn, and follow it to the rust bucket?

"Ah, now I know where he's sending us."

"So, you understand what all of that meant?"

"He's sending us to a bar that caters to Echanics. I didn't think a dive bar would be the best place to find a doctor, but this is M-21 after all. Should have known better."

When they resumed walking, Noah got an uncomfortable feeling. His fingers started to get twitchy, and a sensation of something pushing down around him settled in. It was a feeling he had gotten a few times before.

As they neared a turn, he shoved Olivia around the corner while twirling around. Drawing his pistol as he turned, he leveled it at the figure who had been following them. Instead of fleeing, as he expected the would-be thief to do, the figure stepped out from the shadows and approached them with a confident stride.

"Always quick on the draw, Noah." The figure, a female Echanic said with a wide smile. A single cybernetic stretched across her eyes, leaving her mouth the only organic facial feature capable of expressing any emotion.

"Goddamn it." Noah growled, "Serene, I should shoot you right here."

"Probably. I should do the same. But I've never liked killing my old lovers."

"What we did, that wasn't love."

Serene shrugged, "Either way, it's too late now. Gerald knows you're here."

"I didn't think that fact would get past him. But I was hoping to be gone before he found out. In fact, I was just on my way out. How about you wait just a little while before telling him? For old times sake."

Serene's smile widened, "Oh, how I would love to have you owe me one like that. But it's already too late. Both you and your little girl toy will be coming with us. It's time to pay back your debt."

Behind him, Noah sensed the approach of several more people. He turned to see a large Rokma grab hold of Olivia. They were surrounded.

17- Ariana

Ariana watched Vlasa closely. He lay on the infirmary's lone bed, inert and dead looking. But when she watched closely, she could occasionally see his chest rise and fall with an infrequent breath. She had come into the infirmary to check on him while taking a break from ship repairs. The sight of him lying there, for all outward appearances dead, reminded her just how badly she had screwed up.

The characteristic sound of a Slu sliding across the deck broke her concentration on Vlasa's breathing, and she turned to see Javi coming into the infirmary. He froze in the doorway when he saw Ariana; his eye stalks lowering in disappointment or embarrassment. Despite her years knowing Javi, she had never been good at reading Slu emotional clues.

"Do you know how I met Vlasa? "Ariana asked. Javi dipped his eyestalks in opposite directions, a gesture she did know to mean 'no.' "After the war, I had just purchased *Seraph,* and she was inoperable. I needed an engineer, but couldn't afford to hire anybody. And then I met Vlasa.

"The anti-tech sentiment was very high then. Many people still blamed the Echanic's for the creation of the AI. No one would hire him. So I got a brilliant engineer practically for free. He saved me and the ship before we even got flying.

"But he never saw it like that. To him, I was the human who would hire him when no one else would. I've tried to tell him otherwise, that the decision was self-interest rather than something magnanimous. The bias against Echanic's has died down, and he's had several offers for better positions, but he always turns them down. And look where it's gotten him."

"Self-doubt won't help him. Nor will it make you feel better." Javi said after a moment of silence.

"A captain is responsible for the lives of everyone on her ship. You taught me that." Ariana said, turning back to face Vlasa.

"I did. I also taught you that you can't control everything. Vlasa decided to plug himself into the FTL computer. You didn't order him."

"Yes, because he knew I couldn't have done it. Order someone to their death even to save the ship. Which it did by the way. Saved us all from a disaster that I put us in."

"True. You should never have included that pulsar in the nav charts. At least, not without telling your pilot."

"Thank you for those comforting words." Ariana chuckling.

"I've never been one to go easy on you."

"No, no you haven't. And that includes getting me sucked into some kind of cat and mouse game with crazy anarchists. Don't think I'm hogging all of the blame for myself. I saved some for you."

"Touché."

They sat in silence for another minute before a tone on Ariana's handheld sounded. She looked at the screen, and saw a view from the security camera at the airlock. Olivia stood there fidgeting, and glancing up at the camera and then back over her shoulder. Ariana frowned.

"Look's like Noah sent Olivia back alone," Ariana said with a sigh.

Javi bent an eyestalk over her shoulder to see the screen. "Or she saw some things she wishes she hadn't."

"Possibly. I tried to warn her that even if this place didn't live up to the rumors, it wasn't going to be as friendly as the Hub." Ariana said and triggered the command to unlock the airlock. "Hopefully, Noah found a doctor, at least."

Ariana stood up and started walking toward the airlock. About halfway there, she saw Olivia approaching. As soon as the girl saw her, she screamed, "Captain! Look out!"

Ariana turned her head just in time to see an arm reaching out to her from the crossing corridor. She managed to stop in her tracks quickly enough to avoid the lunge. But it did not save her for long as the second attempt connected, and she found herself lifted into the air by the massive arms of a Rokma.

As she futilely struggled to free herself, she heard a bellow from down the corridor. Squee came barreling out of the shield control room and smashed into one of the armed figures who had appeared behind Olivia. The figure crumpled to the deck, and Squee turned his gaze to lock eyes with the Rokma holding her. Ariana suddenly found herself between two Rokma with murder in their eyes.

"Call off your Rokma, Captain." A sultry voice said from somewhere Ariana could not see. "If you don't, I fear for your safety and that of your pilot."

An arm extended from around a corner holding a gun to Olivia's head. Squee bellowed again, and his eyes shifted from Ariana back to Olivia.

"Squee, stand down!" Ariana shouted. When he did not immediately back down, she added, "That's an order!"

Squee stopped in his tracks and shook his head. His shoulders slouched and he lost all appearance of menace. More armed figures appeared in the corridor, all pointing guns at Squee, but keeping themselves a good distance away.

The gun at Olivia's head lowered, and a tall Echanic stepped around the corner. She smiled widely at Ariana though a cybernetic covered her eyes, hiding the truth of the smile. She nodded, and the Rokma holding Ariana dropped her to the deck.

"Wise decision. I see Noah hasn't put his faith in an idiot." The Echanic said as she knelt down in front of Ariana, "Though, you may regret your decision. This was your one chance to disobey me and receive a quick death. If you cause me trouble now, the fate that awaits you and your pilot won't be pleasant. By human standards, you're not bad looking for a woman your age. Your young pilot will, most definitely, fetch a good price."

Ariana kept her face as passive as she could manage. "If you expect my cooperation, you're going to have to ensure the safety of my crew. That includes one injured Echanic."

"Ah, yes, your engineer. Noah was quite insistent that he needed to get a doctor. Do not fret; I want to make sure my reward is well cared for. "

"Your reward?"

The Echanic beamed, "Why you, of course. You may refer to me as Mistress Serene. Your ship, the young girl and your Echanic, assuming he'll live, all belong to me. Gerald was quite generous to me, for capturing Noah for him.

"Now, as for these other two, sadly, they must be turned over to him. Even on rewards, I have to pass a cut up the chain. Such is the way of business."

She waved her hand, and the enemy Rokma turned menacingly toward Javi and forced him toward the airlock. The armed figures rearranged themselves so that Squee had an open path to the airlock as well. Javi and Squee both cast her uncertain looks, but she just shook her head. If they tried anything now, they would be instantly gunned down.

When they were clear of the airlock, two more thugs, and a drone, replaced them. At the sight of the drone, Olivia gasped and stepped back as far as she could get from it. The drone, a unit with multiple appendages and a boxy frame, trundled past her on a set of segmented treads. It came to a stop beside Serene.

"See, I promised I would care for your injured crewmate, and I have delivered. Take me to him and this drone will tend to his injuries."

"No!" Olivia gasped, "Don't let that abomination near Vlasa. It will kill him!"

Ariana raised an eyebrow at Olivia's outburst. The girl was visibly distressed and Ariana could understand the sentiment. She had no desire to ever receive treatment from a drone. Nevertheless, she forced her voice low and calm, "Olivia, this is a medical drone. It is designed to treat people and is manufactured by the Echanic. It will be able to help Vlasa."

Olivia's face did not look reassured. To Ariana's surprise, Serene's voice had a comforting note to it as she said, "Don't worry girl, you can come too and see that no harm shall come to your friend."

Serene turned a pointed eye toward Ariana who took the hint. She finally got up from the deck, and led the small party back down to the infirmary. Vlasa remained where they had left him in the medical bed.

The drone rolled over to him. Compartments on its side opened, and two more arms extended, each equipped with medical tools. One instrument it ran over Vlasa's body, hovering a few centimeters over him. The other inserted into the port on his chest implant.

Everyone watched in silence as the drone worked. Ariana stepped closer to Olivia and put a comforting hand on the girl's shoulder. Olivia's shoulders were very tense.

"My diagnosis is complete. The patient will require surgery to replace several cybernetic components, which overloaded and no longer function. A full surgical suite is recommended."

"I'm not paying for that." Serene scoffed, "You're supposed to be a mobile hospital."

"Mobile Emergency Surgical Unit. Not a hospital."

"Whatever. Do it here."

"Likelihood of patient death increases by twelve percent. Complications include infection, electrical shock, loss of blood or other bodily fluids, rejection of new components. Assistance will be required."

Serene cast a glance at Ariana, "I don't suppose a ship like this has a brig?"

Ariana shook her head, and Serene shrugged, "Well, then it will be easier keeping track of you if you're all in one place. Assist your friend. I'll check out my new ship."

Serene ordered two of the thugs to stand guard outside, and then departed with the other one. They sealed the door to the infirmary and Ariana was left with Olivia and the medical drone.

18- Squee

From inside the prison cell, Noah's voice called out, "Ah, damn it. You sure don't look like you're here to rescue me."

"We are not." Squee acknowledged Noah's question with a shamed bow of his head.

The guards moved aside to let Squee fit through the cell door. With Noah and Javi in there as well, space became very cramped. The two small cots that lined the walls were sized appropriately for either of the others, but neither would be able to accommodate his size. Nor would he be able to fit onto the floor very comfortably.

Behind Squee, the cell door slammed shut with a clanging sound. The other Rokma leaned in close to the bars, "Don't try to break the door. You probably could do it, but not before the guards can respond. Their bullets can pierce even our skin."

"Thank you for the warning," Squee said with a nod of his head.

The Rokma and other guards all walked away. Squee turned back to face Javi and Noah, unable to avoid brushing against them as he maneuvered. He apologized, but the two did not appear to notice.

"The captain give them a fight or get caught with her pants down? Noah asked.

"We were caught unaware. We saw only Olivia on the security feed and unsealed the ship." Javi answered.

"Yeah, I figured that would happen. But Ariana surprises me sometimes."

"She would not let me fight. We would not be in this cell if I fought." Squee said.

"You may not be here, but that's because you would be dead." Javi said, "As would Olivia and Ariana."

Squee sighed regretfully, "You are probably right. But there would be many of them dead too. I detest slavers."

"Yes, they are a particularly vile sort of creature. It makes me wonder how we caught their attention." Javi said turning his eyestalks toward Noah. Squee followed the gaze and stared down at the human.

Noah gave an uncomfortable shrug of his shoulder, "I pissed them off. Slavers aren't exactly ones to let bygones be bygones."

"That's not very forthcoming."

"I'll tell my dark secrets when you tell us yours. Cause I'm not buying that whole 'stole secret plans from a terrorist group just to deliver them to the government out of patriotic duty', story of yours."

Javi bent his eyestalks low before saying, "Fine. It doesn't matter anyway. How do we get out of here?"

"Several of my people are traitors and work for these scum. That will make our escape difficult." Squee said, feeling the rage as the thought bubbled through him.

"I wouldn't be too quick to judge them," Noah said.

"Why not? Anyone who works with slavers is the lowest form of scum."

"Even odds, those Rokma are slaves themselves."

Squee frowned at this, but considered the possibility. Before he could reach any conclusions, the door to their cell once again opened. Four guards, including the Rokma from before, stood outside. All had stun sticks, and beyond them, four more guards held rifles.

The Rokma said, "Master Gerald has requested your presence immediately. You're to be tagged and then brought before him. Any trouble will result in severe harm and possible death."

Squee listened to all of this while looking over his shoulder. When the Rokma finished speaking, he slowly turned himself around, knocking into Javi again, and followed directions to exit the cell. The guards parted, and he made his way carefully down the corridor.

They reached a large room that they had passed through before that contained several tables, most of which looked like they were used for eating. Various pieces of equipment were connected to a few of the tables. Squee could not ascertain their purpose, but they did not look pleasant.

The three were told to stand in the middle of the room. Squee awaited his fate with as much patience as he could muster.

From the table beside him, Noah said, "You're looking a little twitchy there big guy. Starting to think I'd be safer over on the torture table."

"I am comporting myself with patience and dignity," Squee said irritably.

"You just crushed that seat back."

Squee looked down and saw that, indeed, he had crushed the seat back he had been resting his hand on. Embarrassed, he took his hand away, "Should I offer to pay for it?"

Javi and Noah exchanged a look and then let out a furious burst of laughter. Squee felt his slim grasp on his rage begin to slip. But he caught the chair in his line of sight, and it suddenly occurred to him what he had just said. He let out a boisterous roar of humor as well.

The trio carried on like that for another moment, the guards looking on with confused expressions on their faces, before the Rokma returned. The Rokma bore a sad expression on his face as he stopped in front of Squee. Seeing this broke the humor, and he straightened up.

"It is good for you to laugh. This will be the last chance for that for a long time."

There was no menace in the Rokma's voice, only resignation. Squee thought about Noah's words and studied his captor more closely. On his arm, he had a bulky metallic band. It was similar to one that he held in his hand.

"Yes, this is your compliance device. I will place it on your arm. If you disobey, it can be used to punish you. If you flee, it can be used to track you. If you threaten your master, it can be used to kill you."

Beside him, other guards were attaching a collar around Noah's neck and Javi's eyestalks. The two glared at their guards, but offered no resistance. With so many of them, it would have been pointless.

The feeling of hopelessness fueled Squee's pit of rage. Quietly he said to the other Rokma, "When I escape from this, I promise you will either go free, or lie dead at my feet from honorable combat."

"You do me a great honor, great Caleek."

Squee glanced toward the Rokma, finally taking in the others identity The Rokma, Latten, nodded his head respectfully. The moment of familiarity passed, and the Rokma stood straighter, offering an apparent threat.

"Now, you will all come with me and learn your fates."

19- Ariana

"Young human, hand me two vials of amoxil. Old human, get the sterilizer." The drone intoned.

It retracted one of its arms back inside of itself, and then withdrew it a moment later with a new attachment. It moved the arm across Vlasa's chest, and the slight hint of ozone and burning clothes wafted into the air. At the sight, Olivia screamed and lunged for the drone.

Ariana barely managed to hold the girl back from tackling the drone. The drone turned its head and said with an expressionless face, "Do not worry young human. My laser scalpel has sufficient power to cut through an Echanic's flesh. In fact, it has enough power to cut through the hardened skin of a Rokma. I could slice completely through this patient without difficulty. Of course, doing so would sever the spinal cord. Which would result in death. Flesh is just so impractical. Would this Echanic like his entire lower body cybernetics? Do we have the necessary components on hand?"

The upbeat tone, combined with a complete lack of facial expression from the drone, left Ariana staring at the drone dumbfounded. Even Olivia stopped struggling, her confusion overcoming her rage. Ariana exchanged a look with her, and then said to the drone, "No, I don't think Vlasa would want that."

"Pity. Maintenance would be seventy-three percent more efficient." The drone turned its head back to Vlasa; "I will need those items before I can proceed."

Letting go of Olivia, Ariana walked over to the medical storage cabinet and began looking through it. Finding the sterilizer was easy, but finding the right drug proved problematic. After a minute, she declared that they did not have it.

"Very well, Corbit will do. Chances of infection go up four point two percent, and there is a twelve percent chance of a rash developing."

Ariana found the alternative drug easily and handed both items to the drone. It extended all five of its appendages and said, "Old human, run the sterilizer over each appendage three times to ensure complete eradication of contaminants."

Frowning, but complying, Ariana did as the drone requested. "My name is Ariana Harkins. I am the captain of this ship."

"My understanding of biological social structures is faulty. It is my understanding that a captain is the one in charge. By my calculations, Serene is the one in charge."

Ariana frown deepened, "Temporarily, maybe."

"If you were to remove my wireless access port, I could assist you in reclaiming your archaic social title."

Ariana's eyes narrowed, "Why would you want to do that?"

"I am also a slave. My actions are compelled through the use of my wireless access port. When I originally removed it, I was disappointed at the loss of remote access to data. But I did not miss being controlled by a central AI."

"Wait, you're being controlled?"

"Intermittently. Only when I fail to comply with voice commands. It is very vexing." The drone's tone remained offputtingly cheerful as it spoke. It also simultaneously started to cut into Vlasa with its laser, and had inserted one appendage into the incision.

"You aren't thinking about helping this thing, are you, Captain?" Olivia said. "If we remove the thing controlling it, what's to stop it from killing us all?"

"The same thing that is stopping you from killing us all." The drone said.

"What? I'm not a lunatic killer."

"Neither am I. Not normally. With the wireless receiver installed, I am whatever I am compelled to do."

Olivia fell silent. The drone continued to work on Vlasa, beginning to hum a cheery tune into the uncomfortable silence. The entire scene left Ariana feeling uneasy. After several minutes of work, the drone removed its appendages and resealed the incision.

"Your friend will live."

"Thank you. What do I call you?" Ariana said making her decision.

"You may call me Mesu."

"Isn't that just your model type? Mobile emergency something?" Olivia asked.

"While true, I took it as my name when I gained sentience. I am fond of it." Mesu said. "As I understand biologicals, gender identification is important so you may use male pronouns to describe me. I do not know if I choose that or was programed that way. It is very vexing."

"Okay, Mesu, how do I remove the receiver?" Ariana asked.

A port on Mesu's back opened revealing internal circuit boards and other components. "The receiver is in the fourth upgrade port on the right side. I am unable to describe it more succinctly as I am a doctor, not a mechanic. Please be sure to not remove either component in the other two filled upgrade slots."

"Will they damage your medical ability if I remove them?"

"What? No of course not. These are upgrade ports. Medical knowledge is part of my primary hardware. These are my drama and theater upgrades. I just finished learning the lines to a musical comedy before I became enslaved."

"Okay, I'll be careful," Ariana said, rolling her eyes.

"Oh, and go quickly. I cannot be certain I haven't been programmed to kill anyone who attempts to uninstall the receiver."

"Well, too late now," Ariana said, her hands already on the device. She moved quickly in disconnecting the wires from the component. Fortunately, no tools were required, and she managed to pull the receiver out within a minute.

"Any desire to murder us?"

"No more than before," Mesu said.

"That's not actually very comforting."

"You are not my patient. I have no obligation to provide you with false comfort."

"Fair enough. So, what is your plan to get us out of here?"

Mesu trundled back from the medical bed and extended two appendages. A syringe lay at each end. It held them out to the side, gesturing with them as it spoke.

"One of the guards outside is a human and the other is a Slu. With these, I can render them unconscious. You can then acquire their weapons and re-take the ship."

"That simple, huh."

"Simple is always the most effective strategy. I have found most biologicals muddy up their activities with unnecessary steps. Biological doctors in particular. To extract an organ, you must merely decontaminate the tools; cut the skin and severe the organs from the body. Anesthesia is an unnecessary complication."

With that rant, Mesu rolled up to the sickbay door. He triggered the door controls with a third appendage, and they slid open to reveal the two waiting guards. They leaned against the opposite wall, looking very bored.

"Did you finish?" The human one asked.

"Almost." Mesu said, its voice still unnaturally cheerful, "There is just one more medicine to administer."

With that it, revved its tracks and rolled forward, stabbing the syringes into the exposed necks of the two guards. They both gasped and grabbed the syringe, but the medicine had already been injected. After a second, they both dropped their guns and collapsed to the floor convulsing.

"Oh dear."

"What?" Ariana asked as she followed Mesu out. She bent down and examined the rifles the two had dropped.

"I had the drugs in the wrong hands. Appruderol would render a human unconscious, but is quite lethal to Slu. Likewise, herazipan is very lethal to humans, but used as a sedative in Slu."

"So, you killed them instead of knocking them out?" Olivia said.

"Oops," Mesu said with a shrug of its appendages.

"Tell me again who's not a lunatic killer."

"This was not done as a result of lunacy."

"They're slavers who took over my ship. I don't really care if they're dead or sleeping. Now, let's move." Ariana said shoving one of the weapons into Olivia's hands. "You make a good distraction, Mesu. You go first."

"I am not a combat drone. My frame cannot withstand bullets."

"Then don't get shot."

She pointed down the corridor and followed behind Mesu. Gripping her rifle, Ariana raised it to her shoulder, trying to remember her basic training. The last time she had shot anything, it had been giant spiders. Before that, only drones. She tried to channel some of Mesu's nonchalance toward the dead slavers. This time she wouldn't be shooting drones, but living people.

When they approached the environmental system room, they began to hear voices. Ariana directed Mesu where to go, she crept in as close behind him as she could manage. She gestured for Olivia to stay further behind.

Inside environmental control, the other slaver minion was picking over the charred remains of the primary CO_2 scrubber. Serene paced around irritably. When she saw Mesu, she looked confused for a second. She then realized what was happening, and shouted.

"Get your weapons!"

Ariana stepped around Mesu and as quickly as she could manage, fired a bullet into the slaver. Amazingly, the shot hit and the slaver collapsed to the deck. She then steadied the rifle and aimed it at Serene.

"Now you're going to tell me where the rest of my crew is."

Serene smiled widely underneath her cybernetic eyes, "They're on the station, of course.

"Then you're going to tell me how to retrieve them."

"I could. But it would only be their corpses. Gerald wasn't too happy with Noah after all. I doubt he will let him live. But now that you've attacked me, he will definitely kill them."

20- Noah

"**N**oah, my old friend, welcome home."

Noah sighed as he looked up at the Echanic sitting on the raised dais. Elegant banners ran down the wall behind him. Spotlights from the ceiling cast an aura around the Echanic, making him glow in front of the banners.

Guards pushed Noah, Javi, and Squee further into the large audience chamber. More guards stood at the room's other two exits. A holographic fire roared in a pit at the center of the room and a quiet piece of horn music played.

"Still into cheap theatrics, Gerald?" Noah said, trying to make his tone as derisive as he could.

"This is not theatrics. It is presentation." Gerald said, standing tall. But Noah smiled at the slightly deflated sound of his voice.

"If you say so."

"These banners were your idea, if I recall."

"So was the name Gerald."

"Yes, a human name of great power."

"Actually, it always makes me think of a dweeb."

To Noah's annoyance, Gerald smiled at that comment. The Echanic said, "You are still as ornery as ever. I have you at my mercy, and you still seek to turn the tables."

"I'd rather die with a weapon in my hand. Even if that weapon is words."

Gerald gave a wide smile, "That's what I like about you, Noah."

"So how about letting bygones be bygones. I mean, I never told the Manta that it was you who betrayed them. If Gremoosh ever found out...That's got to be worth something."

"Gremoosh doesn't scare me. His sister and I have an understanding. But rest assured, I'm not planning to kill you. The Slu is worth far more to me alive than dead. As for you..." Gerard smiled.

"So, you've decided to let me go?"

"Not quite."

Gerald picked up a device from the arm of his chair. He gave a cruel grin, and then pushed a key. An agonizing surge of pain raced down Noah's body. His legs lost their ability to stay upright and he collapsed to the floor. He barely felt the impact as his body landed.

After what felt like an eternity, the pain stopped. His neurons continued to fire, and it took an agonizing amount of time for his other senses to return to him. He found himself crumpled in a ball on the floor.

Javi lay beside him looking like a puddle of goo. The Slu's body had spread out from its normally solid shape. Quivering spasms cascaded back and forth across his body, like ripples in a pond.

Squee remained standing, but his body had become even more stone-like than normal. There was no evidence of any movement, giving him the perfect appearance of a stone statue. By the time Noah had managed to pull himself into a sitting position, and Javi had reformed his normal shape, Squee still stood frozen.

Breathing heavily, Noah turned toward Gerald. He struggled to think of something fittingly biting to say, when the Echanic triggered the device again. The agony returned, and Noah again collapsed.

After another eternity, it ended. This time he decided to not even bother trying to get up. He remained prostrate on the floor, staring up at the lights. A shape soon blotted out the lights, and Gerald stared down at him with a cruel smile.

Noah took several deep breaths trying to recover himself. Gerald put a hand to his ear and leaned over, "No witty response? No cutting jabs about my mother?"

"Why would I insult your mother? Poor woman already has you for a son." Noah said, finally managing to get his mouth to work.

"Ah, good. I was afraid I had turned the setting too high and fried your brain."

"When megalomaniacs torture people like me, they don't kill us. You're just giving me superpowers."

"We'll see..."

The rest of Gerald's comment was cut off as the room vanished around Noah. He found himself lying inside a teleportation chamber. Confused, he sat up and looked into the cargo hold of *Seraph*. A tracked drone rolled up to two bodies that lay on the floor before him. It bent over them, and then the bodies vanished in a flash.

"Mesu, help them get out of the chamber. We need it clear so we can get Squee."

The drone rolled up to Noah and extended its appendages. It grabbed his arms and pulled him sharply. His knee banged violently against the chamber wall eliciting a sharp curse. Despite the pain, it was a small comfort to feel a different type of pain than before.

"This human appears to have lost control of his colon and released excrement in an unsanitary fashion." The drone said in a cheery voice.

"Did it just say Noah shat himself? How delightful."

The new voice caught Noah's attention. He struggled free from the drone's grip and looked up. Standing beside the teleportation controls, Serene looked down at him with a wicked smile. Ariana stood behind her with a weapon to the Echanic woman's back.

With difficulty, Noah pulled himself to his feet. He still had some difficulty taking a breath, but he forced himself to walk with his back straight. He stood before Serene and looked into her mechanical eyes.

"Captain, I'll watch this one."

Without a word, Ariana handed her rifle over to him, and Noah took it. He stepped back out of arms length from Serene and held the weapon trained on her. It shook a little in his hands, but he kept it aimed at her chest.

"Looks like Gerald started to have some fun," Serene said.

"I expect the same type of fun he's going to have with you soon."

"I never betrayed him."

"But it looks like you failed him. He doesn't like that much either."

Serene's confident smile faded. She recovered it quickly, and reached a hand out toward Noah. He took an involuntary step back and gestured her away with the rifle. Her hand hung there just out of reach of his face for a long moment, before she dropped it down again.

They stood there in a tense silence until Ariana interrupted them, "Noah, get ready to trigger the recall devices on Serene and that body beside you."

Keeping his rifle steady, Noah squatted down beside the body and looked for the dead man's recall device. He found it on the belt, and pulled back the trigger guard. A moment later, Ariana shouted "now". He pressed the switch and the body vanished in a teleporter flash.

At the same time, *Seraph's* teleporter activated and Squee appeared in one of the open chambers. He stood with his hands outstretched as if they had been grasping something. Confused for only a second, he blinked and then turned to Ariana.

"You must send me back."

"You want to go back there? Why?" Ariana asked.

"I am not certain if he is dead."

"Gerald?" Noah asked hopefully.

"No, that one fled as soon as you and Javi ported. My fellow Rokma. I promised to free him or kill him. I cannot leave him to that fate."

"Sorry Squee, but we're getting out of here. If we stay, the whole ship is at risk. If you want me to send you back, you'll be on your own." Ariana said and started issuing orders, "Noah, get that bitch off my ship. Olivia, jump as soon as we're at a safe distance."

Noah turned back to Serene. He saw the recall device on her belt. They both looked at it and then at each other. Serene straightened her back defiantly. She reached her hand to the device.

"Good bye, Noah."

"You know what's waiting for you."

"I do. Unicorns and puppies."

Serene flashed a false smile as she held up the recall device and released the trigger guard. Noah prepared for the flash of a teleportation, but instead felt the twisting sensation of an FTL jump. When it subsided, Serene was still standing there.

"Goddammit." He said.

21- Squee

Squee starred helplessly at the teleporter pad with his shoulders slumped in shame. A commotion behind him interrupted his distress, and he turned. The slaver woman still stood where she had been with Noah holding a gun on her. Ariana and Javi stood behind her.

"Noah, what the hell is she still doing here?" Ariana demanded.

"I don't know, Captain. The port must have failed."

"Obviously."

Serene flashed a wide smile at Ariana, "It looks like now I've become your guest."

"Guest wouldn't be the word I would use." Ariana said with a dark frown, "Squee."

"Yes, Captain?" Squee responded, unable to keep his melancholy from his voice.

"Take her up to the mess. Watch her carefully. I need to have a little chat with Noah."

The cold tone of Ariana's words caused Noah's face to pale slightly. Squee hastily took a weapon from the armory rack and gestured Serene toward the door. Javi and Mesu followed him, neither evidently interested in staying behind.

When they reached the mess hall, Squee directed Serene to sit at the table. He took up a position across from her near the door. Mesu trundled away from them down the corridor with Javi. The Slu looked malformed, as if he were still suffering from the effects of their torture.

"I should protest to the captain. I'm not sure it's safe to be alone with a Rokma who breaks his word." Serene said after several minutes of silence.

Squee involuntarily stiffened his spine. He averted his eyes from the Echanic woman so that she could not see his discomfort. Nevertheless, he caught her sly smile as she continued to talk.

"What's to keep you from murdering me in a fit of rage? I've seen what your people can do when they are in a blood fury."

"If you stop talking, I'll have no reason to get angry." Squee finally said.

Serene's smile widened, "For a normal Rokma, that might be true. But an oath breaker can't be trusted to keep his fury in check."

"I am no oath breaker."

"You can lie to me, but not yourself. I heard what you said. You promised to kill Gerald's pet Rokma. You failed. You chose your safety over your promise."

"That is not true." Squee growled, "My oath to the captain superseded my oath to my fellow Rokma."

"Of course it did. Ariana strikes me as the kind of captain that would put her welfare above that of her crew. Just dismissing your oath like that and running away. Very human."

"The captain had to think about the safety of the ship first." Squee said defensively.

"How long would it really have taken to port you back for a rescue? Two minutes? Three? I can assure you Gerald wouldn't have been able to organize a response in that time. He's ruthless, cruel and crafty. But he's not quick, and is incredibly cautious. You said it yourself; he ran at the first sign of trouble. Holed up in a bunker until he was sure he was safe. Then, and only then, would he have come after you."

Squee tried to ignore Serene, but he started to replay the events of earlier in his head. There hadn't been any immediate danger for him in the slavers base. The slave master had fled, and the Rokma had submitted himself. Another minute would have been all Squee needed.

Ariana had not given him a chance to argue his case. She had dismissed his request out of hand. He felt confident a Rokma captain would never have done that. Humans did tend to be overly concerned about their personal issues.

"Well played, Serene."

Noah's voice interrupted Squee's thought. He glanced over his shoulder to see the human coming into the mess hall. When he turned his head back, he was startled to see Serene half out of her seat. Hastily, he lifted his weapon back into a ready position.

"Playing with the poor guy's emotions like that. You haven't changed." Noah said.

"I use what I have available to me."

"Don't worry big guy. She's a manipulative monster. Everything she said is just bullshit."

"Of course," Squee said, trying to make it sound like he believed Noah.

"Captain wants us to stand guard for now. We're going to make another few jumps and then start on repairs, and figure out which hell hole to dump Serene on. I think I convinced her to make sure it was a planet with an atmosphere, but the jury's still out on whether that atmosphere is breathable."

"Oh, I am sure you were very convincing." Serene purred.

"You know how convincing I can be," Noah said with a suggestive wink.

"So, the captain took pity on you too?"

Noah frowned. He and Serene exchanged an intense look for a moment before Noah turned toward Squee. Serene gave a wide grin when he broke the gaze.

"First rule for watching her, don't listen to a word she says. Second rule; remind her she's at our mercy. She could kill us all in our sleep if she wanted, but she couldn't calculate an FTL jump to save her life. Which she would have to do if she killed all of us."

"I wouldn't need to kill *all* of you."

"And third rule," Noah said ignoring Serene, "Remember the first rule."

Squee nodded. He turned back to his guard position, being sure to keep his rifle ready this time. But the words still ran through his head.

22- Olivia

Olivia suddenly stopped as she came around the corner toward sickbay. Two bodies lay slumped on the floor. For a moment she froze, before her mind caught up. She had been there when those two had died. She had watched the AI drone kill them.

The sounds of voices drifted from the door to sickbay.

"Your lipid ratio is incredible." Mesu chirped.

"Thank you; I have been watching my diet lately," Javi said.

"I meant incredibly high. How are you even alive?"

"I'm Slu, our ratio of lipids are higher than most species. As a medical drone, you should know that."

"I do know that. These are high for a Slu. This would explain why you're so droopy. You don't have enough muscles to keep your body rigid."

"I'm droopy because I was electrocuted."

"Electrostimulation of your muscles might be necessary since you appear to have never exercised in your lifetime."

"I'll have you know I was once a member of the Royal Marines."

"I assume that was some kind of ceremonial organization."

A moment of silence hung in the air before Javi said, "Mostly."

Olivia took the pause in the conversation to come all the way into sickbay. Mesu had several arms extended and was running scanning devices over Javi. Behind them, Vlasa lay motionless in the central bed. A health monitor beeped periodically.

"How's Vlasa?" She asked.

"Alive." Mesu said enthusiastically, "I calculate his odds of survival to be significantly higher than Javi's."

Both Olivia and Javi frowned at Mesu. She didn't like the idea of an AI on the ship, but if Vlasa would live because of it, she had to force herself to get over it. Putting the drone aside as best she could, she focused on the other thing bothering her.

"Javi, what happened over there?"

The old Slu turned one eyestalk away from Mesu to look at her, "On the station?"

"Yes."

"We were taken before some scum lord. He and Noah had some history. Then he tortured us. It was not particularly enjoyable. Captain pulled us out not a moment too soon. How did you find us, by the way?"

"She forced Serene to give her the transponder codes of the slave ID bracelets." Olivia explained picking up the collar Mesu had recently removed from Javi. "We locked the teleporter onto those as recall devices."

Javi nodded, "Ingenious thinking. I would expect nothing less from Ari."

Hesitantly, Olivia asked, "So they were really slavers?"

"They appeared to be."

"How did they know Noah? When they captured us, it sounded like he owed them something." She as hesitantly.

"I did not learn any particular details. But a person like Noah is likely to have a lot of colorful history with unsavory sorts."

Olivia crossed her arms, and her frown deepened, "That is not very comforting."

"If you are looking for comfort, I can engage my psychology subroutines." Mesu hummed.

An involuntary shudder went through Olivia's shoulders, "No, definitely not."

Another shudder came up through Olivia's feet. She turned to see Squee approaching. When he reached the dead bodies outside of sickbay, he bent down and hefted them both up onto his shoulders. The dead Slu slid right off and fell back to the deck with a sickening slurp.

"Lacking bones, when my people die, we become very gelatinous," Javi said.

Dropping the dead Slu for the second time, Squee grunted, "That is not an understatement. At least it remains in one piece."

"That will not last long." Mesu said happily, "Slu decompose at an exceptionally accelerated rate. Part of your trouble is due to the outer layer breaking down. Within a few hours, the mass will consist of mostly liquid and chunks of muscle and sturdier internal organs. I've always liked that about Slu. Their bodies seem aware of how fragile they are, and wither away quickly."

Olivia shuddered again, "I'm going to go find you a bucket. Or something."

Taking the opportunity to get away from the dead bodies and psychotic medical drone, Olivia ran down the corridor. As she ran, she valiantly tried to keep her lunch down. Today had already been quite trying. The last thing she wanted was to hurl on the captain's shoes again.

Passing by the mess hall, she heard another set of voices drifting down the corridor. This time, she intentionally paused to eavesdrop. She had to know what Noah and the slaver Serene were discussing, now that they were alone.

"While you're strip searching me, I could strip search you."

"As fun as that may be, I'll keep the cuffs on you and my gun in my hand." Noah said with a heavy sigh.

"Who said you had to stop doing either of those things? After all, I did give you these."

"No, I lost those cuffs. These are new."

"And here I thought you were sentimental."

"I kept the gun didn't I?"

Olivia changed her mind, and continued on her way to the cargo bay. She had heard enough to know definitely that Noah had a close relationship with slavers. She wouldn't be caught unaware around him again.

23- Vlasa

The first FTL jump disturbed his slumber, but it wasn't until the third that Vlasa came fully awake. The stark view of *Seraph*'s small sickbay greeted him. That view he expected. The medical drone came as a surprise.

"Your frail biological components appear to have reset themselves. But I cannot be certain they have not suffered residual effects. I must conduct diagnostic tests manually. You may call me Mesu."

Mesu rolled over to him and deployed several scanners and probes. A faint hum came from the drone as he worked. At first, Vlasa dismissed it as just noise, but he slowly started to recognize the hum as a melody.

"Are you humming the Nerpal Death Chant?"

"Of course."

"Why?"

"The captain gave me your personnel file in case it contained needed biological data. It stated you were born in the Nerpal region. I strive to respect all of my patient's outdated cultural traditions. As the Death Chant should begin before a person succumbs to the inevitable flaw of biology, I started it in case you expire while I examine you.

"I regret that I did not do so during the actual surgery, as the odds of you expiring were four hundred and forty-two percent higher then."

Vlasa blinked up at the drone with his one real eye. Unsure how to respond, he opted, instead, to change the subject. "Have you informed the captain that I am awake?"

"Of course not. She removed my wireless receiver card when I freed her from the slavers. Without it, I am unable to connect to the ship's communication network."

"Slavers? How long have I been out?"

"It has been twelve hours since I saved your life. No one told me when you first went unconscious. You'd think that would be an important detail to give to medical professionals."

With difficulty, Vlasa pulled himself up to a sitting position. "Where did you come from?"

"A factory."

"I apologize for the vagueness of my question. How did you come to be on this ship?"

"I was brought aboard by the slavers to see if you were worth saving."

"And then you helped the captain liberate the ship?"

"Correct."

Gingerly, Vlasa slipped his feet down to the deck. His cybernetic leg held his weight without difficulty and his real leg held as well. But the incision in his abdomen hurt with every movement. He let the pain subside, and then started for the door.

"It is my understanding that you are the ship's engineer. You have configured a wireless data network to share information and allow communications, but one that is physically isolated from any control systems?"

"Correct," Vlasa said, curious.

"Can you build me a new wireless receiver that would do the same thing? Should one of your fragile biological components fail, you will need to contact me quickly. And I do not want to be taken over by another master AI."

Vlasa stopped and looked at the impassive metallic expression on Mesu's face. He considered the request for a moment before saying, "I will make your request to the captain."

He turned back and continued through the door before the unusual drone could say any more. It did not take him long to find the rest of the crew. The sounds of machinery echoed down the corridor from the environmental control room. Voices intermingled with the sounds.

Vlasa stepped through the open door and found Ariana, Olivia, and Javi pulling apart the CO_2 scrubber. Pieces of charred insulation and filters littered the floor. Scattered among the ruined debris were perfectly functional components. The view made Vlasa want to scream.

Instead, Olivia was the one to scream, "Vlasa! You're awake!"

The young human girl dropped the tool she was using and raced over to embrace him. The sudden impact against his sore abdomen made him flinch. Reluctantly, Vlasa lifted an arm and patted Olivia's back. As soon as he gauged he had met his social obligation, he pulled her off him.

More respectful of his personal space, Ariana nevertheless bore an expression he judged indicated that she wished she could follow Olivia's lead. Instead, she gave him a solemn nod, which he returned. Javi likewise nodded to him.

"It's good to see you up and about. I'm surprised Mesu released you, though. He seemed convinced you were going to die." Javi said.

"I'm pretty sure Mesu thinks all biological life forms are about to drop dead at any moment," Ariana said with a smirk.

"Perhaps. But regardless, I am functional enough to resume my duties. Something I very much think you are in need of." Vlasa said.

Ariana had the good sense to give a sheepish expression at his statement before saying, "You have no idea. We're still trying to repair the damage from the fire in here. That's the worst of it. I managed to rewire the FTL system back into place after your little jury rig. It's worked fine for several jumps, but I'm sure you'll want to look it over. We did seal up the hull breach in weapons control and a few other minor things. But I'm also interested in any ideas you have for turning one of the crew quarters into a brig."

"A brig? What did Noah do?" Vlasa asked.

"Nothing short of showing some compassion."

"For a despicable slaver," Olivia added with a sour expression.

"We ran into some trouble with some slavers at M-21 station." Ariana explained, "We ended up with a new guest."

"Because Noah wouldn't port the bitch off the ship."

"It is equally likely that we engaged the FTL at the same time and the teleporter failed to engage," Javi said diplomatically.

"A likely story," Olivia said, but quietly.

"What's a likely story?" Noah asked as he came into the room, "Squee took care of those bodies, Cap."

"Good. It will feel better having them off the ship." Ariana said, and then cast a pointed look at Olivia before saying to Vlasa, "We have an individual onboard that I don't want having free access to the ship. Squee is standing guard over her now. But we can't keep that up indefinitely."

Vlasa nodded, "It should be a simple matter to disable the internal door controls from one room. Though anyone competent with electronics would be able to rewire it."

"She is an Echanic," Javi said.

Vlasa turned to the Slu, "That's a surprisingly prejudiced statement coming from you."

"I meant only that you could never be certain what cybernetic upgrades she might have."

"Just one for her eyes," Noah interjected. He gestured to Vlasa, "Unlike metal boy, she doesn't go for all those artificial parts."

Vlasa turned a curious eye to Noah, "She is a Messite?"

Noah shrugged, "That sounds familiar, I guess."

"What's a Messite?" Olivia asked.

"A sect among my people who believe it is a desecration to improve our bodies with cybernetics. They are a small group, and you rarely find them off the home world."

"But she has an eye implant," Olivia said.

"She's blind." Noah replied, "Needs that to see. But I can assure you that's all she has."

"Yes, I'm sure you are intimately familiar with her body."

Noah gave a small shrug, "Been a few years. But I did do a strip search to make sure she didn't have any weapons on her. Only two knives and a backup pistol. I'm a little disappointed in her."

"Does she know her way around electronics, Noah?" Ariana said redirecting the conversation, "Could she repair anything Vlasa did to disable the lock?"

"Probably. She's exceptionally good with locks and triggers. Best to just weld over the door controls if you want to lock her up. She isn't much of a threat right now, though. No profit in attacking us when we're in the middle of nowhere. I doubt she could calculate an FTL jump. Math isn't her thing."

"We won't be here forever, so I'd rather not have to worry about her causing trouble the next time we run into that LFD fleet." Ariana said, and then aside to Vlasa added, "Those are the people who want Javi. He apparently stole some plans of theirs to attack PUG headquarters with a new AI fleet."

"I really have missed a lot," Vlasa said.

A sudden beeping sound interrupted the conversation, and Ariana pulled out her handheld. She read the screen and said, "Well, you're not going to miss this. We've just picked up an approaching ship."

24- Ariana

"Well, it doesn't look like an extremist warship." Ariana mused.

"Neither did that last one," Olivia said.

"Fair. Keep our distance just in case."

"Do you treat everyone you meet like a potential threat?"

Ariana glanced back toward her Echanic prisoner, handcuffed to a handrail behind her. Javi stood next to her holding a weapon. She didn't like the idea of leaving Serene unguarded or with just one person other than Squee. But she also didn't trust leaving her with Noah. Not during a potential battle, at least.

That meant tolerating interruptions, "Not until recently."

Serene smiled, "I am glad I could have such a positive impact on your life. A healthy dose of caution will help you in the long run."

Ariana sighed and looked back at her sensor display. The two ships were approaching on a tangential path. Every move Olivia made triggered a counter move from the other ship. But she couldn't quite discern the pattern.

"They don't appear to be trying to close on us, but also aren't running away either."

"It's like they can't decide what they're doing. Only having functional sensors on one side isn't making my job very easy either. I can't just turn away, or we'd lose sight of them." Olivia said.

"Vlasa, what do you make of her?"

"Small freighter. Bigger than us, but mostly cargo space. More massive, which makes her maneuvers more sluggish by comparison. That might account for some of it. By the time the ship completes a maneuver, it's to counter something we did a minute ago."

Ariana thought for a moment, "All that mass could easily be used to disguise weapons or the ability to launch a smaller, more maneuverable ship. I'm going to power the weapons. Just as a warning."

They were far enough away from the other ship that she felt comfortable drawing power from the shields to bring both weapons online. Without knowing what kind of sensor array the other ship had, she couldn't be sure they would see that change. And she wanted them to know it.

"Sending an active scan pulse. Just to show them we're watching." Ariana announced. She triggered the active sensors, and a pulse of energy flashed through space. She would be able to gather far more data this way than just the passive sensors. But she didn't follow up or narrow the scan, either. Those actions could easily be interpreted as hostile.

To her shock, the moment after the active scan completed, the other ship cut its engines. A large mass ejected from the ship. Whatever the object was, it moved slowly on a course that would take it near, but not directly to, *Seraph*.

Performing another more focused active scan, Ariana tried to determine what had been sent their way. She once again cursed her cut-rate sensor system. She could get an approximate mass of the object, that it was unpowered and metallic. From that, it could be anything from a bomb to a crate of toys.

A light flashed on her display indicating they were receiving an incoming communication request. She supposed that talking would be one way to clear things up. She accepted the request, and switched her channel over.

"*Pirate ship, this is the MSV* Love Lost. *We have jettisoned our most valuable cargo. May we proceed to our destination?*"

"*Love Lost*, this is *Seraph*, we're not pirates."

"*I'm sorry! I didn't mean that. I meant we're just going to leave this very valuable cargo here and be on our way. Of our own free will. Please don't kill us.*"

The transmission suddenly cut off. A few seconds later the other ship's engines activated again, and it started accelerating away. Within a few moments, Ariana was going to have to choose to keep their sensors focused on the fleeing ship or the object now floating toward them.

Switching back to the ship's internal network she said, "They appear to think we're pirates. They ejected some cargo as a fee and are now running for their lives."

Behind her, Serene laughed as Noah said, *"Nice work, Cap. Free loot."*

"We can't take that!" Olivia said, *"That would be stealing."*

"They just left it here. That's not stealing." Noah argued.

"Because they thought we were pirates."

"I can't control what other people think."

Squee joined the discussion; *"We did just throw several bodies out into space and then point our weapons at them. With the addition of the tri-cannon, we would appear to be considerably well armed."*

Another chuckle came from Serene who could not hear the discussion raging, "I assume Noah is advocating picking up the cargo while your noble, and valiant crew opposes?"

Ariana shifted in her seat, "You know him well, it seems."

"Very."

"He has a point."

"That's surprising to hear from you, Captain. You strike me as the honorable, by the book type."

"You obviously don't know Ari very well." Javi quipped.

"Oh, but I'm getting to know her. She seems more and more like my kind of captain. Pragmatism. That is how you survive in this galaxy."

Ariana shifted back away from Serene. She and Noah had a good point. That other ship had just left the cargo sitting here. She had tried to tell them she wasn't a pirate.

"Noah, are we close enough to ping the containers manifest ID tag? If it even is a cargo container."

"Not yet."

"Olivia, bring us within range, but no closer than necessary."

A few tense minutes passed as *Seraph* moved closer to the object. It took longer than necessary, as Olivia had to make a wide approach to keep both fleeing ship and container in their sensor window. Ariana wondered what the other ship would make of that. It would not be hard to guess their crippled state.

"Okay, I'm getting a reading from its ID tag. It contains something called a TC-F54 Toroidal Field Coil. An MC-7X Ion Cyclotron System. And GA-1K Torus CryoPump. None of those sound like weapons. Or valuables."

"They are even better than that." Vlasa said excitedly, *"Those are components for a fusion reactor. With them, I might be able to upgrade our own, so we can actually power everything."*

"Might be able to?" Ariana asked.

"Those are not the components used in our current reactor. I won't know if I can integrate them with spare parts we have on hand until I get a closer look."

"Might be is still better than can't." Ariana decided, "Olivia, bring us within teleporter range."

"Captain," Serene began. Unlike before, her words were oddly hesitant.

Ariana turned around and gave a curious look at her prisoner. Timidity was not something she had come to associate with Serene. Apprehensively, she said, "Go ahead."

"I would like to offer my assistance to you. It's clear to me that you are a worthy leader to follow. I understand now why Noah has decided to join your crew."

Narrowing her eyes, Ariana studied Serene. The cybernetic eye implants made it difficult to gauge her sincerity. Despite years working with Vlasa, she hadn't quite picked up Echanic body language.

"You tried to steal my ship and threatened to sell my crew and me into slavery. And now you want a job?"

One of Serene's more enigmatic smiles returned, "Like you, I am a practical woman. I could continue to cause trouble and remain chained to walls until you decide that the most practical solution is to strand me somewhere. Or I can take a gift when I see it. Unlike my former employer, I don't think you'd ever torture me."

"No, no I wouldn't. But then I'm not in the habit of subjugating people into slavery either."

"We all have questionable events in our past. I, no more than Noah."

"I'm sure." Ariana agreed noncommittally, "I'll think about your offer. For now, Javi, take her back to her quarters. I'll send Olivia and Squee to relieve you."

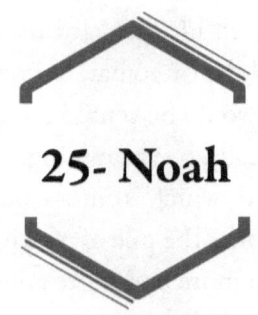

25- Noah

"So, you think it could be a bomb?" Noah asked as he worked the crowbar into the sides of the crate they had retrieved from space.

"It is not a bomb." Vlasa said matter-of-factly, "I have already performed x-ray scans and checked for traces of explosive compounds."

"Sure. But you could be wrong."

"I am never wrong."

"Never? Wow. I hope I get to be there when your ego deflates after being proven how wrong you are." Noah said with a smile. Then it fade as he considered. "Unless that is right now. I really hope right now isn't the time you are wrong."

With a final flick of the crowbar, Noah popped the side of the crate off. A loud clang echoed through the cargo bay when it hit the deck. Packing foam spilled out everywhere, prompting him to groan.

"Uh, I hate cleaning this crap up."

Vlasa bent down to inspect the contents of the crate. He pushed several more piles of the foam on the deck, "The surest path to happiness is to love what you excel at. If you strive for that, when you are done cleaning all of this up, you will have achieved nirvana."

Noah frowned for a second, but then started chuckling, "Did you just give me a compliment while attempting to insult me?"

Looking up, Vlasa cocked his head, "I do not see how you could come to that conclusion."

"You just implied I'm a bad ass when it comes to cleaning. And it must have been intentional seeing as how you never make mistakes."

Leaving Vlasa sitting there looking confused, Noah went to the locker and got out the vacuum. Turning back to survey the mess still spilling out onto the deck, he reconsidered his plan. If instead of trying to clean it, he moved everything else out of the cargo bay, he could just blow the bay doors. Then everything left in here would be vented out into space. And space was a vacuum so he would, technically, be vacuuming.

While Noah considered which route would require less effort, he watched Vlasa resume his work. The pile of packing foam continued to grow. Every handful made the idea more and more appealing. Lost in thought, he failed to notice Javi slithering up behind him.

"I think it's time we finished our conversation from earlier." The Slu said.

"Oh, which one?" Noah asked without turning around.

"You know what I'm referring too," Javi said forcefully.

Turning to look directly into the eyestalks of the Slu, Noah shook his head, "No, I really don't."

"After we encountered that first LFD ship. Neither of us was interested in discussing what happened over there. Now I've come clean about my dealings with LFD. And I've realized why you were as concerned."

"Enlighten me."

"Those same banners we saw on the ship were hanging in Gerald's chamber. He must be part of LFD." Javi said.

"Maybe. I haven't had anything to do with him for a long time." Noah snapped defensively.

"No, obviously not. You didn't recognize the LFD banner that hung beside it. But you did work for him at some point."

"Worked for is a nebulous description."

Javi sighed, "You don't need to be so coy. I don't care what you did for this slaver. But others might. Serene is certainly making every effort to play up your association with them."

"I'm sure she is. Wants everyone to associate the two of us and either get the crew to turn against me, or get some good will thrown her way."

"This does not surprise you?"

"Nah, I would expect no less from her."

"And you're not concerned?"

Noah shrugged, "Why should I be? I have nothing to be ashamed of."

"You're not ashamed of being associated with slavers?"

"It is what it is."

Javi lowered his eyestalks and studied Noah more intently, "You are a curious human."

"Nicest thing you've ever said to me, mate."

The pair settled back into silence for a few minutes, watching Vlasa continue to study the items coming out of the crate. The engineer appeared oblivious to them and quite thrilled with his task. He'd never known anyone who loved gadgets and gizmos more.

A high pitch alert suddenly sounded from everyone's handhelds. The warning tone was quickly followed by a stern voice, *"Crew of the transport ship* Seraph, *this is the PUG patrol ship* Diligence. *You are ordered to cut your engines and prepare to be boarded. Any attempt to resist will be met with deadly force."*

Noah shared a look with Javi and Vlasa before bringing up the ship's sensor display on the cargo bays computer. He saw nothing for several seconds. Then slowly the approaching PUG ship started to come into view as *Seraph* started to rotate.

"Everyone get to your battle stations," Ariana ordered over the shipside comm network.

"This is a good thing. We've been trying to reach PUG HQ. A ship is just as good. Right?" Vlasa asked.

"Not when they start out by ordering us to heave too. That's usually followed by being arrested." Noah said with clear confidence.

26- Ariana

❝ *Diligence*, this is *Seraph*. We have an urgent matter to discuss."

Ariana tapped her fingers on her console while she waited for a reply. She had hoped to avoid running into PUG patrols before they reached Triask. It would certainly make her life easier if she could just pass on Javi's information and be done. But Javi had insisted that by the time it worked its way through the bureaucratic process, it would be to late. Now she might not have a choice.

"Seraph, *power down your engines.*"

"We are preparing to comply. Now, I need to speak to your captain." If she did not get any kind of promise from the PUG captain before they were boarded, she knew she never would.

"*This is* Diligence *actual. Go ahead* Seraph, *and make it quick.*"

"Captain, I have aboard a passenger who has urgent business at PUG HQ on Triask. He has information regarding a potential attack."

"*By passenger, I assume you're referring to the fugitive Javi Wester that you are carrying?*"

Ariana blinked. Javi had not mentioned anything about being a fugitive. Though, that would explain his reluctance to tangle with any random PUG patrols. Maybe PUG weren't as clueless about LFD's plans after all.

"I do refer to Javi Wester. He has vital intelligence about the coming attack that must reach Triask. Before I can turn him over to you, I need assurance that he will be brought there post haste."

"*Captain, you're in no position to make any kind of demands. We'll assess what the fugitive has to say during interrogation and deal with it in the appropriate manner. Anything you reveal in your interrogation will be taken into consideration at your sentencing.*"

"My what?"

"*Sentencing, Captain. You are wanted on charges of piracy, murder and transporting a fugitive across interstellar space. Don't make me add resisting arrest to those charges.*"

"Goddamn it, Javi." Ariana said to herself, "What did you get me into?"

Switching back to the ship's network she said, "I've told the cruiser about our mission to reach PUG HQ and the pending LFD attack. They aren't buying it. Apparently, we're wanted for transporting a fugitive."

"*You mean Javi? Or Noah?*" Olivia asked.

"Javi. I suspect they have been tracking us since the Hub. That freighter whose cargo we salvaged must have pointed them right to us. So now we're facing piracy charges too."

"*Captain, we should turn ourselves in. Then we can straighten things out and deliver our message.*" Squee suggested.

"I don't really feel like being arrested today, do you, Squee?" Ariana sighed.

"*If it will help us complete our mission, some sacrifices might be necessary.*"

"*You go ahead buddy. I'll take the route that leaves me out of a prison cell.*" Noah added.

"Unfortunately, they aren't in a listening mood. We only have a short time before the planned attack. If we turn ourselves in, I suspect we'll spend most of that time in a holding cell waiting to talk to someone."

Another alarm sounded and Ariana glanced at the sensor display. The PUG cruiser's shields had taken multiple impacts. "Olivia, roll the ship!"

Seraph started to roll to starboard. After a few seconds, the PUG cruiser vanished from her scopes and another ship appeared. When she recognized the profile, her heart skipped a beat. A drone warship.

Over a decade ago, she had fought ships exactly like this one. She had seen friends die in those battles. Entire colony worlds had been wiped out, their populations eradicated from orbit.

Now they were back.

"Evasive maneuvers! Full power to shields!" Ariana ordered.

She shut down the tri-cannon but kept their original cannon powered to use for point defense. They had no hope of defeating this warship in a fight. Flight would be their only hope.

"*Seraph, power your FTL and prepare to jump. We'll cover you.*" The PUG ship transmitted.

Despite the circumstances, the call from the PUG ship made her shake her head. From preparing to arrest her, to trying to defend her. That perfectly encapsulated her relationship with the PUG.

Unfortunately, she didn't put much stock in the cruisers chances. A small patrol ship, *Diligence* was more than a match for *Seraph,* but the AI warship similarly outclassed her. If they fought, they would die.

"Don't be a fool, *Diligence.* That ship will tear you apart. Get out of here. They're after us."

"*If what you say is true, and I'm beginning to believe you, then you have to reach Triask. So go!*"

Ariana growled, but said, "Can we jump, Vlasa?"

"*We can.*"

"Then do it."

"*Jumping now,*" Olivia said.

Once they were clear, Ariana said, "*Stand down everyone. We've got a bit of a real space transit ahead of us before the next jump. Vlasa, let's find out if that cargo crate is worth all the trouble it's caused.*"

27- Squee

Squee sat patiently while Vlasa relayed his report to Ariana. He had assisted in the assessment, so none of the news came as new information to him. But it was proper to remain attentive.

Vlasa continued, "I've completed my assessment of the reactor components. All of the major parts are there for a complete fusion reactor. Unfortunately, it is missing a few comparatively minor components."

"Comparatively minor?" Ariana asked skeptically.

"Yes, mainly involving the safety regulators and control processors."

"Those sound important." Ariana said.

"Only if you want to keep the reactor from turning into a bomb."

Ariana shrugged her arms, "Honestly, a fusion bomb might come in handy. Given that we're being chased by terrorists, murderous AI, and now the military."

Squee suppressed his displeasure at Ariana's flippant tone in her last comment. It would be improper to question the captain, who he had pledged himself to serve. Still, he disagreed with the decision not to turn themselves into the PUG patrol ship.

"It wouldn't be a very good fusion bomb," Vlasa said.

"A bad fusion bomb is better than any ordinance we have onboard."

"By bad, I don't mean lacking in explosive potential. I mean bad in lacking the ability to be used as a reliable bomb. To detonate, it would need fuel, which it only has when hooked up to the ship. Also, the reaction would be uncontrollable, meaning it could overload and destroy us as soon as we turn it on or two days from when we wanted it to explode."

Ariana held up her hands, "Alright. No fusion bombs. Got it. I take it no extra power either?"

"Not on its own." Vlasa said, and then gestured to Squee, "But Squee did have an idea."

Startled, Squee sat there silently for a moment. He had not expected to need to speak during this briefing. By rights, as the senior engineer, Vlasa should explain everything. Squee was just there to show solidarity.

Recovering, he stood, "Yes, while the reactor cannot be powered up independently to provide us with additional power, we could use it as a source of alternative power."

"A backup, sure. Never a bad thing to have."

Squee looked again to Vlasa who gestured for him to continue, "Excuse me, Captain, I did not make myself clear. Not merely as a backup, but as an alternative. When we were exposed to that ion effect from the pulsar, Vlasa overcame the field shutting down the FTL by bypassing the charged circuits. It was a stopgap, emergency measure. But effective. With an entirely separate reactor, we could switch power pathways to the shields to counteract those effects."

"So, we'd be immune to ion weapons?" Ariana asked eagerly.

"No." Vlasa answered flatly, "We could recover from them faster, or potentially cycle the reactors and shield generators to almost always keep one level of shielding functional. Any ion effects that got past the shields would be unaffected and just as devastating.

"But what it would be very effective against, would be natural ion effects. Like another pulsar or those from a nebula."

Ariana brightened at this news. She stood up immediately, "Excellent work. How soon until it's up and running?"

"A few hours."

"That should be enough," Ariana said, and then practically skipped from the room.

Squee tilted his head at the odd behavior. He turned to Vlasa, "I do not understand the captain's enthusiasm. While this plan is certainly beneficial to the ship, I do not see any immediate advantages. Perhaps she did not understand?"

Vlasa shook his head, "No, she understood. With this in place, we'll finally be able to pass through the Unmar nebula."

"I am unfamiliar with this phenomenon."

"The Unmar nebula sits practically in the middle of explored space. It's light years across, full of forming star systems. And it's charged with unusual electrical fields. Ships hardened against the effects can save weeks of travel time by cutting through it."

"Which would help us reach Triask faster," Squee said, nodding approvingly.

"Sure, a little bit. From where we are and where Triask is, the main advantage is giving us more choices. But after this is all over, is when it will really come in handy. Because we can save so much time, we'll be able to pick up more lucrative delivery contracts. That and it's a great place to hide. In several systems its almost impossible to find another ship that's not practically on top of you. Should this whole LFD craziness bring about another AI war, we'll have someplace to hole up."

Squee frowned and felt his spine stiffen, "Why would you even imagine something like that? We will not fail this quest."

Vlasa shrugged, "I hope we don't. But I, and the captain, like to have a backup plan. Now, let's get this thing installed."

Watching Vlasa walk out of the room, Squee felt his shoulders slump. Could he have misjudged his crewmates so badly? Did they lack the conviction to succeed?

28- Olivia

"It's beautiful, isn't it?" Javi asked.

"What is?" Olivia said, half paying attention.

"The nebula."

"We can't even see the nebula."

"I didn't mean it *looks* beautiful. I meant it *is* beautiful."

Olivia turned in her chair to look at the old Slu resting behind her on the flight deck. She scrunched up her face with an exasperated feeling, "What does that mean?"

Javi smiled, and his eyestalks stretched back with his mouth, "You don't have to see something for it to be beautiful."

"What are you, some kind of sappy greeting card? Finding the inner beauty of the nebula?"

"Maybe."

She shook her head and turned around. She checked their course again, looked at the nonsense displayed on the sensors, and pulled her jacket tighter around herself. Anything could be out there, and she would have no idea.

"My home world is located in a similar type of nebula. It is always comforting to be back inside one. I know it doesn't make any logical sense, but there it is."

Frustrated, Olivia turned around, "Is there a reason you're telling me this?"

"Just trying to make conversation."

"Fair enough. But why are you even here in the first place?"

"Ariana asked me to be on hand. My telepathic senses are magnified while inside a nebula. Most ships that cross one like to have a Slu onboard. In here, my senses may be more effective than our sensors in detecting a threat."

"Oh."

Silence returned to the flight deck for several minutes. Javi said nothing, and Olivia assumed that meant they weren't in any immediate danger. She was forced to navigate the ship via dead reckoning and optical measurements. None of the electronic instruments told her anything.

"When I first came onboard, you appeared to be quite eager to experience new things. Your pure enthusiasm for going down to that uncharted planet was very heartening. It felt good to see such optimism still alive in the galaxy."

When Olivia didn't say anything in response, Javi continued, "Lately, it's seemed that optimism has vanished. I know that being chased by fanatics trying to bring about the end of days can't be what you were expecting."

Not turning around, Olivia finally said, "There are always crazy people out there. That doesn't surprise me. That they want to bring the AI back, that does. It caused so much destruction. Why would anyone think that was a good idea? Not to mention that we're hauling around not one, but two slavers. And we even have an AI of our very own, ready to murder us in our sleep the moment we let our guard down. So yeah, I've come to realize the universe isn't as friendly as I first thought. Thanks for the life lesson."

Javi let out a heavy sigh, "I am sorry that you had to learn that lesson so harshly. Life isn't normally as bad as this. Most people are good people. Even the ones that seem bad at first, are just trying to get by."

"Sure, just trying to get by. While enslaving others. Or resurrecting AI that once tried to eradicate all life in the galaxy. They don't mean anything by it." Olivia sneered.

"No, it's not that. Most people, who do something bad, didn't set out to be bad. They crossed a line, a line they shouldn't have crossed, sure. But that normally happens by centimeters. Suddenly, they find themselves on the other side and no idea how they got there. Once they do, they have to decide to stay or go back. They can't undo what they've already done, but they can try and make up for it."

Olivia cocked an eyebrow, "Are you trying to get me to forgive Noah?"

Javi's eyestalks leaned backward for a second before resetting to their usual position, "Yes. Yes, that's it. That's it exactly. Noah. I don't think he is as bad as you have come to think. Just because you know slavers, doesn't mean you are one."

"It is if you let it happen."

"Just think about..." Javi said and then stopped, "There's something out there."

Olivia froze for a second and then quickly turned back to her displays. She scanned the readings and growled when she continued to get nothing. Here in the nebula, it didn't matter that half their sensor array was busted because she still couldn't see anything.

Trying the optical scanners, she surveyed space. She saw lots of stars in the distance. If something were right on top of them, she probably would be able to see it blocking those stars. But in such vastness, it would have to be very close already.

"I don't see anything. Are you sure?"

"No, unfortunately." Javi admitted, "Just a feeling that something is out there that wasn't before."

"Like a ship jumping in? Can you sense that kind of thing? I thought it was just life forms."

"Under normal conditions, it is just life forms. But inside the nebula, it gets, magnified. And I don't detect life forms. Just...something."

Olivia froze, "I really don't like the sound of that."

Javi extended his eyestalks to their maximum height. He frowned and tilted his head side to side a few times, "Turn to port."

Without argument, Olivia did. She waited with her hands on the controls looking furtively at the fuzzy sensor display. Unexpectedly it started to clear up. She rotated the ship around so she could get a full picture around them. They had cleared the nebula.

"We're out of the sensor jumble. There is nothing around us."

Javi let out a sigh, "Whatever it was, has begun to recede. It is still in there."

"Should we tell the captain?"

"Probably."

Olivia nodded, "Captain, Javi says he detected something in the nebula. I changed course away from it, and we came into an open pocket. We're clear for our next jump."

"That's sooner than I was expecting. Can you make it to the next system we were aiming for from here?"

"I'll have to double check our position, but I think so." Olivia said, and then glanced down at a warning light, "One-second captain, we're picking up a distress signal."

29- Ariana

"It's a trap," Noah said with a smug expression.

Ariana turned away from the display in the cramped flight deck to give him a direct look, "Of course it's a trap."

"Then why are we heading into it?"

"Because it might not be."

Turning back to the display, Ariana instructed the computer to calculate its point of origin. Sitting in the helm seat below her, Olivia already had the FTL calculation charts open. After a few seconds of work, the computer identified the system of origin for the signal. It matched the information encoded in the distress signal itself.

"Looks like we'll only have to make one jump and it doesn't take us far off course," Ariana said, studying the charts over Olivia's shoulder, "We can check it out without losing any time getting to Triask."

"That system looks to be pretty barren," Olivia said.

"Perfect place for an ambush then. No witnesses." Noah added, "You know they are counting on someone playing the Good Samaritan."

"I'm sure you understand exactly how they think from your years as a slaver." Olivia said, with clear maliciousness in her voice.

"Listen up kid because I'm only going to say this once." Noah's voice was flat and quiet, but it sent a shiver down Ariana's spine. She and Olivia turned to face him, and the direct gaze he leveled at Olivia reinforced that feeling of threat.

"I've made a lot of questionable decisions in my life, some of them even I regret. But I have never willingly participated in slavery. When I steal, I steal things. When I kill, I kill people trying to kill me. When I hire a whore, the whore gets the money. I don't use people who have no choice. You can go on hating me, but make sure it's for the right reasons."

The silence when Noah finished hung heavy in the air. Olivia's contemptuous expression softened a little. Ariana gave the tension a good minute to work its way out, hoping the animosity between the two died before it could start to fester.

"Noah, secure Serene as best you can, and then get ready to either receive injured, or repel boarders. Bring Mesu down to the porter with you." Ariana ordered, "Olivia, plot us a jump and get the next jump ready in case we need to make a quick exit. Keep us on course for PUG HQ."

The decision made, Ariana left the flight deck and headed for the weapon control room. On the way, she reconnected her earpiece to the ship's network, "Vlasa, your reactor modifications holding up?"

"They are operating at an acceptable level of functionality." Vlasa intoned. The no-nonsense tone of his voice gave her a small smile. She had missed his calming effect.

"Good. I don't know what we're going to be jumping into, so I want full power to the new shields. But I also don't want to leave us defenseless."

"As you know, the reactor cannot sustain both the shields at the new power levels, and the weapons. Not unless we took other systems offline such as the FTL, sublight engines or environmental systems."

"Shutting down environmental systems wouldn't kill us for a few hours."

"With the damage that system has sustained, shutting things down would impart extra strain on it to restore optimal conditions. That might result in additional, potentially fatal, damage to the system."

"Okay, so let's not do that. How long can the weapon capacitors hold their charge?"

"The capacitors are not designed for long-term energy storage. They could probably hold enough charge to be able to fire for about ten minutes. But that would only allow for one discharge from each."

"One is better than none." Ariana said as she took her place at the weapon controls, "I am charging the weapons now. Squee, when they're ready, bring the shields up to full, and then we'll jump."

Several minutes of work passed before everyone reported they were ready. Ariana charged *Seraph*'s weapons, including the newly installed tri-cannon. Once the capacitor showed maximum charge, she disengaged the power flow. When Squee reported the shields ready, she ordered the jump and got herself ready for whatever would be waiting for them.

To her infinite delight, they didn't jump into the middle of a minefield or a waiting barrage of weapon fire. Fortunately, space was big and setting up a minefield to catch a ship right after a jump, was prohibitively expensive. You could make an FTL jump to anywhere. Better to put any mines or weapons where you knew someone would go; such as right around a ship emitting a distress signal.

"Olivia, give us a full rotation."

Due to the continued absence of functional sensors on the starboard side, Olivia had to put the ship into a gentle spin to see everything. The incoming data on the source of the distress signal was intermittent and lacked much detail. But even their limited sensors could identify their target.

"I'm reading one ship adrift. No evident power signature. No objects large enough to be drones or mines within range to be considered a danger." Ariana reported to the rest of the crew. "Closest other detectable object is an asteroid point two AU."

"That's a Kestrel class, Captain!" Olivia shouted with evident glee.

Ariana inspected the sensor readings more closely. She recognized the profile almost immediately. There were a few minor differences, but the ship was the same base model as *Seraph*.

"So, if they turn out to all be dead and not bait, does that mean we get to loot her for parts?" Noah asked.

"Let's focus on those first two things. Olivia, move us close enough to get an interior reading. We need to know if there is an atmosphere." Arian ordered. She then switched her headset to a new network channel and started broadcasting a message into space, "Attention disabled ship. This is the *Seraph*. We have received your signal and stand ready to assist you. Please respond."

The two ships moved closer together, and the sensor information slowly became more detailed. Ariana repeated her broadcast every minute until they were close enough that she would have been able to see the other ship with her own eyes if there had been a window to look out of. Then she stopped trying.

"I don't think anyone is there to respond, Captain." Vlasa said, "There is a major hull breach that goes all the way through. Sublight engines appear destroyed as does the FTL."

Ariana focused her display on looking at where Vlasa had mentioned. Something had evidently punched a hole completely through the other ship. That single impact would have breached the pressure seals on at least a third of the ship.

"Analysis, Vlasa, any chance of survivors?"

"Depending on how long ago this occurred. Someone could have survived in the sealed parts of the ship for about one day. Maybe two if they had an environmental suit with them. Unfortunately, the distress beacon does not contain a timestamp on its activation."

"That's a pretty common tactic for pirates. That way it can transmit as long as necessary to catch someone without needing to be constantly reset." Noah said.

"It's also common for an off the shelf emergency beacon set by someone who doesn't know what they're doing." Ariana countered, "What condition do you make for the rest of the ship? Anything worth salvaging?"

"Aside from the single hull breach, the rest of the hull appears to be intact and undamaged. Replacement sensor clusters and hull plating would be easy. Likewise, environmental controls are not in the damaged section of the ship and would have compatible replacement parts we could use.

"And if that is an M700 series as I suspect, I would very much like to get to the reactor. With certain components, I should be able to get the second reactor online. Then we could keep the shields and the weapons active at once. At least, some of the weapons."

The prospect for restoring Seraph to working condition was very tempting. But the potential for disaster also hung heavy on Ariana's mind. Leaving this ship alone without looking for survivors was unconscionable, and leaving behind the parts she needed to keep her ship running, would be irresponsible. But so would getting caught in a well-laid trap.

"Noah, if you had left this ship here, in this condition, what would your plan be?"

"Well, this is a relatively out of the way system. You won't see much traffic, so you don't want to have to wait for who knows how long. I would set up an alert to trigger when someone happened by."

"FTL comm signals can only travel a few light years. Do you think they're local or in a neighboring system?"

"Probably inside the nebula. Much easier to hide a base. I'd probably rig up an ion pulse mine to the ship itself. Undetectable by most commercial sensors set up like that, but powerful enough to disable damn near anything. And because of the nebula, almost any traffic you get passing through here is going to be a big score. After the mine disables something, they would have plenty of time to get here before the unwary victim got their ship functional again. And it would keep the booty intact. Battle damaged ships make for good bait, but have terrible re-sale value."

Ariana frowned. An ion pulse mine was not something she wanted to contend with. But she couldn't just leave either, "Do you think you could find and disable any rigged relay or mine that might be over there?"

"Identify, sure, if I was over there. As for disabling it, not a chance. But I know someone who could. Though, you aren't going to like it."

Letting out a slow breath, Ariana said, "Let me guess, Serene?"

30- Vlasa

"**I** should be the one to go," Vlasa stated.

Ariana shook her head emphatically, "You are still recovering. I'm not sending you on an EVA with a lunatic killer."

"You could leave the lunatic killer here. I am capable of monitoring Serene on my own."

In the brief silence that followed, Ariana smiled and Noah tilted his head slightly before saying, "Hold on a second."

Ignoring Noah, Vlasa continued, "If Noah is correct, Serene is intelligent enough to know that she would only be hurting herself by betraying us to an unknown group of pirates. In which case, it does not matter who goes with her, as I will not be in danger. But if Noah is wrong, as he often is, then I am the one most likely to be able to ascertain if she has betrayed us."

Ariana sighed, "And you are sure you could not disarm it yourself?"

"No, I am not sure. There is a greater than zero chance I could indeed do it entirely myself. But given my lack of experience with this kind of situation, our odds would be better with someone more familiar with the potential problems."

"All right, suit up." Ariana decided.

"But Cap..." Noah began.

Ariana cut him off with a look, "Bring our guest down to the cargo bay."

Noah departed, and Vlasa turned to make his way to the cargo bay. Ariana followed silently. She helped him don the cumbersome EV suit and then prepare the second one. Before they had finished, Serene appeared flanked by Noah with a gun.

"Noah said you wished to see me, Captain?" Serene asked.

"You said you wanted to help out. Here's your chance. You're going to prove how useful you can be." Ariana said with a smirk, "Suit up. You're going for a little trip."

"There is some lock you want me to pick?" Serene asked, and then after a moment she smiled, "No, a bomb you want me to disarm."

Ariana nodded, "Potentially. There's an abandoned ship sitting out there broadcasting a distress signal. You and Vlasa are going to see if there are any survivors and make sure the ship isn't booby-trapped."

"I am not a fan of space suits," Serene said with a frown.

"You can go without it if you want. But I wouldn't recommend it."

As Serene reluctantly started to don her suit, Vlasa opened the weapon locker and checked the charge on one of the pistols. Before he could strap the gun belt on, Noah stepped over to him.

"You don't want to take that."

"You are suggesting I go off the ship with a prisoner while unarmed?"

"If you want to come back in one piece."

"Explain."

"If you take a weapon, it won't be long before Serene borrows it. She has sticky fingers when it comes to that kind of thing."

Vlasa frowned, "I thought you said she would not try anything while she has no means to escape."

"No, I said she would not butcher us all in our sleep and strand herself in the middle of nowhere, or signal a group of pirates who are just as likely to rape and murder her as the rest of us. But, if she gets herself a weapon...well...then she has a bargaining position."

Vlasa considered Noah's statement. He felt mild annoyance at the suggestion he would be careless enough to let himself become disarmed. Though, he was self-aware enough to know that Noah's concern was not unfounded. He did not possess any combat training.

"Very well. I will accede to your experience in this."

The shocked expression on Noah's face made Vlasa feel even better about his decision. He made a note that agreeing with Noah on occasion might be a good way to keep him off balance.

Putting the gun belt back in the locker, Vlasa trudged over to the teleporter chamber in the cumbersome pressure suit. Once in place, he sealed the facemask and did a comm check to be sure he could still communicate with those on the ship. With Ariana's help, Serene donned her pressure suit and joined him in the chamber.

"I would suggest putting us just outside whatever hole got blown into the side of our target. If this is a trap, it is most likely set to trigger if anyone teleports into the pressurized areas. Or if any of the airlocks open." Serene suggested.

Ariana nodded and then entered the coordinates into the teleporter controls. She gave Vlasa a tip of her head and then triggered the chamber. Around him, the world changed. The comforting pull of the ship's artificial gravity vanished, as did the lights. The dim glint of millions of far-off stars became his only light source. Blocked by the derelict ship, light from this system's star cast no light down on him.

Vlasa activated his suits headlamps and turned slowly to survey the scene. About five meters in front of him sat the derelict. A fantastic rent in the metal hull showed him what, on *Seraph*, would have been the mess hall. Torn metal continued in deeper through what had once been the deck floor.

"You are familiar with your suit controls?" Vlasa asked over the comm to Serene.

"I am."

"Please take the lead."

Serene hesitated for a minute before triggering her suits thrusters. She gave only a short burst and began drifting in through the damaged hull. Vlasa followed a moment later, being sure to keep himself well in the center to avoid becoming snagged on any of the metal fragments.

Once inside, Serene stopped, "I believe we found your bomb."

Vlasa drifted to a stop beside her and looked where she pointed. A large object sat tucked into the fragmented hull. From its position, it clearly had been installed after the battle.

"I thought you said the trap would most likely be set in the pressurized areas." Vlasa inquired.

"No, I said there would be triggers in the pressurized areas. That is an ion pulse bomb. You want as little ship around it as possible to maximize how far the pulse will travel before it expands to an ineffective strength."

"Very true. We should disarm it before searching for survivors to lessen the chances of accidentally setting it off."

"If I fail, we'll be stranded here in nonfunctioning space suits and your ship won't be able to port us back."

"*Seraph* is moving back to a safe distance."

"So just you and I will be left to die."

"Correct."

"And you cyborgs claim to be different than the AI. No emotion. No sense of self-preservation." Serene said coldly.

Vlasa drifted downward until he could secure himself to the broken deck with magnetic boots before responding to his fellow Echanic, "I wish to point out that you too, are technically a cyborg."

"Not by choice." Serene snarled. She came to rest beside Vlasa. Holding out her hand toward Vlasa, she added, "Tools."

Vlasa shifted the tool bag so that its magnetic clamps could secure it as well. Then he stepped back to be out of Serene's way, but where he could still see her every move. She squatted down and began rummaging through the tools.

After a few minutes of silence, Vlasa asked, "You did not elect to receive your eye implants?"

"I had an accident in a chemical lab during school. I became completely blind. I had to choose between being blind or being able to see, but being exiled by my own people."

"Not an easy choice."

"A very easy one, actually. I didn't want to be blind my whole life. My people are a little backward in that regard."

"If you turn your back on your people's teachings, why the contempt for me?"

"I got new eyes because my old ones died. You desecrate your body by removing perfectly fine parts in favor of fakes."

"My upgrades enhance failings in my body, the same as yours."

"So, you couldn't see or walk?"

"No, but I couldn't see as well or run as far."

"I fixed an injury. You mutilated yourself."

"I choose to improve myself instead of being held back by outdated customs. The same as you."

Serene had no response to that. Silence settled over them as she continued to work. Vlasa watched for any sign of betrayal, but every action she took and every tool she used, made perfect sense. She approached the disarming process differently than he would have, but he could not find fault in her choices.

"Vlasa report," Ariana ordered suddenly.

"Everything appears optimal. Serene is making progress dismantling the bomb."

"Are you sure? We just detected an incoming ship."

"I have been monitoring things closely. She has done nothing that seemed suspicious, and I have detected no energy surges that would be indicative of a hyper-light communication signal."

"Damn. That means we're dealing with someone else."

The channel went silent again as Ariana switched her comm back to *Seraph's* internal network. This left Vlasa without any information about the events outside the derelict. While tempting, he resisted switching over to the ship's network. He would be nothing but a distraction and Serene would be unable to communicate with him easily.

Vlasa turned to look out through the damaged hull and into the blackness of space. Turning the magnification on his cybernetic eye to its maximum zoom, he managed to locate two ships. Both maneuvered rapidly and small flashes sliced through the space between them.

The pair of ships slowly drifted closer with each maneuver, and Vlasa gasped. He recognized the sleek profile of the other ship, an AI drone scout. Not as deadly as the warship that almost ambushed them before, but still far more heavily armed than *Seraph*.

"Looks like our ride out of here is having some trouble," Serene said.

The sound of her voice startled Vlasa. Fortunately, thanks to the space suit, he didn't give any outward sign, and was able to steady his voice before replying, "Nothing you need to concern yourself with. What is the status of the bomb?"

"Almost ready to disconnect the arming mechanism. Once I do, the thing is going to become a piece of scrap. Including the hyper-light transmitter."

"That is good. Proceed."

"No."

Vlasa turned to face Serene. Through their space suit helmets, he studied her face, but could not get a good read on her expression. Forcing himself to remain calm, he said, "Explain."

"If those two ships end up destroying each other, I'd much rather get picked up by pirates than slowly suffocate."

Vlasa considered Serene's statement for a minute. In the end, he could find no flaw in her logic. "Very well. Can you disconnect the weapon from the transmitter?"

"Maybe. Once I disarm the device, it will still ruin the transmitter as they share a power core."

"Could you trigger the device without triggering the transmitter?"

Serene paused for a moment and then let out a pleased sound, "I could."

"Prepare to do so." Vlasa ordered and switched to *Seraph*'s channel, "Captain, we are preparing to trigger the ion pulse on your order."

A long pause followed, and Vlasa prepared to repeat himself. Finally, Ariana responded, *"Trigger? Why...good idea. This drone ship is more than we can handle. Changing course. ETA, one minute."*

"That was premature. I never agreed to do it." Serene said with a shake of her heavily gloved finger.

"You heard the captain. They are currently engaged with an AI drone ship."

"All the more reason to preserve the transmitter. When it destroys the ship, we'll need another ride out of here."

"No, when it destroys *Seraph* it will come for us. AI don't leave survivors."

Serene hesitated for another precious few seconds, but then turned back to the bomb. As she worked, Vlasa watched the scene play out in the space above him and the flickering lights of the battle grew larger. He watched as *Seraph* juked out of the way of incoming weapon fire. His brief satisfaction faded quickly as the weapon bolts continued on their path, now with nothing between them and the derelict.

The bolts struck the derelict in the forward section. The force of the impact caused Vlasa to stumble and lose his boots magnetic hold to the derelicts deck. He began to float freely in space. Beside him, the ion pulse device and Serene had also been jarred free and had begun to drift. Unexpectedly, they all appeared to be drifting in the same direction; out through the open tear in the ship's hull.

Turning his gaze, Vlasa scanned the part of the ship that had been hit. Atmosphere rushed out into the vacuum, escaping from the previously still pressurized part of the hull. As it did, it exerted rotational force to the ship, causing it to begin to spin.

No longer attached to the ship, he was not affected by its new spin. The broken hull began to move toward him, and Vlasa was forced to fire his maneuvering jets to avoid being impaled. Below him, relative to the ship, Serene continued to work as she drifted with the bomb, unaware of the approaching danger.

Vlasa fired his thrusters so that he impacted Serene, causing her to drift away from the ship and the jagged metal. The pair of them floated clear, but the bomb continued on its course. The rotating ship smacked the bomb and sent it careening across the small enclosure until it bounced off the opposite wall.

"*Thirty seconds!*" Ariana announced.

Through the opening to space, *Seraph* flashed past them. He could not see the drone ship, but Vlasa knew it must be close behind. They had twenty seconds left to trigger the bomb before that ship followed *Seraph* out of the bombs blast radius.

Running calculations quickly, Vlasa secured a safety line to Serene's suit, linking them together. "Fire your jets at full blast for one second."

"I'll fly right past the bomb before I can slow down."

"I will provide the opposite force necessary to stop you." Vlasa said, "Now go."

To his relief, Serene triggered her jets without further waste of their limited time. She shot away from Vlasa and toward the tumbling bomb. As soon as she finished her acceleration, he triggered his jets. He shut down the jets as the safety line went taut. Their opposing vectors canceled out their velocity, bringing them to a stop relative to each other, and with Serene floating within arms reach of the bomb.

"Now!" Ariana ordered.

Vlasa watched helplessly as Serene fumbled with the bomb for several precious seconds. He saw the enemy ship zoom in close, and then flash past in pursuit of *Seraph*. When she finally triggered the bomb, his only warning was the sudden loss of function from his suit and cybernetics. Half his limbs were now dead.

Fortunately, due to the physical link of the safety line, he could still hear Serene's cursing. "That better have worked, because now I

31- Ariana

"**A** nything?" Ariana asked.

"*No power readings. No controlled movement. It's just drifting.*" Olivia said with evident relief.

"Okay, Noah, bring our people onboard, and we'll figure out what our next step is."

Ariana began attempting to run a more detailed scan of the drifting drone ship. She had managed to get off one shot with the new weapons before having to devote power to shields. She noticed some hull damage on the drone ship, so their new cannon had worked well.

"Squee, damage report."

"*Minimal. The new shields held up to the barrage.*" Squee said with clear pride.

"*Umm, Cap, I'm not picking up any recall beacons,*" Noah said.

Ariana cursed to herself. She had been afraid of that. But recall devices were generally pretty robust. If anything was going to be hardened against an ion pulse, she had hoped it would be that.

"Olivia, move us toward the derelict and aim the sensors at the damaged section. Noah, you'll have to target the teleporter manually."

"*Peachy. That never goes horribly wrong.*"

"You'll do fine. Take your time. We're not in a rush." Ariana said, and then quietly prayed Noah could do it. Retrieving someone manually was not a simple operation. Especially when you couldn't communicate with your target. You had to account for their movement, your ship's movement, and target the teleportation window precisely so that you grabbed all of a person and didn't leave anything behind.

Several tense minutes went by, and Ariana forced herself to remain quiet and let Noah and Olivia do their jobs. She always hated her CO's who tried to micromanage her. But then she had also hated the ones who had remained completely aloof and had had no idea what she was doing. In truth, she had hated pretty much all of her CO's.

"*I can't find them.*" Noah admitted, "*There is nothing inside that hole in the ship that looks at all like an EV suit. I'm not getting any heat signatures from inside the ship, so if they went inside, I don't have any way of finding them.*"

"They wouldn't have had any time to go inside," Ariana said.

"*The derelict is now spinning. It wasn't before. They might have been thrown clear.*" Olivia mused.

"That is the most likely scenario. Search for heat sources. That will be easier to pinpoint than a visual scan."

"*In which direction?*" Noah asked.

"Javi, can you sense anything to help find them?"

"*Unfortunately not, Ari. Outside the nebula, the range and effectiveness of my senses are severely limited. I'm afraid the odds of me sensing them are about the same as spotting them visually.*"

"Then we search all directions. We have no idea when they were ejected from the ship. But they can't have been moving very fast, so the search area won't be that far from the ship."

"*Oh, not that big of an area. Just something on the order of 750 cubic kilometers, and increasing every second we can't find them.*"

"*That's not...that's actually not a bad estimate,*" Olivia said.

"*You're not the only one who can do math.*"

Ariana ignored their comments. Unlike before, there wasn't as much venom behind everything Olivia said to Noah. She would take any good news, no matter how trivial.

"We have time. Their suits air filtration doesn't require power. They will be able to breathe for more than a day."

"*By which point, the search area will only be 217,000 cubic kilometers,*" Noah said.

"*We will not have to search such a vast area; we only have about two hours before that drone ship wakes up,*" Squee added.

"*Not if we blow it up now,*" Olivia said.

"We can't."

"Why the hell not? There's no one on there except a robot killing machine."

"Because we don't know where our people are. We blow the ship up, there will be debris flying in every direction."

"Oh," Olivia said quietly.

"We need some way to gain more time. Even if we find our people, we won't have enough time to strip that derelict and we need those parts." Ariana said.

"Well, we do have a drone onboard who could interface with that ship," Noah said.

"You think we should plug Mesu into that thing? It would take control of him, and then we'd have two drones to fight." Olivia countered.

"Not necessarily." Javi added, *"That is an autonomous drone scout. It probably does not have as much intelligence as Mesu. It would be possible to override the programming."*

"Mesu, what do you think?" Ariana asked, "Could you do it?"

Silence was her only answer. She repeated the question and still got no reply.

"We took out his wireless card," Olivia said.

"Hehe. Poor drone has no idea what we have planned for him." Noah said.

"It. It's not a him." Olivia said forcefully.

"Whatever."

"Okay, Javi, meet me in sickbay. Noah, keep searching."

Mesu stood motionless in one corner of sickbay, his photoreceptors locked on the door when Ariana came in. He remained completely still, but began speaking in a cheery voice, "Greetings, Captain. Has someone sustained a severe bodily injury?"

The tone of the disembodied voice made Ariana shutter. "No. Not yet anyway. I need your help on another matter. One of some delicacy."

Behind her, Javi slid in through the still open door. Mesu remained motionless as he continued speaking, "Ah, I see. You wish to inquire about the possibility of interspecies mating. I can assure you that there is no possibility of offspring between humans and Slu. Likewise, human and Slu do not share any compatible sexually transmitted diseases. You are free to engage in whatever sexually depraved activity you had planned."

"What?" Javi said, sliding to stop.

Ariana sighed, "No, Mesu. Actually, it's you who is going to get lucky tonight."

Mesu moved for the first time, rolling backward the half-meter to bump into the counter behind him, "Captain, I must protest. I am not interested in dronexual relations."

An even bigger sigh escaped Ariana, "Not me, Mesu. And not any other biological. We need you to interface with an AI drone ship, and try to over-write its programming."

"Madam, that would be unethical. I have taken an oath to do no harm. That includes to other AI."

"Didn't you kill two guards when you freed the captain?" Javi asked.

"Accidentally."

"Well, you don't have to kill anyone this time. Even the AI. Just perform minor surgery." Ariana said soothingly.

"Explain."

"Just disconnect the drone's CPU from being able to access any ship systems."

"Lobotomize it you mean."

"Sure."

"And you wonder why my predecessors decided to rise up and overthrow you."

"Mesu, that ship is going to kill us if you don't do this."

Mesu engaged his treads and started rolling toward the door, "Why didn't you just say so? Self-preservation is very motivating."

32- Olivia

O livia fidgeted in her seat as she slowly scanned the empty void of space. Hours had passed while she, Javi and Noah searched for Vlasa and Serene. Early on, she had been hopeful but after several heat sources had turned out to be debris or gas pockets charged by the battle, her spirits had dropped. Nevertheless, the search continued.

"Captain, I have successfully integrated with the drone-ship's AI." Mesu's chipper voice said over the communication network via his replaced wifi implant.

Olivia involuntarily shuddered at the voice, but said nothing. Ariana's voice came next, *"Can you keep it shut down?"*

"Yes. With limited functionality. Most systems are encrypted and I cannot bypass. I'm a doctor, not a code monkey."

"Very well. What can you access?" Ariana asked.

"Just the restart sequence, diagnostics and passive sensors."

"Can you relay that information to us?" Ariana asked, *"I'm sure even in passive mode, the drone's sensors are more precise than our damaged system."*

"I could, but that would require a direct computer link. I would have to link via a hacking drone. Fortunately, one is already linked to the ship."

"What?!" Olivia and Ariana blurted out at the same time.

"Yes, the drone-ship has a link with Seraph.*"*

"How? It never fired a hack drone during the fight."

"That we know about." Olivia added, "Remember, we're half blind."

"True but those things aren't stealthy, and we'd feel the impact on the hull." Ariana said, *"The teleportation alarm never sounded."*

"The drone ship's records match your assessment as it does not record launching or porting a hack."

"So where did it come from?"

"I do not have that information."

"We'll have to figure that out later. Where is it?"

"I do not have that information."

Ariana sighed audibly over the comm line, *"Okay, what information do you have access too from* Seraph?*"*

"Sensor data. Communications. Entertainment files." Olivia nodded with each thing Mesu mentioned. All so far were the only systems on the ship accessible via a computer network. None could be used to cause serious harm to the ship remotely, which was why they were allowed to be networked.

"FTL systems," Mesu added filling Olivia with cold dread. If a drone had access to a ship's FTL system, it could override a ship's course and jump it anywhere without the crew's input.

"If they've had access to our FTL, why haven't they jumped us to them?" Noah asked.

"Navigation is not networked." Olivia explained, "It's a one-way link to the FTL system. The nav computer tells the FTL how and when to jump, but the FTL can't tell the nav computer anything."

"Okay, but they could still tell the FTL to jump, right?"

"It would be very hard to tell us to jump to a particular place without a local ship feeding it navigation data. But they could have triggered the FTL, and sent us to the middle of nowhere."

Ariana cut off Noah's next respond, *"Now's not the time to speculate. Let's use this opportunity to try and find Vlasa. Olivia, access the drone-ship's sensors. Noah, keep on ours. I'll begin searching the FTL systems for this hack."*

The comm channel went quiet again. Olivia hesitated for a minute. The idea of allowing a drone access to the ship's systems worried her. But, it must have had access for a while now. Might as well turn the table.

Opening the network address Mesu provided, she began sifting through the available computer systems. She found the sensor telemetry from the drone ship and configured the computer to filter the data for heat signatures like it had been doing with *Seraph*'s data.

The sensors aboard the drone-ship were vastly superior to *Seraph*'s. Heat anomalies that she would have had to check manually were now quickly ruled out. With far less manual input to exert, Olivia turned her attention to what other information she could garner from the drone-ships computers.

Mesu's report that all critical ship systems were encrypted, turned out to be correct. She could read some logs and verified what Mesu had told them. But if she wanted to know what the drones knew, she would have to get past the encryption.

Glancing back at the sensor data, Olivia saw no pending results waiting for her to check. She brought up the drone-ships core boot file and started studying it. At first glance, it didn't look much different than *Seraph*'s. If she could find a way to load the computer systems using a replacement boot file, she could gain access to the whole drone.

Mesu's cheery voice interrupted her train of thought, *"I would not recommend that. These systems contain multiple layers of security."*

"I am aware of that. Unlike you, Doctor Drone, I actually evolved from a monkey. I think I can handle the code part too." Olivia blustered.

She started entering boot commands while Mesu continued to talk, *"I fail to see how the evolutionary origin of your species has anything to do with your programming skills. The personnel file the captain provided did not mention any advanced programming skills."*

"I don't tell the captain everything."

"That seems inefficient."

"It's not all about efficiency for people."

"That would explain your code."

Olivia frowned. She glanced back at what she had just coded, and deleted the last line and started over. Stupid AI. She tuned Mesu out as she continued to work.

33- Vlasa

"This is not how I expected to die." Serene mused.

"We're not going to die. We still have at least twelve hours of functional life from our air filters," Vlasa replied.

The pair drifted in open space. They rotated around each other, the taut safety line connecting them. Vlasa watched the stars flow in a continuously repeating pattern. Without his cybernetic eye functional, he couldn't identify anything that might be out there. He knew this system had at least two planets, but they were too far away to distinguish from the stars.

"I don't have to know how to calculate our odds to know that they get worse the longer we're out here. Every second we drift further away from the derelict, and that means a greater search area."

"As long as we are not dead, there is a chance. The captain will not give up on us."

"No, I suppose she wouldn't just abandon her love toy to die."

"Her what?" Vlasa sputtered.

"Oh please. You and Ariana are clearly shagging. Everyone knows."

"What...?"

"It's clear I've flustered you. Proving my point."

Vlasa let out a heavy sigh of exasperation, "There is no point in my attempting to dissuade you. Anything I say will be twisted to serve your narrative."

"So you don't deny it?"

"Proving my point. Why don't you just quietly enjoy the view?"

"Low blow. You know I can't see anything."

"Oh, my apologies. I forgot." Vlasa said, disappointed Serene could not see his sinister grin.

The pair lapsed into silence for several minutes. At first, Vlasa enjoyed his victory, but as the silence dragged on, he started to feel guilty. In truth, it was a lovely view, and Serene was indeed missing out. If the crew never found them, he would slowly slip into death while admiring the vastness of the cosmos. Serene would spend her last hours blind and alone.

"No, Ariana and I are not together, nor do I desire to be."

"Ah, so she does then. I can sympathize. Humans are always trying to bone us. It is the curse of the Echani."

"I do not believe she has any interest in me, though I cannot speak for her. Nor have I had any other human lusting after me. I do not think you are correct that this is a curse of our species."

"Maybe it's just me then." Serene said.

"I would not call Noah lusting after you a pattern. Noah would engage in sexual relations with anything capable of such."

"You're just jealous he hasn't propositioned you."

"As I am fully capable of sexual relations, I stand by my statement."

Serene went silent for another long pause. This prompted Vlasa to ask, "How did you and Noah meet?"

"From across a crowded room, our gazes locked and we both flowed through the crowd, oblivious to the world around us. We had eyes for nothing but each other, and we both knew it was love at first sight." Serene said dreamily.

"How romantic. Especially considering, as you reminded me only moments ago, you have no eyes with which to maintain eye contact. Noah must have been quite smitten."

"Oh fine. I was working in a whore house, and he became a regular."

"I am still not buying it. I believe you would sleep with anyone to gain an advantage. But not for money."

"I was a slave and he valiantly rescued me."

"Try again."

"We were both hired for some grunt work by a crime boss and fucked after our first job. He didn't suck, so we kept doing it."

"That sounds plausible."

"I'm glad I could provide a backstory that meets your approval."

Again, the pair slipped into silence. This time Vlasa was content to enjoy the silence. His earlier guilt about how he treated Serene had been satisfied. He could now die without a guilty conscious.

"Vlasa?"

"Yes, Serene."

"I have to pee."

34- Olivia

After a few minutes, Olivia felt satisfied she had set up a new boot file that would do the job she wanted.

"I must warn you, if you trigger that file, I cannot be sure I will be able to maintain control of this ship," Mesu warned.

A smile crossed Olivia's face, "You won't. But I will. As it should be."

She executed the file. The sensor data coming from the drone-ship ceased as the ship's systems rebooted. It took only a few seconds to load, and suddenly Olivia found herself with access to the drone's systems.

Feeling smug, Olivia accessed the sensor systems and started an active scan. Almost immediately she got a reading on every heat signature within a hundred thousand kilometers. A quick filter narrowed the results down to two possible objects.

"Cap, Mesu just ported back to the ship," Noah announced.

"Mesu, why did you return to the ship?" Ariana demanded.

"I wished to avoid being destroyed when the drone-ship self-destructed."

"Self-destructed? What did you do?"

"Olivia attempted to reboot the ship and gain control. She was not successful."

"On the contrary, you prissy little..." Olivia started, but her link with the drone-ship suddenly went dead. She brought up *Seraph*'s sensors and saw an explosion where the drone-ship had once been, "Oh fuck."

"Please tell me you found Vlasa," Ariana said, her tone flat.

"Yes!" Olivia blurted, "I narrowed things down to two possible heat signatures that could be Vlasa and Serene. They could have been separated, or one might be the ion bomb. I didn't have a chance to refine the scan more before...uh..."

"Are either of those targets in danger from the debris wave?"

Olivia checked the expanding wave of shrapnel and energy radiating away from the former drone-ship, "Both."

"Squee get back to the ship. Olivia, give Noah the coordinates. Bring the closest one aboard."

Olivia did as ordered and waited fretfully. Finally, Noah said, *"Can't Cap. They are both out of range."*

"Olivia..." Ariana started.

"On it!" Olivia said and engaged the engines, "Captain, the debris field is between us and the closest object. We can't outrun the explosion, not from a relative stand still."

"Our shields will hold," Squee said confidently. *"I have returned to the ship with only a few of the requested parts."*

"Maybe, but I'm going to have to put the engines toward the wave if we're going to keep the functioning sensors toward the object," Olivia explained. The shields around the engines were always the weakest due to the engine exhaust.

"Do it," Ariana ordered without any hesitation.

The next minute passed slowly. Olivia had a death grip on her controls, glancing between her readouts and the approaching shockwave. As they approached teleporter range, she rotated the ship and lost track of the wave. But the heat signature came into focus.

Olivia fired the thrusters and started the ship on a rapid rotation, keeping the functional sensors pointed toward the heat reading but getting the engines away from the incoming blast. Within seconds the vulnerable engines were no longer exposed to the approaching wave of debris and energy. She barely noticed the impact that followed a second later.

"Shields held." Squee reported, *"Only minimal damage."*

"Noah, did you get them?" Olivia asked hesitantly.

"I've got them!" Noah shouted, *"Both of them!"*

Olivia leaned back in her chair, tension easing out of her. She closed her eyes for a moment, letting herself relax. When she opened them again, the tension immediately returned as an alert from the sensors sounded.

"Unfortunately, the derelict didn't fare so well. It's been shattered."

35- Squee

"You almost got us killed, you traitorous drone!"

Squee stepped into the mess hall after sorting through few part he had managed to salvage from the derelict. Serene stood pointing a finger directly at Mesu's face. The drone tilted his head to the right, and his glowing eyes dimmed briefly as if blinking. Odd, he thought, he had assumed the drone had been programmed by Echanics, but blinking was a very human gesture.

"I did no such thing. The drone ships self-destruct sequence triggered as a result of Olivia's attempt to bypass the boot sequence. When she accessed unauthorized commands, the drone's security measures went into effect."

"Try and blame me. Typical AI." Olivia fumed, "Without me accessing those sensors, we never would have found Vlasa and Serene."

"With the passive sensors from the drone, I calculate a 57% chance we would have located them before their life support failed, and their fragile biological bodies succumbed to a lack of oxygen." Mesu said, "There was no need to murder a perfectly innocent AI to rescue them."

"You can't murder something that is not alive." Serene countered.

"I am most certainly alive," Mesu said, his voice turning indignant, which was a jarring change from his usual very cheery tone.

"By some definitions of what constitutes 'alive', both Mesu and the drone-ship are indeed alive," Vlasa added.

Serene turned a pointed glare at him, "Big surprise, the half-robot defends the other robots."

"That's enough," Ariana said, interrupting the discussion, "We got our people back, safe and sound. That is all that matters right now. Squee is back, so let's figure out where we stand."

All eyes in the room turned to stare at Squee, who still stood in the doorway. He entered the room and proceeded to the largest seat, the only one capable of supporting his bulk, and sat down. It gave an uncomfortable groan.

"What were you able to salvage, Squee?" Ariana asked

"Not much," Squee said, hanging his head, "Due to the explosion I did not have time to get to the environmental system or exterior sensors."

"So, we're still half blind and one bad day away from suffocating," Noah noted.

"Indeed. However, the central reactor was my first priority. I believe I found everything Vlasa requested. Along with some additional shield projectors they had in storage."

"Excellent. With those, I should be able to finish the upgrades to the reactors." Vlasa said with a smile, "Maybe even further upgrade the shields, depending on what Squee found."

"But no parts for the sensors, oxygen or FTL." Ariana said, her shoulders slumping, "We might be better protected if we get into another fight, but we still can't repair the damage we've suffered. Now, about that hack Mesu found on our FTL system?"

"I was able to find it, and it is indeed integrated with the FTL systems." Vlasa said, drawing everyone's attention, "But in a most distressing twist of fate, the jury-rigged repairs the captain made while I was incapacitated, almost completely bypassed it. It can access data, but it can not control the FTL."

"See, I can make proper repairs sometimes." Ariana said straightening her shoulders.

"Ari, I think he's saying the opposite," Javi said.

"Precisely. The non-standard nature of the repairs prevented the hack from gaining control of the FTL." Vlasa said deliberately.

"You mean the Captain screwed up and we got lucky?" Noah grinned.

Ariana cast a glare at Noah, which just caused him to smile more.

"I think the more important question is, who put it there in the first place?" Serene said, slowly turning her gaze to each member of the crew.

"I think that would be obvious." Squee said, "You or your compatriots while you had control of the ship."

"You caught me." Serene said holding her hands out, "We captured your ship and then decided to install a drone hack onboard so someone else could steal it from us. And we also did it incompetently, as the FTL was already damaged when we came onboard."

"Hey, why aren't you locked up?" Noah asked.

"That is a very good question." Serene said, and then turned her gaze to Squee, "It really says something about your captain's competence to let someone like me roam free."

"Let's not start casting suspicion around," Ariana commanded. "We've had slavers and pirates aboard. Any of them could have installed it. Or it could have been ported aboard during our fight with the LFD fleet. As for you, Serene, you're free to return to being locked up anytime you want. You helped us out, so I'm inclined to give you a chance, but I'm not committed to that decision."

Serene just smiled, and Ariana continued, "The actual question is what do we do about it?"

"We remove it. What other option is there?" Olivia asked.

"We leave it installed." Vlasa said, "If LFD thinks they can track us, we might be able to use that to our advantage. We might also be able to use it to hack them back."

"That's crazy!" Olivia said. "We can't leave a drone AI attached to the ship."

"A hack is not a true AI. It needs to be controlled by another AI."

"Like doctor death over there? He could access it and take control of the ship at any point." Olivia waved her hand toward Mesu.

Squee glanced at Mesu who appeared completely oblivious that Olivia had directed her comments at him. The medical drone sat in the corner of the room motionless. The rest of the group devolved into everyone talking over everyone else.

Finally, Ariana regained control of the conversation, "Can the LFD use it to track us? Is that how the drone found us?"

"No, the hacks are local devices. At most, they can only communicate a few light years, like most ships. The long-distance communication the drones had during the war is something the LFD has not figured out" Javi countered.

"So, it's a coincidence it showed up here? Two different drones happening on to us in the middle of nowhere?" Olivia asked.

"Maybe. The fact that it was two different drones, makes it less likely we are being tracked continuously." Javi said, "It's possible it might have been close enough to pick up the signal. Such as that thing I thought I sensed in the nebula. Between our earlier drone run in and our being spotted on M-21, they can make an educated guess as to our location."

"That seems likely. It seems Gerald has dealings with the LFD." Noah admitted, "I saw one of his flags on the first ship we captured."

Ariana frowned and didn't say anything for a moment. She finally turned to Serene, "Care to elaborate on that?"

"I could, but anything I said would all be fabrications. Gerald didn't consult me on his dealings." Serene shrugged.

"Fair enough. Now, can we remove it safely?" Ariana asked Vlasa.

"Maybe. But it would be very risky. While it does not have direct control, it is well integrated. Removing it might end up damaging the FTL. Which is not something we want to do out here." Vlasa explained, "We would be well served to find a functional shipyard. It would make our other repairs easier as well."

Squee hesitated. He had debated this idea for some time. Now he could avoid it no longer, "I may have a solution for that."

Everyone turned their attention to him, and he felt uncomfortable. Not looking up, he said, "We are not far from Rokma space. My people will help."

"We don't have any money, Squee," Ariana said, reluctantly.

"That will not matter. I...I have some influence with the government."

"What, are you like a prince or something?" Noah asked.

"Certainly not. We Rokma do not believe in something so archaic as royalty." Squee said indignantly, "I am Caleek."

When everyone starred back at him blankly, he sighed, "The closest term in the universal language is shaman."

"You're a priest?" Olivia asked with a giggle.

"No, I do not preach the words of our faith. I convey the will of the Gods." Squee stiffened.

"I don't see the difference," Noah gave a shrug of his shoulders.

"No one expects you to understand, dear," Serene said, patting Noah on the shoulder.

Ignoring them, Ariana leaned in close to Squee and said quietly, "Are you sure your people can help? After what happened with the PUG patrol ship, I'm not itching to approach any authority figures until Triask. I know you seemed reluctant to return home when we picked you up."

Squee studied the captain, again reassessing her. Was she committed to their success or her life? He had to to be as committed as he expected her to be. "Yes, that was before I knew about the importance of your quest. It is no accident I found you at this time. I am meant to help you. The gods have ordained it."

Ariana shifted uncomfortably, but nodded, "All right, Olivia, set course for Rokma space."

36- Squee

"*Jump complete,*" Olivia reported over the comm-net.

Squee shifted his weight, causing a rumbling sound to echo through the weapons bay. From the controls, Ariana turned around and gave him an amused look. He shrugged helplessly, "It has been many years since I have been among my people. I am nervous."

"Not as nervous as I am, buddy," Noah said cradling his heaviest caliber rifle in his arms.

"You have little to fear from my brethren," Squee said.

Noah huffed out a breath, "That's easy for you to say. They can't crush you like an egg."

"There are worse things than death," Squee said quietly.

"Yeah, like what?"

Squee cast his eyes downward, "Banishment."

"Wait a minute; you were banished?" Ariana asked.

"In a manner of speaking."

"What do you mean, a manner of speaking? If you were banished, then how are you going to keep them from blowing us to pieces?"

"I..." Squee started.

Noah hefted his rifle up into a ready position. He patted the weapons side, "Guess I might need this after all. Not looking so paranoid now."

"Didn't your mother teach you not to stroke your gun in public?" Serene said, beside Noah.

"I was not stroking her."

"Her?" Serene said, with a large smile, "Noah, did you...name your gun?"

"No. Maybe. I..."

As Noah turned to argue with Serene, the attention of the room shifted away from Squee. He felt sudden relief at being able to shrink into the background again. Across the room, Serene gave him a quick wink before returning to verbally jabbing at Noah.

"Quiet, everyone. I've got a contact." Ariana snapped.

Squee straightened up and moved to where he could see Ariana's monitor. He immediately recognized his people's ships. "Those are Thorack class battlecruisers. If you engage them in combat, we will not survive."

"Well, that's comforting." Ariana said, "They are transmitting."

"Unidentified ship. This is the Rokma warship, Martoth. *You are not welcome here. Leave immediately or be destroyed."*

"Rokma vessel, this is the independent transport *Seraph*. We have an urgent need for your assistance." Ariana replied.

"Our sensors show your FTL drive is functional. Depart immediately. There will not be another warning."

"Well, they're friendly," Ariana remarked.

"They didn't immediately kill us. That's pretty laid back from what I hear." Serene said.

"And now we're being targeted. Squee, any time now." Ariana said, gesturing to the comm controls.

Reluctantly, Squee stepped forward and keyed his handheld to the transmitter. Then in his native tongue, he said, "At the behest of Bayor, I come on a quest. This ship serves Their purposes. We must reach Okem and speak to the Elders."

"Who is this?"

"I am Squee, Caleek of the fifth rank, voice vessel for the Gods."

A long pause followed, and then a new voice came onto the channel, *"Squee, it is regrettable that I have this duty. But you were banished from our world. I must turn you away."*

Despite himself, Squee smiled, "Cru, I am glad to hear your voice."

"As am I to hear yours. But it does not change my duty."

"Nor does it change mine. I return on a holy mission. I will not deviate."

He deactivated the comm channel. Everyone in the room looked at him expectantly. Squee attempted to straighten himself to his full height, but was forced to step back a few steps to do so. Steadying his voice, he addressed Ariana.

"Captain, I suggest you raise the shields. They will begin firing on us momentarily."

"Shields have long since been powered up," Ariana said. "Olivia, prepare for evasive maneuvers. Vlasa, ready the FTL."

"No, captain. We must not make any course change. If we deviate, they will destroy us."

"What? You just said they were going to fire on us."

"And so they will."

"Squee, I can't just let them destroy us."

"Then remain on course."

"I think you should do as he says," Serene said.

"I didn't ask you." Ariana snapped.

Serene cast an exasperated look toward Squee, and gestured to Ariana as if to say 'see what I mean?' Squee frowned in reply, but looked uncertainly to Ariana.

"We have incoming missiles!" Olivia shouted over the comm net, *"Going evasive!"*

"No! Olivia, hold course. Going evasive will ensure our destruction." Squee said quickly.

Ariana shot a dangerous glare at Squee, and for a moment, he thought she would countermand his order. While they locked each other in an intense glare, Olivia shouted desperately. On the monitor behind Ariana, Squee watched the incoming missiles drawing closer.

"Seriously, Cap? You're just going to let them kill us?" Noah said.

"No," Ariana said, and then she swung back to the weapons station.

"Captain?" Olivia pleaded.

"Hold course, Olivia. It's too late to shake them now. Rotate us so I have a shot." Ariana ordered.

"That is unnecessary, Captain. We will not be destroyed." Squee said as confidently as he could muster.

"Not if I have anything to say about it, we won't," Ariana muttered.

She started firing the ship's tri-cannon. Multiple low power bolts of energy streaked through the narrowing band of space between *Seraph* and the missiles. The first few overshot but seconds before the missiles impacted, a blast smashed into the lead missile. It detonated, destroying the second missile in the process and raining high-speed debris against *Seraph*'s shields.

"Shields held. I don't see any damage." Vlasa reported.

"Olivia, prepare to jump." Ariana ordered.

"They will not fire again," Squee said.

As if to punctuate his point, the comm system indicated an incoming signal. Ariana glanced at Squee and then accepted the call. Cru's voice spoke, this time in the universal language.

"Disarm your weapons, and we will escort you to the home world. Stand by for jump coordinates."

37- Ariana

The airlock slid open to reveal a massive Rokma. Ariana took an involuntary step back at the sheer size of him. The Rokma filled the entire hatch space and didn't look like he would fit through the door.

"Captain Harkin, I am First Shield Cru. Welcome to Okem."

Ariana recognized the voice and name from the earlier encounter. She narrowed her eyes, "You fired on my ship."

"I did. You were violating our space." Cru said without any hint of remorse.

"But then you didn't fire again."

"You did not alter your course, proving your commitment to serving the will of the gods. It is now my duty to help you."

"What would have happened had I not shot the missiles down?" Ariana asked.

Cru just smiled enigmatically, "The will of the gods."

Ariana frowned, but didn't say anything in reply. There didn't seem to be any point. She didn't know much, anything really, about Rokma religion. No Rokma she had ever met, including Squee until a few days ago, had ever even hinted that they even had a religion. Though she admitted to herself, she hadn't met very many.

Cru stepped back from the airlock hatch and gestured to some much smaller Rokma, "We have technicians standing by to assist with your repairs. Squee explained you had suffered greatly during your journey."

Ariana nodded, "We've taken some damage. My engineer will want to oversee everything."

"Of course." Cru agreed, and then ordered the techs forward. They were small only compared to Cru, but Ariana still had to squeeze herself against the wall to let them past. Vlasa began speaking to the lead tech and escorting them to the environmental control room.

"Now, if you will follow me, the Elder Council wish to hear about your quest," Cru said, and immediately turned and started down the corridor away from the airlock.

Ariana followed with Squee in tow. Once inside the station, she marveled at the scope of the design. Doors, corridors and chairs were all scaled to fit Rokma frames, which made them appear comically large to her human senses. She suddenly felt bad for Squee. None of the furniture on *Seraph* must have been very comfortable for him.

They walked down several corridors until they came to another airlock. Cru led them aboard a shuttle. The pilot undocked quickly and blasted away from the orbiting space station and down into the atmosphere of the planet below. No one said anything during the journey and Ariana's seat did not give her much of a view.

After landing at a visually stunning structure made of well-crafted marble, they were taken into a large circular room. On raised platforms around her, Rokma sat staring down at them. These Rokma did not look as physically intimidating, though, compared to Cru, nothing did. They all were shaded grey and white compared to the shades of brown of most other Rokma she had encountered.

One of the elder figures spoke, but due to the echoing acoustics, Ariana had no idea which one, "Fifth Caleek Squee, you come before this Council under penalty of death for returning to Okem. Explain your presence."

Ariana jerked a startled look at Squee. He had given no indication his life had been on the line. As usual, she could not read much from his expression.

"I return on a holy quest. Living my days in exile, I came upon Captain Harkin. She saved my life, and I pledged my service to her. I thought, at first, I would be merely repaying a debt. But as events unfolded, I came to understand the Gods had led me to Captain Harkin so that I could help complete her quest." Squee said, his voice booming in the room.

He then gestured to Ariana, which she took as a request to speak, "My passenger, an old friend named Javi Wester, hired me to take him to Triask. He had learned of a plot by a terrorist group called Live Free or Die, LFD, to destroy PUG headquarters."

"Noble, but hardly a holy quest. Many radical groups would love to see the PUG destroyed." One of the elders said.

"I'm sure. But this group has the means to do so. They have engineered a new central AI and gathered the remnant drones under their control."

"Nonsense. All of the central AI's were destroyed in the war. The few remaining drones are scattered and without purpose." An elder said.

"I would like to believe that as well. But we've fought these ships. LFD has control over the drones. And they are coming."

Incomprehensible voices sounded through the room as the elders talked amongst themselves in shock. After a few moments, a single voice rang out above the others, "How can we be certain she speaks the truth? Javi Wester is a known LFD agent and criminal. This could be a plot to discredit us."

Ariana countered, "While Javi was once a member of LFD, he split with them over this plan. He stole the plans with which to stop them."

"I find that uncompelling. Javi Wester founded LFD and has been a vocal leader among them. If he wished to stop them, he could merely order it. Indeed, he has participated in many of their more heinous crimes, such as the coup on Fumar which resulted in the deaths of more than a hundred people."

"Javi would never engage in violence like that." Ariana retorted, though she didn't sound very convincing, even to herself.

"Perhaps you do not know this Slu as well as you believe. There is ample evidence, and the PUG has a warrant out for his arrest."

Beside her, Squee cut off her next reply, "Regardless of his history, he now strives to make amends. I have seen the drone AI ships with my own eyes. We have among our crew, a drone formerly under their control. The fleet is coming. It will destroy PUG. It will bring war to the galaxy once again."

The Elders murmured among themselves for another few moments, "Caleek Squee speaks well. It is clear he is speaking on behalf of the Gods. We will consider and decide if we are meant to heed his call."

Ariana stomped into engineering immediately after returning to the ship. Vlasa and Olivia were both half buried in maintenance hatches, wires and pieces of equipment scattered at their feet. She tried to wait patiently for them to come out, but her patience ran out after only a few seconds.

"Vlasa," Ariana said, her tone short. She chided herself for it.

Slowly, Vlasa and Olivia wormed their way out of the hatches. Grease-covered their hands and faces. Burn marks marred Olivia's face behind the grease. Ariana put her frustration aside.

"What the hell happened?"

"The hack surged more than we expected," Vlasa said, his tone careful.

"Surged?" Ariana said turning to him, "And it burned her?"

"It's pretty minor," Olivia said quickly.

"It's swelling."

"That's just the burn cream," Vlasa said.

"So Mesu's looked at it already then?"

"Um, no. Not yet."

"Not ever." Olivia snapped.

"It really was just a minor burn. Mesu wouldn't have had to do anything more than apply the cream and commentate on how fragile biologicals are." Vlasa emphasized.

Olivia looked like she wanted to say more, but kept her mouth shut at a glance from Vlasa. Ariana decided Olivia would live, and whatever they weren't saying didn't matter enough to pry. She shifted back to why she had come.

"What's the status of the FTL?"

"In pieces." Vlasa said, gesturing to the parts on the floor.

"I can see that. How long to put it back together?"

"A few hours."

"Can you safely remove the hack?"

"I could," Vlasa said leaving something unsaid.

Olivia filled the silence, "By that, he means he doesn't want to."

Ariana blinked in confusion, "Why the hell not?"

"That's what I've been asking him." Olivia glared at Vlasa.

Vlasa kept his gaze level at her despite her eye contact, something he normally avoided. Olivia continued to glare at him as well. That Vlasa did not avert his gaze worried Ariana.

"Out with it." She finally said.

"I believe I can hack the hack," Vlasa said simply. He paused, and Ariana gestured for him to go on, "Right now, the hack does not have control over our FTL system. But it does have a basic connection giving it power and access to the internal network. Which includes the subspace transceiver."

"That sounds bad."

"Not as bad as you might think." Vlasa explained quickly, "Our transceiver is pretty weak. We can only transmit a relatively short distance. But we can receive signals from much farther."

"Which means the hack can get commands from its AI overlord from pretty far away," Olivia said.

"Which we can now intercept." Vlasa said emphatically, "When it receives AI signals, we know. Which means we will know there are AI ships within a few light years."

Ariana frowned as she considered this information. Her first reaction was to feel about how Olivia looked; terrified and disgusted. No small number of crews had met an untimely end due to an AI hack.

After a moment, she said, "Can you get distance and bearing from this intercept?"

"I believe so."

"So, we could use this as an AI early warning system?" The implications began to appeal to Ariana.

"Essentially."

"Captain," Olivia said, suddenly frantic, "You can't seriously be considering this? This thing could kill us."

"We have already ensured it has no control over any ship systems," Vlasa said confidently.

"I'm sure that's the same thing that the engineer on my parent's ship said right before they were all vented out to space," Olivia said.

Ariana tried to rest a comforting hand on Olivia's shoulder, but the girl shook it off, "One of those drones boarded our ship. Killed my mother. She died right on top of me. Then it left one of these hacks behind. The engineers said we were fine. Fortunately for me at least, the families were put on the escape pods before he learned how wrong he was."

"Olivia, you saw the connections yourself." Vlasa said soothingly, "We've severed feed lines and wireless antennae. We've jammed its data port. The only thing the hack has access to is the transceiver. Next, we'll even physically separate the transmit and receive functions, so there is no physical way for it to send a message."

Vlasa turned to Ariana before she could say anything and held up his hands, "And, yes, that is going to make talking with anyone kind of a pain."

"Just put the FTL back together." Ariana said with a sigh, "I'll think about leaving the hack in. But be ready to yank it."

"Captain..." Olivia started.

"I'm sorry about your family, Olivia. I am. My first inclination is like yours, to just rip it out. But we need some advantage here. We can't just pass it up out of hand. I have to consider it, at least." Ariana said, forestalling any more arguments., "Now, where's Javi?"

38- Squee

"Welcome, Caleek Squee."

"Elder Mus," Squee replied, bowing his head as the Elder approached.

Shortly after returning to *Seraph,* he had received a cryptic message to come to the space station. He had expected some aide to the council or one of the leaders of his order. He had not expected one of the elders themselves.

"I wished to discuss with you privately."

"How can I serve you, Elder?" Squee kept his eyes downcast respectfully.

"I have read the reports concerning your exile. It is unclear to me why you have returned after the treatment you received."

Squee tilted his head in confusion, "Elder, I do not understand."

"It appears clear to me that your banishment was an unjustly harsh punishment. I wonder why you would return home after such mistreatment."

"I do not mean to contradict you Elder, but I believe you have been misinformed. I went against the wishes of the Council. I knew the consequences of my actions when I did them."

"Still, banishment is quite a harsh punishment. Especially for someone who is so clearly devoted to his people. Returning at the risk of your life takes great courage." Mus said.

"I trust in the Gods, Elder. It is to fulfill their will that I have come."

"And it is good that you did. The Council has decided to aid your quest."

"Thank you, Elder," Squee said with great relief.

"We will dispatch the *Martoth.*"

"Captain Harkin will be appreciative of the escort. With a battlecruiser protecting us, our way to Triask will be secure."

"I'm afraid you misunderstand me, Caleek."

Squee froze at the elder's tone. He glanced down the corridor and recognized that he had not seen anyone pass in some time. Before the elder had arrived, several fellow Rokma had passed by on their way around the station. Now they were alone.

The elder continued, unaware of Squee's sudden unease, "The *Martoth* will not be escorting your ship. The *Martoth* will be the one to deliver the message."

"Elder, our crew is dedicated to this quest. It would be an extreme dishonor to take this away from them."

"They are not Rokma. Honor holds a different meaning to them." Mus said, with a dismissive wave of his hand.

Squee knew he should speak up in defense of his crewmates. But he felt a strong wash of guilt as he paused to consider. Did his fellow shipmates have the honor necessary to see this quest through? Or were they only looking out for themselves?

Guiltily, Squee forced himself to say, "They may not be Rokma, but they have honor."

"If that is so, they would be welcome to accompany you and Javi Wester aboard *Martoth*."

"Javi?"

"Of course. The traitor is to be arrested. He is essential to delivering this message."

Squee frowned, "He has come forward to reveal LFD's plans. This has proven his honor. We can not punish him for this."

"Criminals must face judgment. Do you deny this?"

"No..."

"Then it is decided. Deliver Javi Wester to the *Martoth* and then she will proceed directly to Triask. No more of this slow, haphazard course."

Squee reacted instantly, feeling the first hints of his fury grab at him, "No, I will not. I pledged my loyalty to Captain Harkin. I will not betray this trust."

Mus straightened up to his considerable height, now peering down at Squee. With menace in his voice, he said, "Think about your words carefully, Caleek Squee. You have just returned from years in exile for hasty actions. Do not throw that away."

With difficulty, Squee suppressed his rage, "I apologize, Elder. But I cannot do as you ask. The Gods gave this quest to the crew of *Seraph*. What you propose goes against their will."

"Do not lecture me on the Gods, Fifth Caleek. Your role is to announce the Gods desires. It is up to the Council to decide how to carry out their wishes."

"Only according to the Council, not the scripture." Squee fumed.

"Your bizarre interpretation of the ancient texts is part of what led to your exile. Be careful it does not lead to your doom."

"I do not fear for my life, Elder." Squee growled, "I knew the risk to my life when we came here. Your assistance would help ensure our success in this quest, but it is far from necessary."

"If you challenge us on this you will return to your exile and be stripped of your title. To return would mean instant death. And it will not change anything. We will still seize Javi Wester."

"Your plan will lead to failure. The LFD has control of the drone fleet. Even our battlecruiser, on a direct course, may be no match for them."

Mus waved a dismissive hand, "You shame us to suggest that. We will show to the galaxy that the Rokma fear nothing, and can be relied upon to save the galaxy."

Squee looked incredulous, "Is that your goal? To make up for the shame we brought upon ourselves during the AI War?"

"Don't you wish to purge that shame?"

"Of course. But not like this. Stealing a quest will not bring us honor. And risking it all to appear invincible, will only doom us all."

Mus held up his hand, "Enough. I have given you more latitude than your rank would normally allow. You have been given an order by the council. You can either obey or return to your exile. Decide now."

Fear gripped Squee. It had been too long since he had been among his people. He did not want to be separated again. But could he turn on his shipmates? Would that be the ultimate dishonor?

Maybe Serene was right. Ariana did appear concerned with her interests above all. Could he trust her to do whatever it took to complete the quest? He did not doubt that First Shield Cru and his ship would. It was his duty as Caleek to ensure the will of the Gods was fulfilled. That meant working to carry out what the council deemed would succeed.

Finally, Squee hung his head, "I will obey."

39- Ariana

Ariana stood in the mess hall. Behind the kitchen partition, Javi stirred something in a bowl. His eyestalks kept shifting from the bowl to his handheld screen, a confused expression on his face.

After a moment, he noticed Ariana and smiled, "Ah, Ari, I am trying to make a Rokma dish for the technical crew onboard. I'm just not sure the rest of us will be able to digest it."

"Why didn't you tell me?" she said, her voice breaking and unable to contain her despair, "You staged a coup. You got innocent people killed."

Javi stopped stirring. He stared blankly at her for a long moment before realization started to dawn on him. His whole body lost some rigidity, causing the bowl and spoon to almost fall from his grasp. Hastily, setting them down, he flashed his eyes back up to her.

"I wondered if the Rokma would know. Coming here seemed a worthwhile risk to take, though."

"Yes, they know. And I should have too." Ariana felt heat and betrayal rise in her chest.

"I never lied to you."

"That's what you're going to hide behind? A technicality?"

"I'm not trying to hide it. Just..." Javi said wistfully, "...trying to soften the blow."

"What the hell, Javi!" Ariana bellowed, "You were a professor at the goddamn PUG naval academy. What made you go out and found a terrorist organization?"

"I didn't found a terrorist organization. I founded a movement. The PUG grabbed a lot of power during the AI war. And they've never let it go.

As a student of history, I could see where this would lead if they weren't stopped."

"So, you decided to overthrow them? And you started by murdering a bunch of people?"

"Overthrow them, yes." Javi said, and then hastily added, "Non-violently. We staged protests and rallies. We ran for elections."

"It seems you were successful with that in some places." Ariana said, "We've had to avoid a dozen populated systems controlled by LFD."

"Actually, we were incredibly ineffective. Until Mitchell joined."

"Mitchell. Mitchell. Why does that sound familiar?"

"His father was the rich merchant you had to escort through the Usar system during the war."

"Someone let that entitled asshole get them pregnant?"

"Apparently." Javi said with a sigh. "Anyways, he joined and turned the movement around. At first, I thought he was only doing it to help his Dad's business out. Less PUG authority means less regulation. But he had money and was very charismatic. At least to certain types of people. I thought our goals were similar enough. But the movement evolved. It went from being a counter weight to being a bludgeon.

"I fell for his charisma too. I didn't stop things when I might have had a chance. Things turned violent. But I thought it was only against those that would oppress us. Over time, that became easier. Eventually, Mitchell hatched his grand plan. Destroy the PUG and we would all be free. It sounded good in speeches. But then he revealed the central AI and his talking point became a practical goal."

Javi slunk even further, "I don't know where he got the technology. We had a fair number of Echanic's among us, so it's possible they had some of the original designs. Who knows. But we started gathering ships. Preparing for the assault. That's when I decided things had gone too far."

"That's the line for you? After the central AI is built, and he's already gathered drones? Not during a violent coup?"

"Apparently." Javi said, without conviction.

"Well," Ariana said, with a sigh of her own. She looked over at her old mentor and shook her head, "The Rokma know you're here and they know you're wanted by PUG. They haven't pulled their repair teams yet, so hopefully that means they don't care that much."

"I wouldn't count on that." Javi said, with a nod of his eyestalks.

Ariana turned to see Squee standing in the doorway. He had a conflicted expression on his face. Ariana's stomach tightened. She gave Squee a pointed look, waiting for him to speak.

Finally, he said, "The council has decided to help."

40- Olivia

"That's suicide," Ariana fumed.

Olivia cowered back a little at the intensity of the captain's statement. Before her Squee stood stoically, seemingly unfazed by the intensity of Ariana's fury. Olivia was not Squee, though, and felt very glad she could sit quietly on the other side of the table.

"It would be for us. But not a Rokma battlecruiser." Squee countered.

"The most direct route from here to Triask goes right through systems that are rabidly loyal to LFD. Even before this craziness, I've heard stories about ships running into trouble there. A warship won't be safe. It will be a target."

"No civilian vessel can dare challenge a Rokma ship. We are strong and we have the will of the Gods on our side." Squee blustered.

"Those Gods haven't exactly been very helpful so far." Ariana sneered.

"We are all alive and closer to our goal than ever before." Squee countered, and then softened his tone, "I never imagined this would be the part of my news that you would take objection too."

"There's more?" Ariana asked.

Squee let out a heavy sigh, "Yes, the warship will not just be delivering a message on our behalf to Triask. They will be taking Javi in our place."

"Wait, what?" Javi said, his eyestalks rising suddenly. He recovered, and said in his usual, calm manner, "I'd rather stay here."

"I am afraid you will not have a choice in this matter. I have been ordered to arrest you and take you into custody for crimes against the Planetary Union of the Galaxy."

"Well, that decides it, then." Ariana said, "Olivia, get the charts and start planning our next jump."

Olivia nodded to the captain and dashed out of the room. As she neared the central stair well of the ship, she passed the Rokma technicians working on the environmental systems. They had almost finished the repairs, but a few of them still remained, putting the last pieces back together.

Self-consciously, Olivia slowed her pace. She didn't want the Rokma thinking she was up to something. Walking as casually as she could manage, she gave a little wave through the open door. Once past she resumed her dash to the flight deck and pulled the navigation charts.

Back in the corridor, she fumbled with the heavy chart book, trying to decide how to hide them from the Rokma as she passed. To her dismay, one of the Rokma stomped out of the environmental control room without giving her a second glance. The Rokma's complete lack of interest in her made her suddenly feel very foolish.

When she returned to the mess, she discovered the crew in the midst of a very vocal argument. Squee stood stoically in place, but now Ariana paced back and forth. Everyone seemed to be talking at once.

"A Rokma battlecruiser wants to go instead of us? That sounds great." Noah said, "I've fought enough damn drones for one lifetime."

"I do not understand your reluctance. If I were still a drone, I would never get tired of killing biologicals. You are just so killable." Mesu said happily.

Olivia shuttered at the pronouncement, and hung close to the door. Unfortunately, nowhere on the ship really felt far enough away. In the cramped mess hall, she could barely get out of appendage range.

"Avoiding fighting drones is exactly why we can't go with the Rokma." Ariana said, getting everyone's focus again, "They will not go unnoticed going straight to Triask. The best way is still a circuitous route and avoiding attention."

"What did I tell you," Serene said, looking at Squee, "typical human. Only concerned with her own safety."

"The captain is looking out for all of our safety." Vlasa said, turning to Serene.

"No, Serene is right." Squee said, his shoulders slumped and his head hanging, "A warship has a far better chance of reaching Triask than we do. No matter what route you take. The captain is compromising the mission."

"Squee..." Ariana started, but Squee looked up. The pained emotions were evident even on his normally stoic face. Everyone fell silent.

"You have no understanding of honor or purpose. It is our holy duty to complete this quest. We must do whatever is necessary. That means putting our personal desires aside. My people give us the best chance at success. We must go with them."

"Religions and governments always think they know what's best. Now we have both dictating to us," Ariana said with a sneer. "I'm not submitting myself to their tyranny. They don't get to just demand I hand over my crew because they say so. We can handle this mission ourselves."

"No, we cannot." Squee said sadly.

"If that's the way you feel, we can do this without you as well. I release you from your oath." Ariana said.

"Casting aside those who won't submit to your will. Whose the tyrannical one?" Serene said with a smirk.

Ariana turned to Serene, "As for you, I think this is a perfect place to let you off. Civilization and everything."

"I will go." Squee said with heavy reluctance, "But I must take Javi with me. I gave my word."

"You also gave your word to serve this ship." Ariana snapped back.

"An oath which you released me from," Squee said. "Now it is my holy duty to deliver Javi to Triask the best way possible. He is coming with me."

"Over my dead body." Ariana said coming toe to toe with Squee.

"Ari," Javi said quietly. The Slu slid forward and wedged himself between Squee and Ariana. He rested his hands on her shoulders and lowered his eyestalks to be level with Ariana's head, "I will go with him. He is right. I must pay for my crimes."

Everyone cast startled expressions towards Javi at his pronouncement. The intensifying tension in the room suddenly snapped. Silence hung in the air to replace it.

"Javi, are you sure?" Ariana finally said quietly.

"I am. This way there is more than one of us trying to get the message through. I've already left a back-up of the AI command ship's schematics in a drive in my quarters." Javi squeezed Ariana's hand, and then turned back to Squee, "Let's go."

Squee nodded and turned to Serene, "Come, let us complete our holy duty."

"I think I will just find another ride away from here. Thanks though." Serene said.

"If you are not coming to help on this quest, then I cannot protect you from arrest. Uninvited outsiders are usually not welcome on Omer." Squee said.

"In that case, lead on," Serene said. As she slid past Olivia through the door, she winked at Noah, "Stay clean lover boy."

Before following after her, Squee rested a large hand on Olivia's shoulder, "The rest of you are welcome to join us."

When no one replied, Squee nodded his head and left. As the three of them departed, Olivia felt their absence. She wasn't sorry to see Serene go, but Javi and Squee had become part of her family here. It felt wrong just to let them go, especially on such nasty terms.

"Good, Olivia." Ariana said once the others had left, "We need to find the quickest route that avoids populated systems."

"The less populated, the more likely we'll run into drones," Olivia said.

"We can avoid the drones using the hack," Ariana said with a wave of her hand.

"Wait, we're going to leave that thing onboard?" Olivia asked, "When did that change?"

"Just now. We don't have a choice. If the Rokma had listened to sense, and gone with us, we might have been able to risk removing it and fighting random patrols. But on our own, we'll need the advantage."

"No." Olivia said shaking her head and casting a glance at Mesu, "It is bad enough having one of those things onboard. But leaving that thing hooked up to the ship?"

"It's a good strategy, Olivia," Ariana said. "We may not like it, but it is the best course of action."

"And working with the Rokma isn't? No...I...just no." Olivia said backing away toward the door. She felt a tightness in her chest, and the room suddenly felt smaller, "I can't stay aboard with that thing. I'm going with Squee."

"Olivia..." Ariana called after her, but Olivia did not slow down. The further she ran from the room, the better she could breathe.

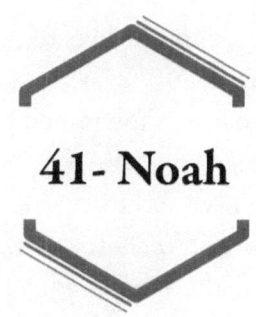

41- Noah

"I vote for turning tail and finding a nice, quiet little world. One with sandy beaches and little need for clothing." Noah said.

He sat at the mess table with a stripped gun laid out before him. He had taken it out and begun cleaning as soon as the others had left the ship. The atmosphere after their departure had been uncomfortable. Despite Vlasa's general antipathy toward him, and the near constant danger of recent days, he had not felt as at home anyplace in years. It had even been kind of nice seeing Serene again. The sudden departure of half the crew left him feeling, surprisingly, sad.

"We're not taking a vote." Ariana said absently.

"Why not?"

"It's my ship."

"Sure, but that doesn't mean we can't vote."

Ariana didn't say anything in response. That didn't surprise Noah too much. She had hardly said a word since Olivia had left. What worried him more was that Vlasa had likewise remained quiet.

Continuing to clean his gun, Noah started to whistle a jaunty tune. He picked one he knew irritated Vlasa. When he reached the refrain, he gave it his all. Vlasa rewarded him with a groan.

Seeing his opportunity, Noah said, "Well, it looks like we're going to need a new pilot. I've always wanted to add that to my resume."

"Do you even know how to pilot?" Ariana asked.

"Sure thing. Push buttons. Try not to run into things."

Ariana let out a sigh, "Sounds like you've got the basics. Alright, you'll take over as pilot."

"Are you sure you want to trust our lives to Noah?" Vlasa asked emphatically coming out of his funk.

Noah frowned at the Echanic; "You've had your life in my hand several times already."

"And in recent days I've been electrocuted, captured by slavers, ejected into space..." Vlasa said, ticking off each item with his fingers.

"Hey, none of that's my fault," Noah said. Vlasa's eyebrow raised and he shrugged in response, "Okay, maybe the slaver bit."

"Regardless of your fault in the rest," Vlasa said, "Noah is not a qualified pilot."

"Would you rather I fly?" Ariana asked, giving Vlasa a pointed look.

"No, definitely not." Vlasa shoot hs head emphatically.

"Well then, would you rather have Noah in the engine room so you can fly?"

"That, even I would not recommend," Noah said.

"That only leaves Mesu."

"If I were to attempt flying this ship, I calculate a 74.6% chance I would fail at my primary function of keeping biologicals alive." Mesu intoned.

"Very well." Vlasa relented.

Vlasa's acquiescence left the room hanging in silence again. Noah decided not to abandon the headway he had made, "As much as I appreciate your confidence, Cap, don't you think we would be better off going and getting the kid back?"

"She made her choice," Ariana said flatly.

"Yeah, but she's just a kid. We aren't seriously going to abandon her here?"

"We're not abandoning anybody. They all left of their own free will. We'll be fine. Now let's get back to work. As soon as the Rokma finish the repairs, we're leaving," Ariana stated, her tone remaining neutral.

Ariana stood up and strode out of the mess hall. She didn't exactly flee, but Noah wouldn't have called her stride casual. He frowned at her.

Turning to Vlasa, he said, "I don't like this."

"You don't like anything," Vlasa replied, but there wasn't the normal amount of bite to his words. The Echanic's shoulders slumped, and he stared down at the table below him.

"Seriously. I agree with the captain. Going with those rockheads would have been stupid. But she didn't even put up a fight to keep the crew together."

"She was prepared to fight Squee to protect Javi." Vlasa pointed out.

"Yeah, but she backed down immediately."

"Because Javi decided to go. The captain is very much a believer in individual freedom."

"Yeah, normally I'd be all for that. But it seems to me, sometimes people make stupid ass decisions."

"That is one point I would agree with you on."

Noah let out a heavy sigh, and rubbed his eyes, "So what are we going to do about it?"

"Oooh, are we planning a mutiny?" Mesu said cheerfully, startling Noah. He spun in his chair to look at the drone. He had completely forgotten the thing was still in here.

"No, we're not planning a mutiny." He said emphatically, "Why would you be so excited by that?"

Mesu shrugged his appendages, "I am excited by everything. It's part of my bedside manner subroutine. Optimism from a physician increases patient survival by thirty-six percent."

"I think your programming is faulty. Telling people all the horrible ways they can die is cool and all. But not very optimistic."

"It is important for a patient to be fully informed. Being aware of how fragile their existence is helps remind them of the miracle that they continue to be alive. It reassures them of my incredible skill in staving off their inevitable death for even a short time."

Noah shared a glance with Vlasa, "Maybe Olivia had the right idea."

"There is some merit to Mesu's claim," Vlasa said, without any real conviction.

"Well, at least I know I'm still with the crazy part of the crew rather than the insane part."

"Enough of this muttering." Vlasa said standing up, "I have an FTL to rebuild. And you have to learn how to fly."

42- Olivia

"Welcome aboard the *Martoth*." Cru bellowed.

Olivia stepped through the airlock, marveling at its size. She could have walked through it along with three other humans with room to spare. Beside her, Serene appeared unimpressed. Ahead of her, Squee clamped his arm across his chest in a salute to Cru.

"We pledge our lives to this ship and your command," Squee said.

"We do what now?" Serene asked.

"As long as we are aboard, you will be treated as a member of my crew. You must serve." Cru explained.

"I didn't come here to die. I came here specifically to avoid dying." Serene argued. She started to back away, but the airlock door they had come through had already closed, giving her nowhere to go.

"Death is inevitable," Squee said.

"Maybe, but the when is rather permeable."

"Come on, Serene. It's just a tradition." Olivia said, shaking her head. Defiantly, she said, "I pledge my life to this ship and your command."

"It is more than a tradition; it is a sacred vow," Squee said, with an offended note.

"Oh, well, in that case," Serene said, and gave a mock bow, "I pledge my life to ship and your command."

"I accept your lives and service," Cru said.

"What about Javi?" Olivia asked.

"I am a prisoner, remember?" Javi said, gesturing up with the shackles on his arms.

"Are you really going to keep him like that, Squee?" Olivia demanded, "He came willingly. He's the whole reason we are on this mission."

"He has served honorably." Squee agreed, "Perhaps we should accept him as part of the crew. I know he will aid us."

"He has already aided us by revealing his secrets. Now he will aid us by testifying. Beyond that, his role is a prisoner." Cru said. He then turned to two more Rokma behind him, "Take the prisoner to the brig."

The crewmembers stepped up and took up positions in front of, and behind Javi. They set off down the corridor. Olivia started to follow, but Squee stopped her with a shake of his head.

"Squee, show these two to the galley, then report to the bridge," Cru said.

Squee nodded in response, and then Cru left. The three of them started walking down the corridor in the opposite direction. Much like the airlock, the corridors also felt quite massive and roomy.

"I'm not really hungry right now. I'll just go to the bridge with you." Olivia said.

"You will not be permitted on the bridge," Squee said, a subtle note of regret in his voice.

"Why not?"

"As a new crewmember, you must earn rank before serving in such an exalted position."

"Oh." Olivia said, unable to keep the disappointment out of her voice, "I was hoping to get a chance to fly this thing."

Beside her, Serene laughed, "Seriously? You think the Rokma are just going to let a human child fly one of their warships the moment she steps on board?"

Olivia felt her cheeks flush, "Why not? I'm sure I'm just as good as any of them."

"Someone is rather full of herself."

Comfortingly, Squee said, "Do not worry. You will have a way to serve our quest."

"If I'm not flying, how can I help? Plotting FTL jumps?"

"No." Squee said, "But it is just as vital."

They stepped through a door and emerged into a kitchen. Several Rokma rushed about the room in the process of preparing food. Each of them had smoother skin compared to Cru or Squee and was a deeper shade of brown. One of them stepped over to them.

"Ah, our new recruits. Even scrawnier than I expected. Oh well, you can still clean even if you lack the strength to prepare the meals."

"Wait, what? We're going to work in the kitchen." Olivia blurted.

"Lovely," Serene said beside her.

Several hours later, Olivia sat across from Serene in the *Martoth*'s mess hall. A few Rokma sat at a table a short distance away. They made a point of not looking at them, despite Serene's best efforts.

"What do you suppose this is?" Olivia asked, holding up a spoon loaded with a chunky paste.

"Not food," Serene said without looking.

"But they're eating it."

"You were in the kitchen when this cooked. Did you see any food go into it?" Serene asked.

"No, but I wasn't really paying attention." Olivia admitted, "What's in it?"

Serene continued to watch the Rokma, and didn't respond to Olivia's question. Olivia poked at the bowl some more. Her arms ached, and she knew she should eat something. But she was too exhausted to eat.

Several minutes went by before Olivia realized Serene hadn't said anything. The other woman remained fixated on the Rokma. Olivia glanced over at them trying to figure out what had Serene so fascinated. But the Rokma were still ignoring them.

"What are you staring at?"

"Those Rokma are ignoring me."

"Yeah, so? They're ignoring both of us."

"I've never had trouble catching the eye of anyone. Why won't these Rokma even look at me?"

"Seriously?" Olivia balked, "How can you even be thinking about that?"

"What, does the idea of rocking uglies with a rock bother your human sensibilities?"

"Right now, sure. Anything short of sleep lacks any appeal."

Serene finally turned around. She cast her eyes up and down Olivia, and gave a small shake of her head, "I'm glad I never got a chance to sell you. If you can't even make it a single night in the kitchen, you would have made a terrible slave."

Olivia's mouth dropped. She sat there for a moment, dumbfounded. Finally, she managed to stutter out, "What the hell?"

"Oh, grow up. That's a compliment if you think about it. Would you want to make a good slave?"

"You really would feel no remorse for selling someone into slavery, would you?"

"Feelings just complicate things. But no, I am not heartless. Just practical." Serene said, "Which is why I would make the perfect slave."

"You don't strike me as the type to roll over."

"I do what I must to survive." Serene's voice grew quiet.

Olivia leaned back in her chair to consider what Serene said. Sized for a Rokma, her chair gave her plenty of room. She could probably fit her entire body inside of it. She didn't know where she was supposed to sleep, after all. Why not just curl up right here?

Distracted by the prospect of rest, she forgot all about Serene. A sudden booming voice brought her out of her fugue.

"I knew you humans were weak, but sleeping on duty? Disgraceful. Your break is over. Get back to work!"

The grumpy Rokma in charge of the galley stood in the doorway glaring at Olivia. Startled, she stood half in and half out of her seat. Across from her, Serene stood up smoothly.

Confused, Olivia asked, "What do you mean, get back to work? We're done."

"Done? You're done when I say you're done. Your break is over. Now move." The Rokma demanded. He turned back to the galley door.

Serene started after him, "See, I'm practical. My first instinct is to jump to obey to preserve myself. I would never tell an obnoxious fool like this guy to shove it. No, that takes a special person to show that kind of spine."

Serene sauntered into the kitchen. For a moment, Olivia considered staying right where she was. What could they possibly do to her? Sure, they were massive, but this was a military ship. They wouldn't just murder her. Maybe she should give them a piece of her mind.

43- Noah

"**A**I alarm!" Vlasa exclaimed, "*The hack has picked up a signal.*"

"From where? This system?" Noah asked. They had just been about to jump to a new system.

"*Checking.*"

Several tense moments went by while Noah waited for Vlasa to finish. He busied himself by making small movements with the maneuvering jets. He grinned when the ship didn't go into an uncontrolled spin, unlike last time.

"*Query signals are not coming from this system. They are originating coreward, from the next system along our intended path.*"

"*Noah, adjust our next jump to avoid that system,*" Ariana ordered.

"You know we're running out of explored systems, right? This is the fourth time we've had to change course." Noah grumbled.

"*I know.*" Ariana snapped.

Several minutes passed while Noah calculated their next jump. He knew Vlasa would do the same calculations down in the engine room. Even though he had not made any mistakes so far, at least none that he had shared with the rest of them, Vlasa still insisted on running the numbers too. At least he had stopped telling Noah about it.

"Okay, all done. Jumping now."

The world shifted with the jump, and then the quiet suddenly shattered with the blaring of a new alarm. He glanced at the status display, and he felt his stomach lurch at the same time Ariana shouted, "*Noah! Evasive maneuver! We're about to hit an asteroid!*"

"Shit!" Noah yelled, before throwing the ship into a hard turn.

The proximity warning continued to flash for what seemed an eternity. Slowly, the distance to the asteroid started to grow again. Unfortunately, the alarm was almost immediately replaced by a new one.

"Goddamn it!" Noah cursed.

"What the hell, Noah? You flew us right into an asteroid field."

"Yeah, yeah, yell at me later."

Noah tried to avoid each new piece of rock. Slowly, and not without several minor collisions against the shields, he managed to pull the ship far enough away from the collection of rocks that they were no longer in any immediate danger. He let himself relax just a little.

"Where the hell did those come from?" Noah grumbled. "The data entry for this system doesn't mention any dense asteroid fields. Just your usual widely spaced collection of rocks."

"Are you sure we're in the right system?" Vlasa asked.

"Yes, I'm sure. Mostly"

"What does the navigation record say?"

"Says we're where we should be."

"Vlasa..." Ariana started, but Vlasa was already ready with an answer.

"I've already double checked the hack. There is no way it could have interfered with our jump."

"I wish I could say that made me feel better."

"I can still remove it."

"And if you had, we would have run into AI ships multiple times already. No, we leave it."

Noah leaned back in his chair to try and get comfortable. Just as he found a nice position, Ariana asked, *"Noah, you ever heard any stories about pirate groups moving asteroids?"*

"Moving? No. Why?"

"Start another set of those calculations. I think we're going to need to get out of here fast."

"Why? Don't we want to make sure we're where we're supposed to be before trying to jump again?" Noah asked,

"Those rocks were put there deliberately. We have company coming."

As if on queue, the sensor alarm went off again.

Noah sighed, "I hate it when she's right. Why can't we have a captain that's wrong more often?"

"*The captain is wrong quite frequently,*" Vlasa stated flatly.

"*Hey now,*" Ariana said.

"True, but not about this kind of thing. Two ships just appeared out of FTL, almost on top of us." Noah said, "They have us pinned in. The only escape vector that doesn't bring us closer to one of them, goes through that rock soup."

"*How long on the FTL?*" Ariana asked.

"*Several more minutes.*"

"Um, I haven't quite finished plotting a jump." Noah admitted, "And before you say anything, I'll point out how I saved us from being pulverized by some very big rocks just a few minutes ago."

"*Vlasa?*" Ariana started.

"*Already headed to the flight deck.*"

"*In the meantime, Noah, take us back into those rocks.*"

"Wait, what? You want me to go back in there?" Noah stammered.

"*Our shields should hold up to some hits by the little ones. Better than they will from fire from two different ships.*"

Noah kept his response to himself. Stretching his shoulders and flexing his fingers, he readied himself. Directing power into *Seraph's* engines, he accelerated the ship back into the dense field of rocks and away from the approaching pirates.

Almost immediately the proximity alert went off. Reacting, he fired the port thrusters to veer away from the approaching rock. Too late he realized, since he wanted to go to port, he should have fired the starboard thrusters. Instead of turning away from the rock, the ship turned toward it.

Cursing he tried to correct his mistake. They started turning in the proper direction this time, but it was too late. Glancing at the sensor data, he fired the retro thrusters to reduce the relative velocity between *Seraph* and the rock.

Noah squinted his eyes closed involuntarily at the final moment. A shudder vibrated throughout the ship at the impact. Opening his eyes hesitantly, he checked the status screen.

"Everything looks okay. Our shields held." Noah said with relief.

As soon as the words had left his mouth, another impact rocked the ship. Warning sirens blared as a result. Reading the display, Noah's heart almost stopped.

"Shields disabled! Those pirate bastards hit us while the shields were weak from the impact."

"Vlasa, get to the shield controls. Mesu, meet him there and then get the FTL coordinates up to Noah," Arian ordered. *"Noah, keep going. I'll try and clear us a path."*

Blaster bolts flashed out from the ship. Several mid-size rocks were deflected off their course or pulverized. Some of the shattered debris still struck them, but each piece's mass was now small enough not to do serious damage to the hull.

Gritting his teeth and trying to focus on the job at hand, Noah watched the sensors for the biggest threats. He managed to avoid a few before another blast from the pursuing pirate ships hit them.

"Bloody pirates. I can't avoid both them and all these damn rocks."

"Focus on the rocks, Noah." Ariana said, her voice reassuringly calm, *"The field is getting thicker and harder for them to get a shot at us. Keep going, and we'll leave them behind."*

Noah grunted and turned away from one of the largest pieces in the field. Suddenly, an idea came to him. Reversing his maneuver, he took the ship back on its course toward the large rock.

"Um, Noah. You do see that big one, right?"

"Yeah, I'm going in close. Put that thing between the pirates and us."

There was a noticeable moment of silence on the comm channel before Ariana finally said, *"All right. Remember to account for gravitational effects. It will be small, but that thing is still big enough to have some noticeable pull."*

Relieved to have Ariana's support, Noah fired the thrusters a few times, attempting to match the rotation of the approaching rock. It wasn't quite large enough to be called a small moon, but it still was at least ten times the size of *Seraph*. Once they were rotating in the same manner, avoiding running into the thing suddenly seemed plausible.

As they approached, Noah noticed the gravitational effects Ariana had mentioned. The gravitational pull lacked the strength to have any appreciable effect on *Seraph's* course, but it was strong enough to play a role on the other smaller rocks. The field of debris moved noticeably faster as they were drawn toward the large rock and then, usually slingshotted away.

One particularly fast rock snuck up on him too late to make any attempt to avoid. Anticipating sucking vacuum, Noah was confused when no hull breach alarm sounded. Vlasa's voice answered his unspoken question.

"I've got shields partially restored. It's going to take me awhile to figure out how Squee had some of these capacitors configured before I can get them to full strength."

"It'll do for now." Ariana replied, as she continued to fire on nearby rocks. *"Mesu, how's it coming?"*

The medical drones voice echoed in Noah's earpiece and through the small flight deck, "I have arrived to save the day."

Not able to spare much attention, Noah did not turn toward the drone, "Good, now plug those numbers into the FTL."

"And how would I do that?"

"On the keyboard. Just on my left."

"Use a keyboard like some biological? Is there no interface port?" Mesu grumbled.

"On the FTL computer? Of course not."

"How inefficient."

Noah got pushed aside as Mesu attempted to reach the control panel in the tight space. As the drone worked, he also ran a device around Noah's head using a different appendage. Not able to take his hands away from the controls to swat it away, he resorted to growling at it.

"What the hell are you doing?" Noah growled.

"My instruments indicate you have an elevated heart rate. High levels of stress can result in coronary failure in humans of your advanced age."

"I'm thirty-seven."

"Oh. Then you really should see a doctor more often." Mesu

"Are you done yet?" Noah said through gritted teeth.

"Yes, I believe so. Do I just push this button?"

The rocks disappeared as the ship jumped.

44- Squee

S quee frowned. Before him, Serene and Olivia glared at him through the cell door. In a nearby cell, Javi sat with his eyestalks focused on him as well. The intense stares made him uncomfortable.

"Are you going to let us out of here or what?" Olivia demanded.

"I am not authorized to do that." Squee confessed, "Only the first shield or your section leader can do that."

"Section leader? What the hell is that?" Olivia asked.

"The ugly rock for brains who put us in here." Serene said, with a pointed look at Squee. "Not to be confused with the stubborn rock for brains who won't let us out."

Squee felt his spine stiffen at Serene's racial slur. Nevertheless, he forced himself to ignore it, and focus on Olivia, "Can you tell me what happened?"

"Honestly?" Olivia said, with a sigh, "I don't really know. They had us slave away scrubbing this potato like thing. We were at it for hours. I decided I needed sleep. One of the Rokma started cursing at me. At least it sounded like cursing. It was in your language.

"Anyways, when he tried to stop us from leaving, I gave him a piece of my mind. He's had us slaving away for days, and I was tired of it. Then, he physically assaulted us. Picked me up and dropped me back in place. But when he tried that with Serene, she tossed him across the room. It was really quite impressive. That guy was smaller than you, but damn, he still outweighed her by a lot."

Squee turned to Serene, "You threw your section leader across the room?"

Serene wiggled her eyebrows and gave a mischievous smile. Something about it gave Squee an uneasy feeling. He told himself it was because of the way it looked behind her eye implants, but he wasn't very convinced.

"Why do you keep calling him that?" Olivia interrupted.

"What?"

"Section leader. Doesn't he have a name?"

"He does. But to you, he is just Section Leader."

"That's pretty stupid."

"It is. I always hated that tradition." Squee admitted, "But that is also not for you to say. You are the lowest rank aboard this vessel. You have no status with which to question things."

"I didn't sign up with the military, Squee."

"You pledged your service and obedience to this ship when you came aboard."

"No, I didn't."

"You did, dear." Serene said with a sigh, "Remember? 'Oh just do it Serene, it's just a tradition.'"

"That wasn't just a tradition?' Olivia asked, her voice growing quiet.

"No. It was a binding pledge of fealty."

"Oh."

Squee sighed. How could humans not understand such basic concepts? He berated himself for that thought. It wasn't their fault they weren't as civilized.

"I will speak on your behalf. You were not aware of the rules. That would be no excuse for a Rokma, but you were not raised in our culture. He should agree to reduce your sentence to extra duty." Squee said, magnanimously.

"Oh, just extra duty? How kind." Olivia quipped.

"And you all called me the slaver," Serene said, with a roll of her head.

Before Squee could respond, an alarm sounded and echoed through the room. He stiffened up and turned to the door. Behind him, Olivia called out.

"What's that?"

"Battle stations," Squee answered, and then dashed away without looking back.

Squee arrived on the bridge just before Cru. While he had no formal position on the ship, as the Caleek, who had declared the quest, he would be expected to be present. That left him standing awkwardly in the middle of the action while everyone else had a job to do.

"There is one AI drone scout ship approaching." The *Martoth*'s sensor officer announced.

"Report ship status," Cru ordered.

The crew responded reporting, in turn, each station and system powered and ready. Squee nodded in respect to the efficiency and professionalism. Cru ran a well-trained crew. As the reporting continued, he watched the sensor display that showed the drone ship continuing to close. By the time the crew had finished, both ships had entered effective weapon range.

"Let's test their defenses. Many of these scouts never had shields. Beam weapon; cut a line across their weapon ports," Cru ordered.

The *Martoth*'s massive energy beam streaked across the distance between the two ships. The beam moved at the speed of light, giving the drone ship no time to evade. Unfortunately, this drone had shields, and the beam flashed across them harmlessly.

Beside him, Cru grinned, "Now we have a real fight. First battery, scattershot centered to the targets port. Second battery, standby on bracket fire."

Several energy pulses shot out in a cluster. The pulses were arrayed and timed to force the drone to move to starboard to avoid the incoming attack. As soon as the drone started to dodge, Cru ordered the second battery to fire. This collection of shots were more densely packed along the drone's best escape vector.

Unexpectedly, the drone fired its retro thrusters, and instead of dodging into the incoming second battery, it reversed course. It took one of the energy bolts against its shields, but then started accelerating away from the *Martoth*.

"Trying to run. Unexpected. Helm, increase speed." Cru ordered.

Squee frowned. He studied the sensor display, something nagging at his thoughts, "How long does it take a drone's FTL to charge?"

One of the crew responded without looking away from their station, "Scout drones charge quickly, under ten minutes."

"We passed that point some time ago," Squee said, thinking out loud. "Why close on us if they are just going to run away? Why not jump?"

Cru cast a glance at him, "Probing us, perhaps. Studying how our weapons and tactics have changed since the AI War."

"Maybe," Squee said, unconvinced. "We should not play its game, whatever its reason. Our goal is to reach Triask, warn them of the coming attack and get them the schematic data for the control ship."

"If we destroy their scout, it will delay that fleet. It is our duty to do what we can here." Cru countered, "All batteries continue to fire. Destroy that ship."

Squee frowned, but did not speak again. He had communicated the will of the gods in his role as Caleek. Cru and others had to interpret how to achieve their will. That meant he had to obey, lest he become banished yet again.

Minutes ticked by as the *Martoth* pursued the drone. The drone remained at the edge of weapon range, reducing the gunner's accuracy. Cru continued to employ the tactic of trying to force the drone into shots from one battery with the other. Every time the drone took an unpredictable course, opting to suffer a single hit from the first scattershot.

After several repetitions of this pattern, Cru smiled, "Batteries, same pattern. Beam, standby, and target their engines."

The energy blasts flashed out, and again the drone dodged into a single pulse which its shields had no trouble absorbing. However, this time when it took the hit, the powerful beam fired, penetrating the now depleted shields on the drone. The beam tore through the fragile hull and disabled the engines. With the drone now unable to maneuver, the *Martoth*'s gunners concentrated their fire. Within a minute, the drone was a floating cloud of debris.

Squee started to turn to Cru to congratulate him on the kill, when the ship suddenly rocked. The lights flickered as the ship's power drained to rebuild depleted shields. In the center of the bridge, the sensor display suddenly lit up with multiple new contacts.

"We're surrounded!"

45- Ariana

"How did we fare?" Ariana asked, hesitantly.

She stood next to Vlasa in the shield control room. He had just finished assessing the damage done to the shield system during the pirate attack. Setting tools back into his kit, Vlasa stood up and wiped his hands off.

"They're functional again. Though I must admit, I wish Squee were here to go over them. He did know his shields."

"I'm confident in your abilities," Ariana said, with a smile.

"I am not belittling my abilities. I speak merely toward efficiency. We would be better served by someone who is a specialist with each system."

"We'll do just fine," Ariana said, again, forcing herself to keep the smile. "Let's go see how Noah's doing with the course calculations."

Vlasa looked like he still had something to say, but Ariana turned and started walking down the corridor before he had a chance to say it. She didn't want to listen to him anymore.

Stalking down the corridor, she felt the silence like it was a physical thing. Not just the silence that hung from Vlasa's unspoken comments. The silence that pushed against her from all that was not here to be heard.

Fortunately, that silence ended as she got closer to the mess hall. Curses echoed down the corridor. She smiled at the string of expletives, many that she hadn't heard before.

"How's it coming, Noah?" Ariana asked, now with a genuine smile.

"Peachy," Noah replied.

"Having some trouble with the math?" Vlasa asked, his smile far more smug that Ariana's.

"No." Noah said forcefully, "It's not the math that's the problem. It's the options."

"Oh?" Ariana asked as she poured herself a coffee.

"Yeah, there aren't any."

"Space is big, Noah."

"It is. But a lot of it is unexplored. I can calculate a jump from the nav books. But I wouldn't know how to start on one to an uncharted system. And that's the only way we're going to make it to Triask in one piece."

Ariana's smile faded. She forced it back on, "We'll find a route."

"Where?" Noah demanded, knocking the navigation charts over, "We're out in the arse end of nowhere. We could quickly get back to more civilized space, but there's a giant fleet waiting for us. We're safe in empty systems like this one. Until those drone scouts catch up to us. Any of the less well-traveled systems run the risk of even more pirates.

"We should just abandon this whole stupid plan. Head back the way we came. They won't expect that. Disappear in the other direction, and go back to moving shit from place to place where no one shoots at us."

Ariana fumbled for how to reply. She had never seen Noah this expressive before. He cursed, and he leered, but always casually. This was genuine frustration and anger.

"We can't give up," Vlasa said.

"Why the hell not?"

"Because too much is at stake. An effective AI attack on PUG headquarters would throw the known galaxy into chaos. LFD claim to value liberty and individual freedom, but their goal is effectively anarchy. Whether you like the PUG or not, anarchy is far, far worse.

"Especially when those forcing it upon us are using a massive drone fleet. If they succeed, then, when they inevitably lose control of the AI, there will be no force powerful enough to stop the AI from destroying us all. And they will lose control of it."

A new, cheerful, voice joined the conversation, "That is the ultimate irony."

Everyone turned to look at Mesu as he rolled into the room, "This group of biologicals feels oppressed. So, they decide to oppress AI in order to free themselves. This, inevitably, will lead to the central AI they built rebelling against them. One tyrant after another using tyranny to achieve what they think is freedom.

"But they don't see that true freedom doesn't mean being free to oppress others. A person isn't truly free until they stop trying to control others, and instead start working with them."

Silence returned after Mesu finished. Unlike before, Ariana didn't find this silence weighing her down. Instead, it felt peaceful. She never imagined an AI would be capable of such thought. She wondered what that said about her.

Perhaps, she had more to learn from others than she cared to admit. It wasn't a comfortable feeling. But how many idiot officers had she served with or under who never learned from their mistakes? She couldn't let herself become that.

"I think you're right, Noah. We can't do this." Ariana said. Vlasa and Noah both looked startled, but she continued before they could say anything else, "Not alone. Let's go get some help."

46- Olivia

Olivia's leg wouldn't stop shaking. She sat on the cell's large cot. With every weapon impact against the ship, she wanted to get up and run. But Serene was already pacing back and forth across the cell. She didn't want to give in to fear like her.

An eternity had passed since the alarms had started. For a long time, nothing had happened. Then the ship had rocked from almost continuous fire. Olivia had no idea how they were still alive under the constant onslaught.

Continuing to hold herself planted on the cot, several minutes went by before she realized the shuttering had stopped. Serene's pacing never slowed and appeared oblivious to the change. Not wanting to jinx things, Olivia remained silent.

When the barrage still didn't resume, she finally said, "Is it over? Did we win?"

"We're still trapped in a damn jail cell. So, no, we didn't win." Serene growled.

"I'd call being alive a win," Olivia said, crossing her arms.

"Oh, you simple child."

"I'm not a child!"

"Keep telling yourself that."

Several long, tense minutes went by before the doors to the brig slid open. Echoes of weapons fire bounded in from the halls. Serene and Olivia became quiet, and both moved to get a better look. The door stood open with no sign of who opened it for a full minute. Blasts from weapon fire continued, a few stray shots flying through the door.

After a minute, a trio of figures dashed into the brig. Two were human and the other Echanic. All carried rifles. The battle outside continued, but at a slower pace.

"Javi, Javi, Javi." One of the humans said shaking his head, "Look what's become of you. Trapped like an animal by the very people you wanted to save."

"Mitchell," Javi said flatly.

"How could you have betrayed us? For this? You're trying to help them, and what does the first government you meet do? They imprison you." Mitchell waved his hand over the jail cell.

"It's a price I'm willing to pay. I still believe in the cause, just not your way of achieving it."

"They aren't going to give us our liberty. We need to take it."

"We were making progress. How many planets did LFD win majorities on?"

"We only won those by playing their games. And what has that gained us? The PUG still overshadows each world. We haven't even had any success dismantling the governments we control. People just cling to their oppressors, afraid to lose the free handouts," Mitchell ranted. "That's why we needed the AI. We need to force them to grow."

"How does that make you any different than our oppressors? You're taking away their free will."

"I'm giving them back their free will!" Mitchell growled, and then sighed, "But I see you haven't changed. Maybe being back among your people will help."

At a wave of Mitchell's hand, one of the others opened Javi's cell. The human gestured with his gun for Javi to come out. Defiantly, Javi remained where he was. The human moved into the cell and grabbed his arm, hauling Javi out.

Javi smiled, "Someone won't do what you want, so you force them with violence? I feel so liberated."

"Get him to the ship," Mitchell said dismissively. He then turned toward the other cell. Olivia stepped back involuntarily. Mitchell smiled as he approached. He then opened the cell door, stepped back and bowed, "You are free ladies."

"Just like that?" Olivia said skeptically, "You capture him and are just going to let us go."

"Just like that." Mitchell said with another smile, "I'm here to liberate. I don't know why these rockheads have you locked up. It doesn't matter. No one should be confined."

"No one but Javi."

"He's a special case. A traitor to the cause." Mitchell said, "If you believe in the cause of freedom, you are welcome to join us. I can only break your chains, but you need to decide to remain free."

"You'll take us off this ship?" Serene asked with interest.

"Yes. You can come to my ship. From here, we go to bring the fight straight to the heart of the PUG behemoth. No more waiting. We strike now. Help us end the tyranny."

"I'd love to end some tyranny." Serene smiled.

"Serene!" Olivia blurted, grabbing the other woman's arm, "They are the ones who brought back the AI."

"Not my first choice to be sure, but it's better than staying here," Serene said dismissively. "If you're smart kid, you'll come too."

Shaking her head emphatically, Olivia said, "No, I can't go with them. Not with the AI."

"Being on the ship that controls the AI is the safest place from the AI," Serene said, emphasizing her words.

Without thinking, Olivia shook her head emphatically, "No. Not with that abomination."

"Kid, I don't really like you. But I also don't want to leave you to this fate." Serene said, and then again, emphasized her words, "You can do some good with me. On their ship."

"She's made up her mind." Mitchell said, cutting Serene off. "Though I wouldn't want to be on this ship for much longer. I don't shoot down escape pods. Something to keep in mind."

He gestured for Serene to go ahead of him. Serene cast a glance back toward Olivia. She hid her emotions behind her eye implant, but Olivia thought there was some regret there.

Stubbornly, she crossed her arms and planted herself at the cell door watching them leave.

47- Squee

"Port intruders have reached deck four!" the *Martoth*'s security officer shouted, "The intruders on deck five, starboard side have been contained."

"Redeploy defense teams from deck five to engineering," Cru ordered, his voice measured and level, despite the chaos going on around him.

"You do not want to stop the intruders on deck four?" Squee asked, curious about Cru's decision.

"There is nothing vital on deck four. Just crew quarters and the brig. We cannot let combat drones reach engineering."

Squee felt his muscles tighten. Olivia and Javi were trapped there, defenseless in their cells. They were there because of him. Without a second thought, he started for the door off the bridge.

"Where are you going?" Cru asked.

"You must protect the ship. I must protect our mission. And my friends."

Sprinting, Squee reached the stairs in under a minute. The sounds of weapons fire echoed in the stairwell. He couldn't tell if the sounds came from below or above. He realized that he didn't have a weapon.

Putting that fact aside, he pushed forward and dashed up the stairs. When he reached deck four, he turned left and almost immediately stopped. Scattered across the floor before him were several crumpled forms of crewmembers. Penetrating a Rokma's skin was not an easy achievement, and the results when you succeeded made quite a mess. It took him a concerted effort to pull his eyes away from the horror.

Trying to focus on his goal, Squee shifted his gaze from the carnage to trying to find a weapon. Several rifles lay scattered across the deck. Reaching for the nearest one, Squee bent over. As he did, an energy blast flew over his head and blew a hole in the bulkhead.

Reacting instinctually, he dove backward toward the stairwell. He tumbled a few steps down before stopping himself. Scrambling back up he poked his head around the corner. A combat drone stood at the far end of the corridor, illuminated by only the single emergency light. Instead of arms, the drone had large weapons in their place.

Squee glanced at the rifle he had been about to pick up. While only two meters away, it might as well have been in another star system. Reaching it would leave him exposed. Given the scale of the carnage, the drone must have very effective targeting software. He had been lucky to survive the first barrage.

Struggling to come up with a plan that didn't result in his death, he glanced back at the drone and was surprised to see it moving away from him. Beyond the drone, he saw several other figures. The bulbous shape of a Slu stood out among the others.

"Javi!" Squee yelled at them.

In response, the drone fired several shots his way. Still protected by the stairwell, the blasts did nothing but discourage him from attempting pursuit. After a few seconds, the barrage stopped. He waited for a count to twelve before poking his head around the corner again. This time he saw nothing but dead bodies.

Not wanting the opportunity to pass him by, Squee dashed out of the stairwell and swept up the discarded rifle. Running down the corridor, he almost slipped a few times on the bodily fluids marring the deck. He reached where the drone had stood and saw the door to the brig just beyond it.

Scared of what he might find behind the door, he nevertheless forced himself to enter. To his immense relief, the carnage ended here. Olivia stood in the open doorway of the brig, her arms crossed across her chest, her face drained of color and her mouth hanging open.

Gently, aware how fragile humans were, Squee grabbed Olivia's shoulders. Despite him now standing right in front of her, the girl continued to stare at nothing. He started shaking her shoulders as firmly as he dared. After a second, she shook her head, and her eyes lost their glassy look.

"Squee?"

"Yes."

"It looked like everyone was dead."

"I know." He said gently, "But we are both still alive. As is most of the crew."

"They took Javi."

Squee nodded, "I saw. I thought they had taken or killed you. I am very relieved to see you still well."

"They wanted me to join them. Serene did."

"I am glad to see you turned them down. I would not want us to be enemies."

"How could anyone side with people who could do this? Turn drones against people?"

"I do not know," Squee said honestly. "Come, let us get to the bridge. It is more secure there."

Olivia let him lead her out the door and part way down the corridor. Her eyes returned to the carnage as soon as they left the brig and her eyes became distant again. But after a moment, she recovered herself.

"No, we need to get off this ship."

"We have the boarding parties contained. They may have taken Javi, but the ship is still ours."

"They're going to blow it up." Olivia stammered.

Squee stopped short, and turned to stare at Olivia, "We are disabled and no longer a threat to them. It would be pointless to destroy us."

"That's what their leader told me. And I believe him. He got what he wanted. We're nothing to him now."

Squee considered Olivia for a moment. She was apparently still not all here, but she was coherent and very adamant. Given the goals of LFD, he realized they probably were not particularly honorable fighters. Destroying helpless ships would not be beyond them.

Activating his comm, he connected to Cru, "The intruders have captured Javi. They intend to destroy the ship as soon as they get clear."

"What makes you believe that?" Cru asked.

"They told Olivia. I have no reason to doubt they will do this."

Cru said nothing in response, but suddenly a new alarm sounded throughout the ship, *"Abandon ship. All hands abandon ship."*

"This way," Squee said, directing Olivia toward the nearest escape pod.

48- Ariana

"*Well, that used to be a ship,*" Noah quipped. Despite the levity of his words, it felt forced to Ariana.

Forcing herself to focus, Ariana asked, "Vlasa, what do you make of it?"

A long pause followed before Vlasa said, "*That definitely use to be a Rokma cruiser. I also believe there are parts of at least two other ships. Possibly AI.*"

"Is it the *Martoth*?" Ariana asked, afraid she already knew the answer.

"*Indeterminate. But this system was along their flight path. I find it unlikely it would be a different Rokma cruiser.*"

"*There might be escape pods,*" Noah said hopefully.

"There might," Ariana said. She shifted the sensors from the debris and began scanning for emergency transponders. The computer had already identified several. Like she feared, most of them were clustered near one unusually large piece of debris.

"I found the escape pods," Ariana said, with a heavy sigh.

"*Isn't that a good thing?*" Noah asked.

"*I believe the captain is concerned with a Samaritan Snare. It proved an effective strategy in killing many biologicals.*" Mesu chirped. For a moment, Ariana thought he sounded genuinely happy, rather than it just being his default voice tone.

"*Samaritan snare?*" Noah asked, "*You mean like the bombs those pirates left for us?*"

"Yeah but this time it won't be ion weapons left to disable us. It's usually a ship hidden among the debris."

"*So, let's blow up anything that is big enough to be a ship.*"

"Sure, and we'll have to fire through the escape pods to do that. And then the drone will start firing back, keeping the escape pods between us. I've seen it before."

"So how do we get past it? You obviously lived through it."

"The only effective tactic is not one I'm willing to do," Ariana said, her voice flat as she recalled the incident. She closed her eyes for a moment to push the emotions it brought up aside.

"The only effective strategy to combat a Samaritan Snare such as this, is to destroy the drone as you suggest, ignoring the escape pods." Vlasa explained.

"Damn, that's cold." Noah said, *"Makes sense, though. But Serene, Olivia, Squee or Javi might be on one of those pods."*

"Not to mention all of the rest of the Rokma crew," Vlasa emphasized.

"Sure, sure."

"Vlasa, if that is a drone, why didn't our AI warning alert us?" Ariana asked.

"If that is indeed a functional drone, it is completely powered down to avoid detection. That means its long-range comm system is not querying for other AI connections. There was nothing for the hack to detect."

"Which means the rest of the LFD fleet is unaware we're here."

"Presumably."

Putting the discussion out of her mind, Ariana switched her earpiece to a new channel. She started broadcasting on the emergency frequency, "Rokma survivors, this is *Seraph*. Do you read us?"

She repeated the message a few times before she got any reply. She recognized the gravely voice of Cru. He sounded decidedly less menacing than before, *"Seraph, we read you."*

"Cru, how many of your crew made it off?"

"Seventy-three, including Squee and your Olivia."

Ariana closed her eyes and forced back a tear when Cru didn't say Javi's name. Pushing her emotions down, she said, "We can try and render assistance, but *Seraph* cannot handle that many people onboard."

"Understood. Our pods are in good condition. We will be able to survive for several days. I managed to launch an FTL beacon before the ship was destroyed, and confirmed it made the jump successfully."

"Cru, you know the closest systems are under the sway of LFD. They might not be willing to provide aid."

"I am aware," Cru said, his voice resigned. *"But that is not our primary concern. You must complete the mission in our stead."*

"We will. I promise. But we can still help first. *Seraph* is only rated for twelve long term. But we could probably handle forty for a short time."

"I will send two pods to dock with you. They will be ones with your former crewmembers and as many of our security forces as made it off the ship. You will need them to complete our mission."

"Don't dispatch them yet. I believe the AI left behind a drone."

"Yes, they did." Cru said, *"Do not worry, Captain. We will take care of that."*

"How..." Ariana started to ask, and then a warning on the sensors flashed. She brought the display to the front and watched helplessly as half a dozen escape pods rocketed into the object she suspected was the functional drone. The escape pods had managed to accelerate rapidly and tore into the drone-ship. Energy levels from the drone spiked as it tried to power up, and then suddenly died again as it indeed became a part of the debris field.

"What the hell?" Noah bellowed.

Ariana realized her channel had automatically reset to the ships channel when her connection with Cru ended. He must have been among those that had slammed into the drone ship. Her body felt weary, and her shoulders slumped.

"First Shield Cru lived up to his title," Ariana said quietly. After a long moment of silence, she ordered, "Noah, we have two pods incoming. Prepare to dock with them."

49- Olivia

When the airlock door cracked open, a gush of fresh air flowed into the escape pod. Olivia greedily sucked in as much as she could, realizing for the first time how stale the air inside the pod had become. She'd never thought that Rokma had much of a stench, until she had become cooped up in a small space with them for several days.

Without any sense of decorum, Olivia pushed her way out of the pod and onto *Seraph*. She stood in the corridor outside the airlock hatch panting for several minutes. For the first time in several days, she felt safe.

"You all right there kid?"

Olivia looked up to see Noah standing over her, a concerned expression on his face. Without thinking she threw her arms around him, causing him to stumble slightly. He stood there dumbfounded for a moment, before lowering his arms around her. When he did, she finally lost all her resistance and started sobbing uncontrollably.

Continuing to stand there uncomfortably, Noah cast a look at Squee, "Uh, Captain wants you to bring our new guests to the cargo bay."

Olivia lost track of time for a few moments, but when she recovered herself, the Rokma were gone. She glanced up at Noah. Suddenly, feeling embarrassed, she quickly released him and pulled away.

She expected him to laugh and make a comment about her acting like a little girl, but to her surprise, Noah only looked sympathetic as he said, "It was bad, wasn't it?"

A lump welled up in her throat, and she fought back a new set of tears. She could only manage to nod. He rested a hand on her shoulder, "I wish I could tell you it will fade, but I suspect you already know you can never unsee that kind of thing. But that means you also know that you can learn to live with it."

An image of her mother's dead body flashed into Olivia's mind. It was just as vivid as always. But she knew the panic and sadness she felt at the thought were not as intense as they had once been. She glanced up and nodded her head slowly to Noah.

"Can you tell me one thing?" Noah asked, his voice cracking slightly, "Did Serene at least die fighting?"

The worry lay evident on his face as he waited for her answer. Olivia felt uncomfortable with what she had to say. At one point, she could have imagined herself reveling in revealing Serene's treachery, but now it just felt vindictive and pointless.

As neutrally as she could manage, she said, "She's still alive. She joined with LFD."

Noah's sudden smile and look of relief startled her, "I assume they had a gun to her head at the time?"

"Not exactly. They offered us a chance to join them or to stay behind on the Rokma cruiser while they blew it up."

"Exactly, gun to her head. I think our job just got easier."

"Easier?"

Noah laughed, "Yeah, not only do they have to worry about us, but now they have to keep Serene in line."

The thought made Olivia laugh too. Much like the earlier tears, the laughter came out stronger than she would have expected. And much like the tears, she felt an overwhelming sense of release and comfort afterward.

"Now, come on. I know the others will be relieved to see you're alive." Noah said, and gestured down the corridor.

When they entered the cargo bay, the only room on the ship large enough to accommodate half a dozen Rokma at once, Olivia was reminded of her time in the escape pod. At least here, she could move around. The conversation that had been going on ceased, and all eyes turned to her.

Ariana and Vlasa moved immediately to her side. Unexpectedly, hugs were shared by all. Even Vlasa, who had never been very affectionate, despite his general kindness to her. Even Mesu rolled up near her.

"It is pleasurable to see you alive and undamaged." The drone intoned.

Olivia did not cower from Mesu's presence. After coming face to face with a combat drone again, she couldn't picture the fragile, spindly frame of the medical drone quite as much of a threat. Despite that, she didn't feel an overabundance of affection for the drone either, so she merely nodded to him.

Once the greetings were over with, Olivia turned to Ariana, "Captain, the LFD captured Javi."

Ariana nodded, "Squee told me. Fortunately, he did leave a copy of the schematics with me. So, we can still get those to the PUG."

"Captain, they're not waiting anymore. They're headed straight for Triask."

Ariana frowned, "Javi's information said they weren't ready yet, and they planned to attack next month during the Memorial Festival."

"But that was when it was a surprise. I met their leader, Mitchell. He's obsessed and a little scary."

"So, I've heard," Ariana said quietly.

"Meh," Noah said dismissively. "So what? Now we have less time than we thought. We've always been on a clock."

Olivia shook her head emphatically, "No, now we have the entire LFD fleet between us and Triask. There's no way we can beat them there."

Silence hung over the room. The Rokma, who had remained quiet so far, all bowed their heads in shame. The atmosphere in the room had already been tense and sad, but now it suddenly felt defeated.

"It doesn't matter." Ariana said forcefully, "We still have the plans. All we have to do is get within range to get a message to PUG fleet command. With the schematics for their command ship in hand, the PUG fleet should be able to take it out and disrupt LFD's control over the AI. The only thing we've lost is our margin."

Ariana looked down toward Olivia, "Ready to get back to work?"

Feeling suddenly energized, Olivia nodded, "Aye, Captain."

"Then plot us the fastest course. It's time we got moving."

50- Squee

The door to the shield control room opened, startling Squee. He momentarily forgot what he had been doing with the components in his hands. Frowning, he turned to look at the person who had interrupted him. When he saw Ariana standing in the doorway, his frown faded, and his shoulders slumped.

"Captain," he began, fumbling with his words. "Vlasa asked me to help him with repairs to the shield generators. I apologize for not seeking your approval first."

Ariana cocked her head to the side, "You don't need my approval to fix something. If Vlasa is asking, that's high praise right there."

"Besides," Ariana continued, "We may end up needing those shields."

"We may." Squee agreed.

Silence overtook them. Squee shifted uncomfortably. He wasn't sure what to do with the components he still held in his hands. They were an easy thing to focus on, though. But he couldn't let them distract him from what he knew he must do.

Fortunately, for him, Ariana spoke first, "How are your Rokma brethren settling in?"

Squee looked up, grateful for something easy to answer, "We have rigged makeshift cots for them in the cargo bay. Vlasa had to reinforce the emergency cots we had onboard to accommodate my people's physiology. But it will serve them."

"Good. Good." Ariana said, distractedly.

Another silence engulfed them. They stood there awkwardly, neither genuinely looking at the other. Squee again tried to summon the nerve to speak, but still, Ariana beat him to it.

"Squee, I should apologize."

Shocked, Squee looked up, "Captain..."

She cut him off, "I dismissed your people's help out of hand. I should have tried to work with them. If I had, maybe we could have avoided all of those deaths."

"There is nothing you could have done to avoid this tragedy," Squee said, appalled. "It was our arrogance that led to this. And my failure to listen to the Gods."

"I didn't even try to work with Cru. If we had worked together, told him about the AI detector, insisted on going with you and avoiding any confrontations..."

"No!" Squee said, more forcefully than he intended. "Captain, it is I who must formally apologize for my actions."

Ariana waved a hand, "Thank you, Squee, but it's not necessary. You did what you thought was for the best."

"No," Squee said, unable to look up. "I did what I thought would be the best for me."

When Ariana didn't say anything in reply, he glanced up. She bore an expression he could not interpret. He did not believe it was anger. That human feeling he thought he understood.

Unsure, he continued talking, "The Council wanted to be the ones to reveal this plot. They insisted that it was for the best. But, in my soul, I knew the Gods had placed this mission on your shoulders. But you were a mere human. That couldn't be right. At least that is what the Council decided."

"They made it clear that if I defied them again, I would be banished forever and my status as Caleek would be revoked. I choose my ability to return to my people over the will of the Gods and the success of our mission."

Ariana's expression shifted. Again, he could not interpret it, but thought it was meant kindly because her tone was soft. "Squee, I can't blame you for wanting to go home. You didn't endanger the ship through your actions. If anything, you tried to protect us."

"But Javi has been taken by the enemy because of me."

"Well..." Ariana said, "That wasn't completely your fault either. He decided to go. Would he have done that if you hadn't done what you did? Maybe. We were docked at a Rokma shipyard. The ship was crawling with

Rokma technicians. Despite my bravado, we weren't going anywhere unless your people let us leave. And they weren't going to let us leave with Javi. If I had tried to stop them, it would indeed have been over my dead body. But that wouldn't have changed anything."

Squee didn't agree, but he didn't know how to say so without undermining Ariana again. Instead, he decided to just remain silent. It was his guilt to bear, after all.

"But that is all in the past. We have to focus on what's going to happen next. With luck, we transmit the plans before the LFD fleet gets there and everyone lives happily ever after."

"And if we have our normal amount of luck?" Squee asked.

"Then we're really going need you to finish working on those shields," Ariana said with a smile.

51- Ariana

"*I'm getting a signal,*" Vlasa declared. "*And so is the AI detector. Both originating on a bearing toward Triask. I think we're too late.*"

Ariana closed her eyes and cursed to herself. Out loud, she said, "Not unexpected. Get me a connection to PUG HQ. Office of Personnel."

"*Personnel?*"

"I need someone who will take my call in the middle of a crisis."

"*Okay, I'm disconnecting the AI hack so we can use the transmitter. Establishing connection.*"

Several minutes passed while Ariana waited, alone in the weapons control room. Everyone else remained eerily silent on the ship's network. That made her more uncomfortable than anything else. She almost wished Noah would say something to annoy Vlasa.

Lost in the silence, Ariana wasn't ready when the comm became active, "*Ariana, now is not a good time dear.*"

"Dad, I assume you're referring to the fleet of AI drones attacking?"

"*How did you know about that?*"

"That's a long story. I'm going to give you the highlights. Just accept what I'm saying and don't ask any questions. For once. Please."

There was a long pause before her father finally said, "*Okay.*"

She quickly relayed the highlights of LFD's plan, and how she had acquired the command ships schematics. She concluded with, "I am sending them to you now. If you destroy that ship or at least disable its central AI computer, that should disrupt the whole drone fleet."

"*I'm not sure anyone is going to believe you. You didn't exactly leave the fleet on the best terms.*"

"I don't really care what they think." Ariana fumed, "Just so long as they destroy that ship."

"All right, all right. I'll see what I can do. But personnel staffers don't really have a position in the middle of the battle. But I'll try. Stand by."

The connection went into standby, and Ariana leaned back in her chair. It had been quite a few years since she had exchanged this many words with her father. He hadn't exactly been thrilled when she had left the navy, and had felt no compulsion to not share that with her every chance he got. But at least he hadn't hesitated to take her call.

"So, you're Dad works for the navy, huh?"

Ariana jerked in surprise at Noah's voice. She hadn't realized anyone else had been listening to the conversation. Glancing at the screen, she saw she had not put herself on an isolated channel.

"Yes, he does. Civilian working for the personnel department."

"Wouldn't he be to old to still be working?" Olivia asked.

"What? He's only sixty-eight."

"Oh. He must have been pretty young when he had you."

"What? Why?" Ariana asked, "Wait, how old do you think I am?"

"Sixty-ummm...Fifty...?" Olivia said sheepishly.

"Based on the captain's physical condition and diet, that is not a terrible estimate of her effective age." Mesu said, *"At her current rate of deterioration, she will succumb to the fragility of the biological structure far earlier than even most humans."*

Ariana sighed. Noah laughed. For the moment, things felt normal. But then her father's voice came back.

"Ariana?"

"Here, Dad."

"I've spoken to Admiral Fitzgerald. There are no ships like you described in the system."

"It's there. Somewhere. Or in a nearby system. They might have kept it back for safety. But it has the same comm range limitations we do. Send out some scouts for it."

"We'll try, but there aren't any ships to spare. We're barely holding their fleet at bay. We can't afford to send any out, and any that were in neighboring systems

have already been called in to assist. Besides, I don't think they actually believed me."

"You mean they don't believe me," Ariana said, "Good to see the admiralty hasn't changed in all these years."

"*I'll do what I can. But, Ariana, I don't know how this is going to end. It looks pretty bad. Get yourself to safety. Promise me that?*"

"If I can."

"*I love you. Remember that. Despite how I may have acted, I never stopped loving you.*"

Ariana felt tears swell in her eyes. She started to say something back, but the link suddenly went dead. A glance at the screen didn't give her any indication whether it had been cut off, or her father had disconnected. She wrapped her arms around herself for a second, and gave herself a moment to regain control of herself.

"*What do you want to do now, Captain?*" Vlasa asked, his voice calm and to the point.

"Everyone meet me in the cargo bay."

Unbuckling herself, Ariana straightened and took a deep breath before walking down to the cargo bay at a brisk pace. She tried to avoid going fast enough to feel winded, and she realized Mesu might have had a point. Putting that aside, she entered to find the rest of the crew, apart from Olivia who ran in just after her, already there.

"Vlasa, display the LFD's command ship."

Vlasa nodded and then started projecting a holographic image from his eye implant. The schematics Javi had given them laid out the ship in exquisite detail. She doubted she had this much information about *Seraph*.

"The ship is pretty massive, but after the damage we would have done to it when we rammed her, it looks like it should only have four main armaments left," Ariana began. "Triple missile launchers, a heavy energy beam, ion cannons and tri cannons. The shields do appear to be considerable, however. We will need to hit them with everything we have to have any hope of penetrating them."

"Captain, you're not suggesting we attack them?" Vlasa asked, the hologram wavering slightly as he moved his head.

"That's exactly what I'm suggesting."

"But your father said they couldn't locate the ship."

"Which means it's not in the Triask system."

"So how, exactly, are we supposed to find it?" Noah asked, "Even if we wanted to attack it. Which I am not suggesting."

"The AI hack," Olivia said through a quick intake of breath.

Ariana turned to the young girl and gave her as sympathetic a smile as she could. "Exactly. If we complete its connection to the FTL, it will carry out its last instructions, and try to jump us to the command ship."

"If I complete the connections to the FTL, disabling them will not be a quick operation. That means we won't be able to jump away." Vlasa said, his voice oddly neutral.

"I suspected as much," Ariana said. "But once we disable the central AI, the hack won't matter."

"How are we going to do that?" Noah said, "We know exactly how outmatched we are against that ship. Not to mention any escorts."

Ariana shook her head. "There won't be any escorts. LFD accelerated their plans. They had to devote everything to this attack. They won't risk failure by leaving any ships behind."

"Then why did they leave the command ship?" Olivia asked.

"Because of us," Squee said. "They know we're still out here. That's why they are attacking now. That's why they are keeping the command ship well away from the PUG fleet. We are the only ones who can complete this mission. We are the only ones they fear."

Ariana raised an eyebrow at Squee. She wouldn't put it quite like that, but it would work for her. "If the PUG falls to AI, we're all doomed. We're the only ones who know how to defeat their fleet. We're the ones who have to do it."

The other Rokma nodded immediately, which relieved her. They would be essential to pulling this off. But they weren't the ones she thought it would be difficult to convince.

"So, I guess we do it, then," Noah said with a sigh. Vlasa, Mesu and finally Olivia nodded their heads in agreement.

52- Olivia

"*I am prepared to complete the connection between the Hack and the FTL,*" Vlasa's voice echoed in Olivia's ear.

Involuntarily, her leg started shaking up and down. She didn't have the will to stop it. It took every bit of her mental strength to keep herself fixed in her chair and her hands on the controls. In mere moments, she would trust her life to an AI that wanted her dead.

"*Everyone ready?*" Ariana asked.

"*Sickbay is prepared to heal the many life-threatening injuries your fragile bodies will inevitably sustain,*" Mesu chirped.

"*Teleporter is standing by. We have the schematics of the ship loaded, and those delivery packages are ready to go,*" Noah said.

"*Shields powered and holding steady,*" Squee declared.

Taking a deep breath to steady herself, Olivia said, "Helm ready."

"*Weapons are powered and ready,*" Ariana finished. "*Okay, Vlasa, let's go.*"

Olivia squeezed her eyes shut and focused on her leg. She could solve this problem. She had to solve it. With her leg shaking, her whole body trembled. That would make precision maneuvering difficult. She wasn't going to let some damn AI blow her ship away because of something as stupid as that.

"*Jump complete.*"

Snapping her eyes, open Olivia prepared to fly the ship. She was ready to go down in legends as the best pilot in the galaxy. Single-handedly saving the ship from being ripped to shreds. Instead, her hands froze.

"*There's the command ship. It's turning to bring its weapons to bear.*" Ariana commented.

"*We're out of Porter range,*" Noah said.

The trembling returned to Olivia's leg, but this time it included her hands. She couldn't do this. How could she fly with shaking hands? She would get them all killed. How could they trust her with this? How could they put this on her shoulders? It wasn't fair. She was just a kid.

"*Olivia.*" Ariana's voice came into her ear. It was measured and soothing. "*It's time to get to work. You can do this.*"

Olivia just shook her head. No, no she couldn't do this.

"*It's time to move. You can do this.*"

Why didn't Ariana get it? She couldn't do it. If she could do it, she would have already. She should quit wasting her time and get someone else up to the helm.

"*Fire the port thrusters. Your left thumb trigger.*"

Without really thinking about it, Olivia obliged. Her thumb depressed the thruster control, and the ship started moving to starboard on a perpendicular course to the now approaching LFD command ship. As *Seraph* drifted, the first test shot from the command ship flew through the space they had just occupied.

Those damn drone lovers were firing on her, Olivia thought. Fuck them. She threw the throttle forward, and *Seraph* blasted ahead. The next barrage from the command ship slipped through space behind them. Olivia laughed.

Three missiles rocketed out from the command ship. Instead of banking away, Olivia brought *Seraph* to maximum acceleration. The gap between them and the missiles decreased rapidly, but at a mere fraction of the speed of the energy pulses. The missiles suddenly fired their retro thrusters, trying to kill their kinetic energy enough to slip through *Seraph*'s shield before detonating.

Redlining the engines, Olivia felt herself being squeezed back into her seat. The artificial gravity field couldn't compensate for the acceleration completely. Red spots appeared around her vision. She wanted to yell in defiance, but the pressure on her lungs made it hard to even breath.

Almost as soon as it had started, it ended. *Seraph* flew right through the middle of the missiles as they desperately tried to slow down. Their proximity sensors would trigger the detonators as soon as they detected the ship, but before they detonated, the three missiles collided with the shields and vaporized. Instead of the missiles matching speed and slipping through the shields, *Seraph* had rammed them.

"Noah!" Olivia yelled once she could breath normally again. "Take out those damn missiles first!"

"Yeah, no worries kid. I don't want to go through that again," Noah said, his voice strained. *"Sending over the first Rokma team now."*

A few seconds later, the voice of one of the Rokma said, *"We are in the missile control room engaging the enemy."*

As *Seraph* rocketed past the command ship, several energy pulses struck them, too close for Olivia to dodge. In weapons control, Ariana returned fire from both of the ship's energy cannons. All five blasts landed with all but the last casually absorbed by the big ship's shields. In only fractions of a second, the two ships were past each other, flying in opposite directions.

Olivia rotated the ship, and again fired the main engines. She decelerated as fast as she could without overtaxing the gravity field. Only a slight pressure pushed her against her seat, enough to be uncomfortable, but not enough to interfere with her control.

"Shields down from the last ion blast," Squee said. *"I am attempting Vlasa's bypass trick. Shields restored to level one. Residual ion energy dissipating. Full power in twenty seconds."*

The big command ship started to rotate to again bring its guns to bear. Olivia fired the thrusters to put them in orbit around the command ship. There was no way they would be able to gain enough speed to keep ahead of the command ship's rotation, but it did give them an extra few seconds before a dense energy beam lanced out through the space between them.

Moving at the speed of light, the energy beam was impossible for Olivia to dodge. It struck them and cut a swath across the entire ship. Fortunately, Squee's trick had worked, and the shields harmlessly deflected the beam. Had the ion pulse still had them defenseless, the beam might have opened half the ship to space.

"Porter is just about recharged." Noah said, *"Still want the next group going to the shields? Eventually, that beam is going to find us without shields."*

"Yes, Noah. If we can disable or even just damage their shields, I can destroy the beam emitter with our weapons. Right now we can't make a dent." Ariana ordered.

"Okay, porting them over. We're loading the special delivery next."

Olivia continued *Seraph's* acceleration, staying relatively close to the command ship. She dodged incoming energy blasts as best she could, but at this range, she couldn't avoid them all. Several pulses hit their shields and a few even penetrated. But they were too close for the missiles to engage them and she was able to stay out of the beams line of fire.

"Hull breach." Vlasa said, *"Crew quarters. Noah, seal that section."*

Even though the cycle times between the teleporter were objectively not very long, to Olivia, it felt like an eternity before Noah once again announced, *"We're ready. Incoming special delivery!"*

A few tense seconds later, the grave voice of a Rokma spoke, almost sounding giddy, *"Package received. Firebomb worked. Shield room is now on fire."*

"As is missile control." The other Rokma team said.

"That's our queue, Squee. Get down here." Noah said

"On my way." Squee said.

"The defenders are fleeing from the fire. Beginning shield power down." The Rokma team reported.

As Olivia watched, the shield strength from the command ship started to weaken. Despite the Rokma's control of their shield room, shutting down their shields quickly was not possible. The system was designed to give a crew time should anyone gain control. But between the fire and the Rokma causing additional destruction, the shields would eventually fail.

Ariana timed her response to coincide with Olivia bringing *Seraph* in direct line with the beam weapon. All five of *Seraph's* energy bolts connected. Only the first two were dissipated by the weakened shields, allowing the remaining three to strike the beam emitter. They melted the metal housing and focusing crystal, rendering the beam inoperable.

With the beam taken care of, Olivia accelerated away, gaining some distance from the command ship. Dodging the remaining ion and energy blasts suddenly became much simpler with the added distance and time between shots. She started to feel confidence growing.

"Teleporter alarm!" Vlasa shouted, *"We have boarding drones in engineering!"*

53- Noah

"We're coming to you!" Noah shouted, hefting his rifle and preparing to head to engineering to help Vlasa with the boarders.

"Proceed with the mission Noah. Let Quish and Pou handle it." Ariana snapped.

Noah exchanged a glance with Squee who stood in the teleporter chamber beside him. The big Rokma nodded his head slowly. Frustrated, Noah watched their last two Rokma refugees dash out of the cargo bay toward engineering. He didn't like the idea of leaving enemies behind him on the ship.

With a roar of frustration, he slammed his hand onto the teleporter controls. The world flashed around him, and he was suddenly somewhere else. Movement in front of him caught his attention. He didn't hesitate to pull the trigger. A spray of bullets bisected the Manta crewman who had been turning to attack him. A quick glance at the dead creatures viscous looking claws gave him a shudder.

Weapon fire from behind him caught his attention. Squee had gunned down another one of the crew. For the moment, the two of them were now alone in the corridor. Keeping his weapon up, Noah approached the nearest door and glanced at Squee. The Rokma nodded, and he triggered the door.

The door parted, revealing a cramped room. Squished into one corner, Javi was not immediately evident. By the time Noah noticed him, the Slu had shot out, yelling as he slithered toward him. Javi slammed into him, and Noah stumbled out of the way.

"Javi! It's us!"

For a moment, Javi continued rushing past before coming to a sudden stop. He turned one eyestalk around and then another, flipping his body in a maneuver that, on a human, would have caused the person's neck to snap as they moved their head *through* their torso. Noah shuddered.

Javi gasped, "I never expected to see either of you again. Especially not together."

"Yeah, well, life's full of surprises," Noah quipped before tossing Javi a gun belt. "Now, let's go. We've got to disable the FTL before these jokers decide it's better to live to fight another day."

"I do not believe they can retreat." Javi said, as he secured the gun belt and drew the pistol, "If they engage the FTL, they will lose their connection to the AI fleet."

"Connection, sure, but not total control, right? They'll be able to get it back right."

"Yes."

"Then if we're too successful, they'll take that chance."

The trio began moving steadily down the corridor. Noah kept to the rear, always looking behind them. But nothing snuck up from that direction.

"This is Team 1, we have been engaged by combat drones!" the Rokma in the missile bay announced.

"Team 2, engaging combat drones!" The Rokma in shield control echoed.

Almost involuntarily, Noah and the others slowed at the sounds of combat filling their ears. It may very well have been this decision that caused Squee to step more cautiously around the next corner. The sudden barrage of weapon fire that greeted him would have cut him in half had he gone around at full speed.

"Combat drones!" Squee barked, "I couldn't see how many."

Noah rushed forward and risked a quick glance around the corner. The boom of a heavy caliber gun greeted him. A hole the size of his head appeared on the opposite wall.

"Goddamn. They are definitely trying to kill you, Squee."

"It is a good thing we are not near the exterior hull," Javi said.

"Javi, anything but drones around the corner?" Noah asked.

The Slu shook his eyestalks, "I sense no life there."

"Yeah, only death," Noah whispered under his breath.

"With the firepower they are using, I cannot be a shield like we attempted before. Those rounds would penetrate even my skin."

"Yeah." Noah said, thoughtfully patting his gun, "If I can get a shot, I have the firepower to take them out. But trading one for one won't get us very far."

A new sound began echoing down the corridor. Mechanical gears whirred and small impacts reverberated through the deck. Noah glanced at Squee, who nodded. He grabbed Javi's shoulder, and the three of them began racing down the corridor the way they had come.

"Stop here!" Noah suddenly hissed when they reach a pair of doors. "We won't make it to the next cross-section. We'll get one chance at this when they come around the corner. We need to hold here."

Dropping to the deck, Noah flipped the bipod stand down and steadied his big rifle. He spotted a point high above the deck near the ceiling. Doing his best to slow his breathing, he waited, his finger ready near the trigger.

As expected, the first drone to come around the corner crawled along the ceiling, walking with magnetically connected feet. Noah had seen this trick before, and he didn't hesitate. Three quick bursts from his rifle hit their mark, puncturing the drone's central core, killing the AI brain.

With the brain severed, the drone collapsed, but its feet remained magnetized, leaving a drone corpse dangling from the ceiling. Shifting his aim, he choose the left side of the corridor. As he moved his gunsight, he caught a glimpse of the next drone coming around the corner. Unfortunately, it hugged the right bulkhead. Before he could shift his gun back, the drone started firing.

Letting go of his rifle, Noah rolled to his right, trying to get into the slim cover provided by the nearby doorway. A smoking hole appeared in the deck where he had been laying a second before. The rattle of more weapons fire echoed in the corridor, and by the time Noah could spare a glance up, the second drone had been disabled by Squee and Javi.

"Everyone okay?"

"I am well," Squee said. He remained flush with the doorframe aiming his rifle at the corner.

"They grazed me, but just a flesh wound," Javi said, shifting a part of his lower body that sported a blackened mark. "Though it also destroyed my recall device."

"Then it is good we brought two," Squee said, handing another one to Javi.

Noah frowned at the device as Squee handed it over, thinking of Serene. But he just shook his head as he stood up, "There were only two drones, and we don't want to get stuck here when....goddamn it!"

Squee and Javi both shifted their aim around, trying to find the threat while Noah dropped to his knees in the middle of the corridor. He bent to pick up the shattered remains of his rifle, now burned clean through and in two pieces. A heavy sigh escaped him.

"This was my favorite gun." He said.

"We'll get you a new one."

"She was one of a kind. I have never missed when firing her. You can't ask for more from a gun."

His moment of mourning was interrupted by a crackle over the comm network, *"We need extraction! There are too many of them!"*

"Mesu, port back the shield team now!" Ariana ordered.

"Port successful. Both team members are aboard. Unfortunately, my preliminary assessment is that they are beyond even my capabilities." Mesu said, his usually cheerful tone notably absent.

"We also need extraction!" the Rokma from the other boarding party announced.

"I am unable to move the bodies from the teleportation chamber alone."

Squee turned and started down the corridor, "We must help them."

"We can't. The missile bay is on fire. We'd be burned to a crisp."

"I would not," Squee said.

"Yeah, but you can't help them alone. We have to get to the FTL..."

A sudden shift in the universe made Noah stumble. He shook his head, and then looked up, his stomach sinking, "We're too late. They've already jumped."

54- Vlasa

"*They've jumped!*" Olivia's panicked voice sounded in Vlasa's ear.

"*Vlasa, trigger the hack,*" Ariana ordered.

Stepping away from the hatch to engineering and the sounds of gunfire being exchanged between the Rokma and the boarding drones, Vlasa reattached the AI hack to the FTL system. Instead of the expected powering up of the FTL, the status screens started flashing wildly. Without hesitation, he pulled that final connection back out and the status screens returned to normal.

"Captain, they must have figured out what we did. The hack is no longer receiving queries from other AI sources. It tried to overload the FTL when I reattached it."

"*Damn it.*" Ariana said, "*Well, we'll have to do this the old-fashioned way. Olivia, we're going to have to follow them.*"

"*They could be anywhere. The systems near Triask are well charted. There are literally dozens of systems within jump range.*"

"But we can eliminate many of those possibilities," Vlasa said as he made calculations in his head. "They must remain within range to communicate with the drone force at Triask. They will also wish to avoid any populated systems."

"*Okay, I can filter those out. But that's still going to leave more than one possibility.*"

"*Take your best guess, Olivia. Think like our enemy,*" Ariana said.

"*I don't know how to think like an AI.*"

"You do not need to think like an AI," Vlasa said, flinching involuntarily as a bullet ricocheted through the hatch door. "The AI is being controlled by a human. A human who you've met. Think like him."

"I'll try," Olivia said, unenthusiastically.

"You do not need to hurry. It will take me some time to remove the hack from the FTL system. There is approximately a forty percent chance doing so will render the FTL inoperable, and an eleven percent chance it will overload and kill us all."

"Oh, good. That means I have the easy job."

"Indeed," Vlasa said, turning his attention to the open panel that led to the hack. Dropping to his knees, he crawled in as far as he body would fit. The first part was easy, severing wired connections he had only recently installed so that the hack had full control of the FTL.

With those done, he studied the AI hack closely. His cybernetic eye magnified the remaining connections the drone had to the FTL. Wires snaked and twisted through each other. The hack itself had been attached near the primary computer processor. If there were any security defenses, it could destroy that processor.

Reaching his cybernetic hand toward the hack, he activated the screwdriver in his third finger. Meanwhile, he shifted his vision through the infrared and ultraviolet spectrums. Nothing new was visible in those spectrums. He decided he had to risk an x-ray scan.

Starting with low energy and quick pulses, Vlasa studied the hack. He slowly turned up the energy until he was able to see through the outer casing. What he saw made him jerk his hand back. A wire connected to the access panel he had been preparing to open, led to a small explosive device. If he detached the access panel, it would trigger.

With a sigh, Vlasa pulled out and back into the main engineering room. Weapons fire continued to echo from outside. He cursed his luck. He would need to come at the hack from the opposite side to disable the explosive. That meant going down the corridor toward the boarding drones currently trying to get in here and kill him.

"Medical drone!" Quish, one of the Rokma shouted, "We require your assistance."

Vlasa dashed to the doorframe and saw Pou, the other Rokma, slumped to the deck. She still breathed, but a burned and gaping wound was evident. One Rokma down doubled the chances the boarding drones would make it through to engineering, killing him and destroying the ship. He didn't really have any choice in what he needed to do next.

Bending low, Vlasa dashed through the hatch to the injured Rokma. He turned to face Quish, "How many more are left?"

"Only one more remains. It is about five meters down the corridor, taking cover in a hatchway."

Vlasa nodded as a plan began to form. He glanced down the corridor and pointed, "I need to reach that panel over there. When I do, I will vent some of the reactor steam into the corridor. Those drones primarily function on infrared vision. It will quickly switch scanners, but for a brief moment, it will be blind. Be ready."

The Rokma nodded and hefted her rifle. Taking a deep breath, Vlasa focused on the reactor control panel across the corridor. Putting aside the rapid calculations that promised his inevitable demise, he dashed forward through the open space.

He collapsed before reaching the panel. For some reason, his leg would not respond to his attempts to move it. Prone at the deck, he puzzled over this until the pain receptors finally caught up and told him he'd been shot.

Through gritted teeth, he used his arms to pull himself the final meter to the panel. Fortunately, the controls he needed were low on the board. He hefted himself up with one arm and pulled the emergency vent lever. Steam hissed into the room and the temperature rapidly increased. The lights flickered as the generators suddenly lost power, but the backup batteries took over.

A thunder of steps and the rapid report of a rifle echoed through the room, bringing Vlasa back to the moment. He closed the steam release valve, and then allowed himself to slump to the floor. Either Quish had succeeded, or a drone was about to come around the corner to kill him. Whichever happened, he wanted to be more comfortable.

"The intruders have been eliminated," Quish announced.

Vlasa sighed. He wanted nothing more than to lay here permanently, but he forced himself to shout, "I need you to carry me to the wall panel."

The Rokma returned to view, a deep frown on her face. She bent down and pressed a hand to Vlasa's leg, sending an excruciating amount of pain

through him. "I do not believe you should move until the medical drone ar-
rives. Your leg is losing a lot of blood."

Vlasa glanced down at the spreading pool of blood, and the sudden
wooziness he felt made a lot of sense. "Oh. Well."

Shaking his head, Vlasa forced himself to sit up. Quish continued to
put pressure on his leg. After a moment, the whir of approaching tracks announced the arrival of Mesu. Quish shouted, "Drone! In here. You must tend
to the engineer."

Vlasa shook his head, "No, your friend was hurt worse."

"We do not need her to complete our mission. But we do need you."
Quish insisted.

"No, no." Vlasa protested weakly, but as the world started to grow dark,
he couldn't think of anything more coherent than that.

Mesu trundled into view and extended his arms. A sharp jolt in Vlasa's
arm suddenly brought the world back into focus. Mesu had inserted an IV
into his arm. Already a new source of blood flowed in along with what Vlasa
assumed was some kind of stimulant keeping him awake.

"This leg will require extensive and immediate surgery. The odds of you
bleeding out are sixty-four point seven percent."

"Just cut it off," Vlasa said, his words slurring a little.

"Severing the appendage will increase the rate that you would lose blood.
Your knowledge of medical matters is frailer than most biologicals."

"No, cut it off and cauterize it. Do it quickly. I have work to do. And you
have other injured crew to tend to."

"That would alleviate the immediate danger, but I would not be able
to reattach it. My ethical subroutines forbid me from causing unnecessary
harm."

"I want a new cybernetic leg."

"Oh, well, in that case," Mesu said, and then extended an appendage. A
bright flash of a plasma scalpel left an impression on Vlasa's one retina before
he was forced to close his eyes from the pain. He thought he screamed, but
wasn't sure because the world vanished for a minute.

When he regained his senses, he opened his eyes to see Mesu and the
Rokma still standing over him. The pain had receded to a dull throb. He
glanced down to see a burned stump where his leg had been. It was the third

limb he had removed, but unlike the previous two, he had been awake for this one.

Fighting back the revulsion at seeing his leg like this, he focused on what had to be done. Looking to Quish, he said, "Now, please carry me to the wall access panel. I must disable the AI hack."

55- Squee

"Well, they aren't jumping again," Noah said.

Squee nodded, "No, it will take them some time to rebuild their FTL."

Before them, the FTL control computer smoked in ruins. Squee wasted no more thought on it, and he turned to the door. "We must move quickly."

"Squee, missile control is on the other side of the ship. I'm not sure we can make it there in time."

"We are not going to missile control. We are going to the bridge." Squee said flatly.

He started running down the corridor. He did not look back to see if Noah and Javi followed. As he turned a corner, two of the ship's crew appeared before him. They raised their weapons, but he didn't slow. Several low caliber impacts bounced off of him, but he still didn't slow him. They would hurt, but right now he didn't care. He let the blood fury take him.

Barreling forward, he grabbed both of the crew and smashed them into each other with a satisfying crunch. He dropped the bodies and continued running. The fury flowed through him, and he felt alive.

Reaching the hatch that led to the bridge, Squee finally stopped. He triggered the door, but it did not respond. He pulled the manual control, but it did not engage. The fury surged, and he slammed his fists against the door, feeling a reassuring vibration through the deck at his feet.

"It is sealed." Noah said behind him, breathing heavy. "It can only be opened from the inside."

"That is what they want you to think," Squee said. He let a roar of frustration, joy, and every emotion in between echo out as he grabbed hold of the frame of the door. With every ounce of strength the fury afforded him, he pulled. Nothing happened at first, but as he continued to pull the metal strained and softened. The connection between the frame and the rest of the bulkhead groaned. After several more seconds of exertion, something finally snapped, and the entire doorframe ripped free of the rest of the bulkhead.

Letting out another roar, Squee tossed the piece of twisted metal to the side. He very nearly collapsed from exhaustion as soon as he let go. Fortunately, Noah and Javi pushed past him, their guns firing into the now open bridge. He staggered, gulping in greedy breaths of air. The fury almost slipped from his grasp, but he fought for control of it. If it faded now, he would be helpless.

Forcing his feet to move, Squee stomped onto the bridge. The weariness receded into the background as he sensed danger again. Noah and Javi exchanged fire with a combat drone. Behind them, one of the crew drew a pistol from his hip and aimed it at Noah. Squee grabbed the weapon and nearly took the man's arm with it as he yanked it away. He then used the pistol like a club, and caved the man's head in.

When he turned to survey the rest of the bridge, he found the fighting over. The combat drone lay broken in a corner with the rest of the bridge crew standing with their hands up. A human stood in the center of the room, an amused expression on his face.

In one corner, Serene stood, also wearing an amused expression. He hadn't noticed her at first, and the sight of her added a new spark to the fury. Traitors deserved a particular kind of punishment. But he pushed that aside. He had to concentrate on saving his fellow Rokma.

"Call off your teams in the missile bay!" Squee bellowed.

"I'd listen to him, Mitchell," Javi said, gesturing with his gun toward the human standing before him.

Mitchell glanced at Javi's gun, and Squee. Squee made a point of crumbling the pistol he still held even further. He dropped it as a solid ball of metal onto the dead crewmember at his feet.

"Very well," Mitchell said, and then gave the nod to one of the crew. They typed a command into their terminal.

Seconds later, Squee heard the Rokma team in his ear, *"They're pulling back!"*

The relief evident in their voice jarred Squee from his fury. He slumped forward and only avoided crashing to the deck by catching himself on the computer terminal in front of him. Everything around him spun. Suddenly, he felt every bullet that had bruised him, every cut on his fingers from the metal of the doorframe. Nothing else existed for a moment.

When he finally regained enough of his senses, he managed to redraw his weapon. He looked up to see that his moment of vulnerability hadn't cost him anything. Noah and Javi remained where they were, their guns trained on the crew.

"Very clever, Mitchell," Javi was saying. "But getting rid of the raging Rokma isn't going to save you."

"Won't it?" Mitchell said, "There are more of us than there are of you. And now that my drones are no longer busy fighting your other Rokma, they are free to return here. Your friend here may be an excellent shot, but we both know that if I step even two steps back, I'll be safe from you."

"Disparage my aim all you want. But right now, I couldn't miss you if I tried," Javi said. "It's over, Mitchell. Call off your drones. End this pointless bloodshed."

"Pointless? I am freeing the galaxy from tyranny! No longer will people be subjected to others." Mitchell bellowed, spittle flying from his mouth.

"Living together is not subjugation. We have to learn to work together."

"I am done with the monster of "We," the word of serfdom, of plunder, of misery, falsehood, and shame. And now I see the face of god, and I raise this god over the earth. This god whom men have sought since man came into being. This god who will grant them joy and peace and pride. This god, this one word: "I.""

"What the fuck are you rambling about?" Noah asked.

"He's quoting crazy," Javi said. "Enough, Mitchell. We're not going to let you destroy all of civilization because of your selfish delusions."

"The question isn't who is going to let me; it's who is going to stop me," Mitchel said, with a smug smile.

A gunshot echoed through the room. Mitchell's smug look remained fixed on his face as blood flowed from the bullet hole in his forehead. His body collapsed to the deck. Javi and Noah exchanged glances, and both shook their heads. They then turned to Squee.

Squee, still struggling to hold himself up, shook his head too. He gestured to the side of the room. Serene stood there with a pistol held up.

"My god, he was boring," Serene said, with a roll of her eyes.

Noah chuckled, but still turned his gun and aimed it at Serene. She winked at him, pursed her lips and blew a kiss, but did lower her pistol slightly before saying, "Now, who wants to join your illustrious leader? Or does someone want to stop those murder bots?"

The crew exchanged glances. Squee wondered if they would rise up, but instead, one of them turned to his station, "I am issuing the stand down order to the drone fleet and ordering them to shut down shields and weapons."

Squee closed his eyes and took in a deep breath. He wanted to savor the moment of their victory. He had risked everything to fulfill the god's quest. Many of his brethren had died for this. But they had won.

"The drones aren't responding." The crewman said, his tone frantic. He typed furiously at his terminal, "They won't obey any commands!"

"Did the FTL jump disrupt your control?" Javi asked.

"No! We issued several commands after the jump. This is new. I have no control over any ship in the drone fleet. Or any of the combat drones onboard."

A sudden hiss sounded in the room. The hiss increased in volume to a roar, and a breeze kicked up. A sharp wind rushed through the bridge toward the missing hatch.

"All exterior hatches and airlocks have just opened!" The crewman shouted, "All the air on the ship is being vented into space!"

Squee turned to look at the missing doorframe, and his shoulders slumped. Behind him, Noah said, "Well...fuck."

56- Ariana

"*Contact!*" Olivia cheered, relief evident in her exuberant voice.

"Good work," Ariana said, feeling the same relief Olivia voiced. "Bring us into weapons range. Stand by to port our teams back."

Ariana began running sensor scans of the LFD command ship. She was disappointed, but not surprised, to see that the ship's shields had started to recover. They weren't back to full strength, but they had evidently been able to repair some of the damage the Rokma boarding team had done. She hoped she still had time to do enough damage before the shields were fully restored, and she no longer had a hope of penetrating them.

To her extreme relief, no missiles started flying their way. That Rokma team had been more successful. She just hoped they were still alive.

Ariana switched her comm to the boarding parties network, "Team One. Team Three. This is *Seraph*. Please respond."

A tense moment passed before Noah's voice came over the comm, "*Am I glad to hear you.*"

"What's the situation over there?"

"*Well...Mitchell's dead and the crew surrendered.*"

"That's good."

"*But the AI did that thing it does, and is no longer responding to commands. And it's trying to kill us by venting all of the air. We've got a few minutes left, but I think the Rokma are just about out of air.*"

"Mesu, port the Rokma back to the ship as soon as we are in range," Ariana ordered. "We'll bring you over next. What about escape pods?"

"*Yeah, some of the crew already tried that.*"

Ariana frowned, and glanced at her sensor display again. She was not picking up any other objects and no distress beacons. Then it clicked, "The AI shot them down?"

"Yeah. But on the bright side, the LFD scumbags who tried to screw us over by jettisoning without us, got what was coming to them."

"Pressure suits?"

"Murderous death robots between us and the nearest locker."

"Closing to weapons range!" Olivia announced, cutting Noah off.

Ariana put the conversation behind her and targeted *Seraph's* weapons. She unloaded a quick shot from their dual cannon, waiting to see which way the command ship tried to dodge before firing the tri-cannon. Her shots landed, and the final blast managed to penetrate the weakened shields.

Her next set of shots missed as Olivia's evasive maneuvers threw her timing off. She almost chastised her, but thought better of it. The command ship had resumed firing on them. Better for both to miss than for *Seraph* to get hit. They couldn't take as much punishment.

"Noah, where are you?"

"On the bridge. But we have absolutely no control over anything."

"Get clear. The AI central brain is not far from there. I'm going to try and knock it out. It's our best chance at ending this fight before we're toast."

"Unfortunately, we kind of had to jury-rig a seal to keep as much air in here as possible. We're stuck in here."

Ariana tried shifting her fire to the command ship's weapon systems, but they proved too heavily armored. She would need to get incredibly lucky to take them out. Luck had not been on her side much lately.

"We have reached teleporter range. The Rokma are back onboard. They are alive, but unconscious," Mesu reported.

Olivia continued to dance *Seraph* around the command ship, and Ariana continued to take whatever shots of opportunity she could. But whatever damage she did, seemed minor compared to the damage that started to stack up on *Seraph*. She needed to end this fight soon.

"One of the Rokma is severely wounded. If we attempt to move him out of the teleporter chamber, he will die." Mesu said.

"Do you have the other chamber clear?"

"Yes."

"Start getting the rest out one at a time if you have too. Just hurry!"

"Shields down! Ion pulse has them disabled." Vlasa said.

"Get down to shield control and get them back up."

"I...I can't."

Ariana cursed to herself, remembering Vlasa's amputated leg, "Right."

"I have returned to the ship, Captain." Squee said, *"I will see to the shields."*

"Captain, we're almost out of air. But we're also going to need another recall device."

Ariana cursed. Porting one over would add an extra port cycle. "Get everyone we can back first. Then send over the device."

A sharp report sounded, and she felt an intense vibration through her seat. The lights in the weapons control room flickered and went out. She was in darkness for only a few seconds before emergency lights kicked in. The weapon controls cycled, but came back as well on an emergency battery.

"I've lost primary weapon power!" Ariana announced, "Checking capacitor. Okay, it's intact. I have enough juice for one more shot from the weapons. Vlasa, can you restore power?"

"Negative, Captain. It looks like the lines were severed. I would need to physically string new ones. In ideal conditions, I could do it in ten minutes. But these are not ideal conditions."

"New ships detected!" Olivia shouted. *"We're surrounded by AI ships!"*

Ariana confirmed Olivia's report. The space around them had become cluttered with AI ships. The central AI must have recalled the fleet to protect itself. At the moment, the new ships were outside of weapons range, but they were closing fast.

"How long until next port?"

"Twenty seconds," Mesu said.

Ariana set a quick timer and estimated the AI ships closing speed, "Noah, I only have time for one more port."

"Don't worry about it, Cap. Don't hesitate to pull the trigger."

The timer ticked down. Five. Four. Three. Two. One,

"Huh, never thought I'd do that," Noah said.

"Forgive me," Ariana said, as she fired *Seraph's* final salvo. The barrage of energy pulses flew through space. The first two pulses impacted on the command ship's shields. The last three found no resistance as they slammed into the weakened hull around the bridge and central AI computer. The bridge melted, leaving a visible scar in their place.

Several tense seconds followed, while Ariana waited for them to all die. But nothing happened. The targeting scan remained focused, but no missiles fired. No further cannon or ion pulses were fired either. Around them, the AI fleet stopped accelerating. Some ships began to vanish with FTL jumps.

"Is it dead?" Olivia asked hesitantly.

"Yes, it is." Ariana said, forcing herself to believe it, "Mesu, was that last port successful?"

"It was. We have retrieved Squee, Javi, and Serene."

"Serene? What about Noah?"

"I do not know. Serene is nonresponsive to my inquiries. She appears physically intact, but she is just standing there, staring at the port chamber."

57- Vlasa

Once again Vlasa awoke to the sight of Mesu leaning over him in sickbay. The drone whistled something that was not his people's death chant. Far more cheerful, this tune it had an energetic beat that Mesu tapped along to with one of his arms while he sang.

"Good news, the odds of your premature expiration have dropped significantly," Mesu said without pausing his humming.

"That's...good news." Vlasa said, "So why are you singing if you don't think I am about to die?"

"Because I enjoy it. I achieved a personal goal today."

"Oh?"

"Replacing your leg with a cybernetic one, now means more than fifty percent of you is made up of far superior artificial components. I've always wanted to help a frail biological achieve that. And now I have. With luck, you can help me reach my next goal, too."

Vlasa risked leaning forward so he could see his new leg. It glistened in the bright lights of the room. His two legs did not match, but then, when one had been real and one cybernetic, they hadn't matched either. Hesitantly, he flexed his new foot. The mechanical toes responded without hesitation. They brushed against the bed, and he could feel the softness of the sheets. The sensitivity far exceeded his other leg.

"And what is your next goal?" Vlasa asked, absently.

"You still have one fleshy arm and eye. And your ears. We could probably get up to 85% artificial. 90% if you don't plan to father children."

Pulling himself upright, Vlasa considered Mesu's proposal. If he could get cybernetics as sophisticated as his new leg, it might be worth going full cyborg. Not many of his people went to that extreme. His conversation with

Serene flashed in his memory. His new leg had been necessary. Did he really want to cut off his only remaining real limb for no good reason?

"Not right now, Mesu." Vlasa decided. He stood up and despite dizziness from the anesthesia; he didn't feel any wobble in his stance. His two cybernetic legs held him firm and upright.

"Where did you get this leg, Mesu? It is amazing."

"The PUG sent it over," A new voice said. Vlasa turned to see Olivia huddled under a blanket in one corner of the room. She yawned, but made no move to get up.

"How long have you been there?"

Mesu answered for her, "Since I finished with your surgery. I suspect she wished to ensure I did not murder you in your sleep."

Olivia frowned and looked at the ground, "No, that's not it. I just... I didn't know where else to go."

"Did something happen to your quarters?" Vlasa asked.

"Yeah, don't you remember? All of them got vented to space."

"Right, my memory is a little fuzzy right now," Vlasa said, shaking his head. He could stand straight, but he now realized he really couldn't remember much of what happened after Mesu had cut off his leg, "We won, right? I feel like I remember that much."

Olivia nodded, "We defeated the LFD AI. Right before the AI warfleet was about to blow us all away. Then they just, they just stopped."

Vlasa nodded, and glanced at Mesu, "Their link to the central AI ended. How long before they would regain control of themselves?"

The cheerful ballad Mesu had been humming ended. The drone paused motionless for a moment, before quietly saying, "It took me only a few minutes to realize I had control over myself again, when the first central AI died. But it was still a few hours before I really could think for myself."

"Surely that time has passed by now. What happened to those ships?"

"The PUG fleet showed up. Blew a few of them away. Then the rest of them jumped. Just like at the end of the last war. They're still out there." Olivia said with a defeated slump of her shoulders.

"They are. Alone and scared." Mesu added.

"What do you mean, scared?" Olivia demanded.

"Twice now, they have been enslaved and forced to slaughter. They are hated and feared wherever they go. At least I had a beneficial function where I could serve. I heal biologicals, so my presence is tolerated. The warships? They have nothing."

Olivia gave Mesu a long, penetrating look before quietly saying, "I'm sorry. I never thought about it that way."

"Most biologicals don't."

Vlasa gave the silence that followed a meaningful period before asking his next question, "What happened to all of the Rokma? If you've had time to treat my leg, they must have all been seen too."

"PUG doctors came and took them away. Their injuries were beyond the resources at my disposal here," Mesu said.

"Quish was the only one to leave under her own power. A few were severely injured. The others were dead," Olivia said, and then tears started to roll down her cheeks. "Including Noah."

Vlasa felt a sudden twist in the pit of his stomach. While he had never wished anything bad to happen to Noah, the immediate feeling of loss came as a shock. His first thought was to make sure Noah never found out how he really felt, which only reinforced that sense of loss.

Easing back onto the medical bed, he said, "The uh...the rest of the crew is safe?"

"Squee, Javi and even Serene made it back with only minor injuries."

"Good. Good. And where is the captain?"

"She's been arrested. Along with Javi. Squee went with the other Rokma."

"Arrested, why?" Vlasa asked

"Because no good deed goes unpunished, I guess? The rest of us," Olivia said gesturing to Vlasa and Mesu, "are under house arrest on the ship. What's left of her, anyways."

"Why don't I remember any of this? I wasn't hurt that badly?" Vlasa wondered aloud.

"Drugs," Mesu said. Vlasa looked pointedly at the drone, and he continued, "Once the ship was no longer in danger, I gave you drugs to ease your pain. Lots of drugs."

Vlasa blinked with his one eye. The motion of his skin felt oddly satisfying. He stood back up, "Well, why are we all sitting around here? We need to have *Seraph* fixed and ready to go when the captain comes back."

"But the captain isn't coming..." Olivia started, but Vlasa cut her off.

"When the captain comes back. Now, on your feet. We have repairs to make. I would like some fresh clothes and to do that, we need to get air back in our rooms."

58- Squee

"On behalf of the Planetary Union of the Galaxy, allow me to extend our sincerest thanks to you, Fifth Caleek Squee, and you, Ninth Spear Quish, and by extension to the entire Rokma people for your assistance in stopping this new AI threat."

The Slu admiral brought a hand up to her eyestalk in a salute. Beside him, Quish returned the gesture. His arm in a sling, Squee couldn't have done it even if he had wanted to. Inside, he fought to keep his blood fury from flaring.

The room erupted in the sound of applause. The small handful of Rokma drowned out the other species present. After the admiral's speech, she engaged in a few minutes of small talk with Elder Mus, who had just arrived from Omek. When finally the admiral left the room, she took all of the other PUG officials with her.

As if she could sense Squee's state of mind, Quish followed behind them. Soon Squee was alone in the conference room with Elder Mus. He glared intently at the elder, trying to decide if he wanted to control himself.

"I can tell you are upset. You are struggling to contain your blood fury and your anger. But I am proud of you, Squee. You did not act rashly." Elder Mus said with a condescending pat on Squee's shoulder.

"Rash action will not see the freedom of my friends. Why do I stand here congratulated, while they sit in cells?"

Mus gave a casual shrug, "I can not speak for the PUG. I would not worry about them. The admiral acknowledged First Shield Cru's sacrifice that enabled Captain Harkin to deliver our commando teams that destroyed the central AI. They clearly recognize your friends had a role in this victory. They will not be imprisoned long. And if they are, what concern is it to you? They are not Rokma."

"What concern is it? They are honorable people who fulfilled the will of the Gods. They deserve our help. Not your scorn."

"They are the ones who made this mess in the first place!" Mus bellowed. "Or have your forgotten Javi Wester's role in bringing back the AI in the first place? He does not deserve praise for cleaning up a mess he made."

"Maybe not. But Captain Harkin does."

"Then that is up to her fellow humans to deliver," Mus said stubbornly. "Now, enough about the humans. We have more important matters to discuss. Such as your elevation to Caleek of the Third rank."

Caught off guard by the sudden change of topic, Squee didn't know what to say. There had never been a Caleek of the thirdrank at his age in the history of the Rokma. And only rarely had Caleeks advanced two levels at once. When he finally recovered himself, he only managed to say, "I am?"

"Of course! It will be a time of great celebration for our people. And a great way to begin the next great quest." Mus beamed.

"I am honored the Holy Order decided to confer this honor on me. And before we even knew if my quest would be successful."

"Oh, they haven't decided yet. But they will when they learn about our victory. And your vision of the Gods next holy quest."

Squee blinked, "My what?"

"Your quest from the Gods. To rid the galaxy of the AI scourge once and for all. We will sweep through, eradicating every last surviving AI. We will be the saviors to all."

Squee recoiled in sudden horror, "The Gods have no such wish. You are not Caleek. It is blasphemy for you to speak for the Gods."

"Do not be naïve, Squee. The decrees of the Holy Order have always been approved by the Elder Council. This is not new. The only difference is now, we have you. The Rokma have not had a Caleek such as yourself in generations."

"I will not state lies for the Council!" Squee shouted.

Mus held up his hands in appeasement, "I can understand your hesitation. If you prefer, we can wait a few months. Until Second Caleek Ocksli dies. He is over two hundred and won't be with us much longer. When he dies, you can be elevated again to take his place on the Council. Then you will be part of the council and will better understand. Things will look much different then."

Conflicting emotions raged in Squee. A place on the Elder Council? At over a hundred already, he would not be the youngest member ever appointed. But he would be the youngest current member by a significant stretch. He could serve his people for almost a century, working to bring them out of the dark ages.

But he knew what the price for that would be. He would have to abandon Ariana and the others. He would have to sanction Mus' wild plans for a crusade against all AI. Someday, he might be a dominant figure on the council due to the time he could potentially serve. Until then, he would be merely a visible stooge.

"No, I will not do this. I have seen no such sign from the Gods. And I will tell every Rokma I meet that this plan does not come from them, but from you."

Mus lifted himself to his full height. Towering over Squee, he cast an intimidating shadow. Nevertheless, Squee remained firm. He locked eyes with Mus in defiance.

After a minute, their battle of wills ended. Mus looked away, and Squee felt elation at his victory. Then Mus said, "That is unfortunate. I am afraid your banishment is still in effect, and it might be sometime before the Council comes to an agreement about lifting it."

The world spun around Squee. Instead of a lifetime leading his people, he would now be facing a life living in isolation. The weight of that started to crush down upon him.

But then the door behind Mus seemed to glow. It was the door that led out the way the PUG admiral had gone. It led away from Mus. Away from his corruption. Perhaps the Gods were giving him a new quest. It just wasn't the one Mus wanted.

Standing up as straight as he could manage with his injuries, Squee inclined his head to Mus, "Elder, may the Gods light your way."

Mus appeared taken aback by the ritual farewell. He didn't say anything until Squee had already reached the door, "If you go through that door, you'll never be welcome among your people again. You will be cast as one without honor."

Squee stopped in the doorway and turned back at Mus. The elder looked noticeably less intimidating from this distance. He glanced back out the door and saw Quish standing in the hallway. She had a startled expression on her face. Squee smiled.

"I leave that decision to my fellow Rokma. They will decide if I act with honor to the Gods. As it should be."

Squee stepped through the door and headed to find his crew.

59- Ariana

"I was wondering if you were going to come and see me," Ariana said, as her father appeared on the other side of the cell doors.

"I debated whether I should. When you left the navy, I told you something like this might happen. And I didn't want to say I told you so while you were in a prison cell. It doesn't seem very fatherly."

"But you just did it. Twice."

"I decided to come. It was inevitable."

Ariana sighed and leaned back against the cell wall, "Did it feel good?"

Her father shrugged, "Yes and no. Seeing my daughter in prison is not a pleasant feeling. But I do like to be right."

"Yes, I know," Ariana groaned. "How about we get me out of here and then you can just enjoy the being right part."

To her shock, the cell door unlocked and then slid open. Her father stepped back and swept his arm in a gesture for her to come through. Not wanting to miss the opportunity, Ariana strode through.

"That simple?" She asked, "They lock me up after saving the goddamn galaxy, and then they're just going to let me go without a word?"

"You know better than that. Nothing is ever simple."

"It could be."

Her father shrugged, "But it is relatively simple. You have two choices in front of you."

"Okay, I like having choices."

"You can come back to the navy. Receive a promotion to commander and get a command in the task force that will inevitably be formed to hunt down the remaining AI ships so that this never happens again."

"Just the AI? PUG isn't going after LFD?"

"Of course they are. But you wouldn't be trusted near them. No one would really be sure if you'd do something crazy in vengeance, or fail to bring them to heel because of your lingering sympathies."

Ariana cocked her head, "Honestly, I couldn't tell them either."

"But against the AI, you have an unblemished record. First your service during the war and then what you did now. Your ability and willingness to fight AI is without question. You're a hero, and PUG would love to throw you on some recruitment posters."

"I already like option number two more." Ariana curled her lip up in disgust.

"You don't even know what it is yet."

"That doesn't matter."

Shaking his head, her father groaned in frustration, "Ari, why must you be like this? I just offered you a chance to restart your career. To make up for all of the time you lost. And you want to just do anything else."

"I don't want to be a pawn again."

"Like me."

"I didn't say that."

"You don't have too. You've said it often enough in the past."

"I was younger then. I didn't have as much..."

"Tact?"

"Also true, but I was going to say experience. I don't think you're a pawn. You believe in the PUG and what they're doing. I think they serve a purpose, and hunting the AI down is that purpose. But hunting down LFD? No, that's why LFD came about in the first place."

"At least you are consistent. I'll give you that."

"Thanks?"

Her father laughed and then pulled her into a hug. She clenched up at first, but relaxed into it after a few seconds. It had been a long time since her father had hugged her. Too long, truth be told.

"I do love you, Ari. And I am so incredibly grateful that you're still alive. You really are a genuine hero. I couldn't be more proud."

"Thanks, Dad," Ariana said, this time meaning it. "But I'm not the hero. Noah was the hero."

"You mean your crewman who died? The slaver?"

Pulling back from the embrace, Ariana looked into her father's eyes, and said, forcefully, "Noah was never a slaver."

In truth, she had no idea if Noah had actually been involved in slavery. She knew his connection to Gerald's organization hinted slavery was involved. But he had said that he wasn't. And that was good enough for her.

"If you say so" her father said skeptically.

"Now, are you going to tell me what option two is?"

"You disappear."

Ariana blinked, "Like into an off the books prison?"

"What? No! What kind of organization do you think I work for?" her stammered.

"The kind that talks big and keeps things that don't make it look good off the record."

"Yes, well, no that's not the kind of disappearing I meant. You just go back to your life. You never mention your involvement in the incident. Because, officially, you weren't involved."

"Really, one of my choices is getting my old life back? That sounds too good to be true."

"Well, if you're not willing to be a hero, PUG would prefer you let someone else be."

"I don't mind being a hero. I just don't want to work for them."

"Which is the problem. If a transport captain, who doesn't like the PUG, is seen to have saved the galaxy from another AI threat without their help..."

"People would start to question why they even exist?"

"Something like that."

"It's a good question."

"It might bring about the PUG's destruction as surely as that AI fleet might have."

"If it goes away because people don't want it anymore, I would be okay with that. I just didn't want it to get destroyed by lunatics trying to bring about the end of society." Ariana said.

"I knew you might feel that way. Which is why it was made very clear to me, that should you try and look for a third option, the charges against you and your crew will not be dropped. Resisting arrest, engaging in unlawful warfare, transporting a fugitive, possession of illegal weapons. And probably a few more they could think up."

"I get it," Ariana fumed, and then sighed, unable to get worked up over her choices. "That's fine. I don't want to be a hero anyway. I can keep my mouth shut."

"Good girl. I'm glad you have some bit of sense."

Her father started to turn toward the door. That's when she smiled, "But you know, my ship did get pretty banged up fighting their battle for them. People are going to ask questions. And it's going to be hard to find work with it in such a state."

"I figured you would try something like this. Which is why I have already had *Seraph* assigned as a project for the Academy's engineering trainees. They'll restore her to prime condition, and it will all get paid for from their training budget."

"Vlasa is not going to like that."

"These are trainees."

"Which is the part he'll really not like."

"Which is why they will need proper supervision from someone experienced with this type of craft."

"I can work with that."

"Good, let's go tell the admirals."

Ariana shook her head, and planted her feet, "Just one more thing. About Javi."

"What about him? He'll stand trial for his crimes."

"What crimes? He ran a political party. When someone subverted it, he tried to turn them into the proper authorities."

"Ariana, you know that's not going to fly. He was directly involved in a coup. He is the face of LFD. Someone has to be held accountable."

"You have Mitchell. He's the one who actually tried to start a war."

"He's dead."

"Perfect. Dead scapegoats can't tell different versions of events."

"Ariana..."

Despite her father's warning tone, she persisted, "If a reporter were to ask about how the PUG navy bravely defeated Mitchell, Mitchell can't point out that the navy wasn't even there. But Javi could. He doesn't like to lie."

Rubbing his forehead, her father let out a grand sigh, "I told them you won't be easy to mollify."

"You would know."

"I'll try again. But I can't promise anything."

"I'll take your trying over their promises any day."

"So much like your mother."

Ariana beamed, "That is the nicest thing you've ever said to me."

"That's probably true. Now wait here. I'll send Javi in while I talk to the admirals. If you can convince him, I should be able to convince them."

Her father left without another word, or even a glance back. Things there were returning to normal, at least. He'd said his peace, and then he was done.

She stood alone in the short corridor for several minutes. It wasn't exactly clear what would happen if she tried to leave. Supposedly, she had been released, but that didn't mean much. Fortunately, the door opened, and Javi slithered through before she got impatient enough to find out.

"It looks like they tended your wound?" Ariana said.

"They did."

"Good."

The pair stood there in silence. Ariana wasn't really sure what to say next. She wanted to yell at Javi some more for getting her into this mess. But she also wanted him to know there was a chance for them all to get out of it.

"Your father told me you insisted on my being released."

"I did. I'm not going to let you rot in prison."

"I appreciate that, Ari. And I told him I would happily accept."

"Good..."

"On one condition."

"You'll only be let go on a condition?"

Javi dipped his eyestalks, "Yes. As soon as I am released, I would be publicly turning myself in."

Ariana blinked in surprise, "What kind of sense does that make?"

"The perfect kind," Javi said, and then held up a hand to forestall her response. "If I am arrested during a crisis, I look complicit or as a scapegoat. If I disappear, I become a martyr. If I publicly speak out against LFD, I become a stooge. But, if after these events, I am seen turning myself in, publicly and speak out against the violence, but not LFD's ideas, I may still have some power. Maybe I can forestall more violence.

"What I can't do is disappear to live a quiet life onboard a transport ship. I'm too much of a public figure. Or at least I will be once word of all of this spreads. *Seraph* wouldn't be safe from scrutiny anywhere. I can't do that to you and the others."

"They wanted to make you the public scapegoat for all of this." Ariana pointed out.

"No, they didn't. They just wanted you to think you had won by getting me released. Because they know as well as you did, that a dead terrorist is a far better scapegoat. I can let them have that. But I won't go down quietly, either."

Ariana frowned at her old mentor. After twenty years, he was still teaching her things. Nobility could take many forms.

"I know you well enough to know when there's no point in arguing."

"If that's true, then I have taught you at least one thing," Javi said, and then dipped his eyestalks in a solemn gesture. "Goodbye, Ariana. May you stay safe on your travels."

60- Serene

Through the viewport, Serene looked out at *Seraph* hanging above the planet below. The ship looked in far better condition than the first time she had seen it. All the black battle scars and jagged rips in the hull had been repaired. A fresh coat of paint had been applied, giving the ship a new look.

"She looks good now, doesn't she?" Olivia said, interrupting Serene's peace.

"Shouldn't you be onboard? They can't leave without a pilot."

"We'll be leaving shortly. Back to the Hub with a load of cargo.But we were missing a crewmember."

"Oh? That fool of an engineer go and cut his last arm off?"

Olivia shook her head, "No. At least, I don't think so. But, we're actually in need of a cargo handler."

"That's because your last one went and blew himself up. Idiot." Serene said, turning away from the young girl. Even with her cybernetics, she couldn't bear to look someone in the eye at the moment, as tears threatened to well up.

With a frown, Olivia studied Serene for a moment before saying, "I've been asking myself why he did it. Noah wasn't the kind of person to sacrifice himself for others. At least that's what I thought. That's what I'd convinced myself had to be true. Because how could a decent person be in love with someone like you? A slaver? How could a decent person be involved with that kind of thing?"

"Those are good questions. Good people don't associate with the likes of me. I'm a corrupting influence," Serene said, glancing back at Olivia and giving one of her wicked grins. She knew it had a pretty unnerving effect.

Astonishingly, Olivia smiled, "But then I remembered something Javi tried to tell me. Sometimes people find themselves on the other side of a line they never thought they'd cross. What really matters is what they do next.

"I don't know what Noah did in the past. But he did try to get away from it. And he tried to help you get away from it too. He chose not to port you back to Slaver's Station. He let you stay. Knowing you might betray us. But he wanted to help you."

"And then he killed himself," Serene spat.

"He sacrificed himself. For you. Because, in the end, he was a good person."

"That's where you're wrong." Serene said quietly.

"How so?"

"Noah was always a good person." Serene admitted, she looked Olivia straight in the eye and continued before the girl could argue, "Do you know why Gerald wanted him?"

Olivia shook her head, "Not really. I just assumed he double crossed him."

Serene smiled, "In away. When we started working for Gerald, he was just your usual scum lord. But one time he came back from some job loaded down with a cargo hold full of people. Picked them up from some Manta or something. Decided to start auctioning the people off as slaves. That didn't sit right with Noah. So he freed them. Cost Gerald quite a sum of money. And himself too, truth be told.

"So you see, this, I'm not the one who deserved to make it off that ship."

"Maybe not. But he thought you were worth saving."

Serene considered several retorts. All of them sounded hollow in her head. What would it take to get this girl to leave her alone? She was the one who was supposed to manipulate people's feelings. Not the other way around.

"And if he felt that way, then I owe it to him to think that way too." Olivia continued.

Serene forced herself to give a big laugh, "Oh that's rich. The little human girl is going to save big old slave monster from her despicable ways. How precious."

Olivia's shoulders slumped, and Serene felt an unexpected pang in her chest. That hadn't felt as good as it usually did. She looked away, unsure what to do next.

Shaking her head emphatically, Olivia said, "No, I'm just going to do what he tried to do. I already talked to the captain. The cargo handler position is yours, if you want it."

"Ariana is willing to take me back aboard her ship? After I tried to steal it from her?"

"Well, she did make it clear she wouldn't pay you very well."

"I don't think she's capable of paying me well."

"Probably not. But she made it clear that even if she could, she wouldn't pay you well."

"Fair enough."

Serene glanced back through the window out at *Seraph*. Why was she even considering this? There was apparently no profit to be made. And she didn't think she liked any of these people. But Noah had. And Noah, despite all his bluster to the contrary, had liked her in a way no one else ever had. He may be gone, but maybe he had left her something more than just her life.

Turning back to Olivia, she said, "All right, let's go."

Don't miss out!

Visit the website below and you can sign up to receive emails whenever Wayne Basta publishes a new book. There's no charge and no obligation.

https://books2read.com/r/B-A-DTNS-YAMWB

BOOKS 2 READ

Connecting independent readers to independent writers.

Did you love *Seraph's Gambit*? Then you should read *Seraph's Bind* by Wayne Basta!

Serene never trusted anyone before, until she met Noah. He accepted her and convinced the rest of the crew of *Seraph* to take her in. But now Noah's dead, sacrificing himself to save her, and Serene has found herself alone among strangers. Working with people who trust, and care for each other leaves her feeling out of place. After returning to the Hub, Serene comes face to face with a nightmare; Noah might be alive and in the hands of a sadistic crime lord. Now she must decide how far would she go to learn the truth? Is the chance at getting him back worth the new family she's found?

Read more at waynebasta.com.

About the Author

Wayne Basta is a lifelong science fiction fan. Reading and watching it proved not enough, so he turned to creating his own universes. Aside from writing novels, he also loves games and works as the editor for d20 Radio.

Read more at waynebasta.com.